THE DOUBLE INITIAL KILLER

INSPIRED BY A TRUE STORY

R.R. FRENCH

FRENEER BOOKS PRESS

www.FreneerBooks.com

THE DOUBLE INITIAL KILLER

INSPIRED BY A TRUE STORY

R.R. FRENCH

The Double Initial Killer

For permission requests, email to the publisher,

FRENEER BOOKS PRESS

freneerbooks@yahoo.com

For additional information on the author visit:

Freneerbooks.com

ISBN: 978-0-692-16190-6

Disclaimer:

This book is a work of fiction inspired by the true story of the double initial murders, and loosely on the life of the author. Names, characters, places and incidents have been changed or are used fictitiously.

DEDICATION

It is with my warmest affection that I dedicate this book to:

My husband and best friend, Steve, whose love, support and encouragement got me through the exhausting and daunting process of writing this book. His belief in me pushed me beyond my struggles and his tears when reading my words gave me the strength to keep going when I felt like giving up.

My pride and joys, my children Niki and Alex who are my greatest blessings and my stepchildren, Jessica and Bobby, who complete my family.

Hun, whose inspiring spirit has been by my side through my entire cathartic writing journey.

Lastly, to the memory of three angels, Carmen, Wanda, and Michelle; the hope that your killer will someday be found is still alive.

ACKNOWLEDGMENT

Special thanks to my "village" who helped me through the overwhelming process of writing, editing, designing, and publishing this book; Steve Neerbasch, Mindy Potash-Smith, Mary Beth Egeling, Hugh (Kelly) Gaspar, Thomas M. Hill, Charles Lago, Robert Farruggia Jr., Donna Farruggia, Dorie Jennings, Jon Kerner, Nicolette French, Barb Anderson, and Mary Dougherty-Mueller.

Cheri L. Farnsworth, *Alphabet Killer; The True Story of the Double Initial Murders.*

INTRODUCTION

Even though I have a finance background with a longtime career in the construction industry, I've always had a passion for writing. Several years ago, after lunch with an old friend who had just published her first novel, I decided to pursue my own dreams and write a book. What I remember most about our conversation was when she said, "The best thing about writing is that you can have your story end however you want it to." That resonated with me and it sent me back to a time in my life that I wanted to re-write with a different ending.

I've never forgotten Carmen Colon, Wanda Walkowicz, and Michelle Maenza, three young girls who were brutally raped and murdered in the early 1970s. Having grown up in Rochester, N.Y. when the serial killer was on the loose, and having double initials along with several other commonalities with the victims, I lived in fear of being next.

Still haunted by the fact that the killer was never caught, I set out on an emotional journey back to my own childhood in an attempt to bring by way of fiction, a resolution to the nearly half-century old cold case mystery. It is my hope that in some way the families of the three victims will find comfort in knowing that so many people were affected by these horrific crimes, and still have not forgotten them after all these years.

The road has been long, and the challenges many, but the growth I've experienced is beyond measure.

—R.R. French

CHAPTER 1

WEBSTER, N.Y.
APRIL 1973

Yellow crime scene tape marked the spot where a team of police detectives and investigators converged on a rainy morning in April 1973. Here, just fifty yards from the parking area at a highway rest stop in Webster, New York, a traveler's dog had discovered something lying in the wet grass. When the dog did not obey his owner's calls, the man went after him. Then, upon seeing what had captured his dog's attention, he paused, covered his mouth, and cried.

An hour later, the police fanned out in every direction from the site where a prepubescent girl lay, half-clothed and caked in blood. They scoured the area for any clues that might help them determine how she got there and who was responsible. Detective Sullivan, a ginger-haired man whose fair skin accentuated his pale blue eyes, clenched the collar of his overcoat and knelt near the girl. He retrieved a ballpoint pen from his pocket and pulled back the shirt the girl was wearing near the nape of her neck. He observed the bruises, crimson marks around her neck that were visible far below the superficial layers of her skin, a stark contrast to the pristine lightness of her legs, arms, and hands.

Detective Sullivan urged two of the policeman to turn her over so he could get a good look at her face. He was the father of a young girl, and his daughter couldn't have been much older than this girl. Putting the thought of his own daughter out of his mind, he got back to work, wiping his face of any emotional response, determined to get to the bottom of this senseless crime.

The detective took out a camera, adjusted the flash cube and began taking pictures. He would have to wait for the autopsy report to confirm it, but from the ligature marks on her neck, he surmised that she had been strangled. An initial examination of her genital region revealed more bruised skin and blood, suggesting forced sexual contact.

"What have we got here?" Dave Williams, Sullivan's rookie partner, said as he rubbed his hand over his short military haircut and made his way across the wet grass from the parking lot.

"Sexual assault," Sullivan said. "The girl was obviously raped and strangled to death, then left here."

"Any footprints?" Detective Williams asked, noting the muddy tracks his own shoes had made on the way to the scene.

"Nothing that we can use," Sullivan answered. "Looks like there's some sort of animal hair on her shirt, too," he said. "A cat? Or a dog maybe?"

"Didn't a dog find her here?"

"Yes, but that was a black lab. These are white hairs."

"I see."

Sullivan paused for a minute and then stood up. He took in a lungful of air and then looked curiously at his partner. "Wasn't there a young girl reported missing from the city last night?"

"You're right. There was a call around eight. I think the APB report said that her name is Whitney. Whitney something." Williams reached into his pocket and took a quick glance at his notepad flipping it back a few pages. "Yes, Whitney Walkowski." He confirmed. "Do you suppose this is her?" a distracted detective Williams said as he looked at the other men in uniform who were weaving their way through trees and bushes, hoping to lift something of interest. They found a beer can here, a paper bag there, but mostly garbage, nothing relevant so far as he could tell.

"Hmmmm," Sullivan murmured.

"What is it?"

"I'm not sure, but this reminds me of a case from about a year and a half ago. Back in November 1971," Sullivan said to his partner.

"As you know, I just transferred to Rochester from Maryland last year, but how many young girls are raped, strangled, and left for dead on the side of the road here in Monroe County?"

"Not many," Sullivan said somberly. "But there was another one. It took me months to shake that image from my mind as she lay there in that ditch."

"Who are you talking about, Mike?" He asked.

"Carmella."

"Carmella?"

"Yes. Carmella Candelario. She was only ten years old. A couple of teenage boys were walking through a wooded area off the Route 490 highway and spotted what they thought was a broken doll crumpled up against a big rock. It was a horrifying sight, even for me, and with thirty-five years under my belt, I've seen a lot of shit in my day." Sullivan admitted.

"Oh, shit!" Williams responded.

"What's even worse is that there were witnesses to her attempted escape."

"Witnesses? What do you mean?" He said inquisitively.

"After her death was reported on the news, we received several calls from people who reported seeing a young girl running frantically from a car that was backing up towards her. She was naked from the waist down." Detective Sullivan closed his eyes and shook his head slowly as if he were trying to shake the horrible vision he had formed in his mind.

"Jesus Christ! And no one stopped to help her?"

"No. No one stopped. It was rush hour traffic too. Hundreds of cars whizzing by . . ." Sullivan paused to choke back the lump in his throat. "All it would have taken was one person. If just one person had gotten off at the next exit and found a pay phone to call for help she may have been saved."

"I can't believe it," Williams responded.

"None of us could. We figured it was the bystander effect."

"Oh yeah, the bystander effect. I remember hearing about that in the academy. A person sees or hears a crime yet they don't step up to assist because they think someone else will take care of it."

"That is exactly what happened. One of the witnesses even admitted that she thought someone behind her would stop to help.

"My God, that poor girl. I can't even imagine how terrified she must have been." He swallowed hard.

"It was brutal."

"Where did this happen?"

"Churchville. That is where she was last seen alive and where her body was found. It was in Churchville," Sullivan answered.

"Wait a minute. Carmella Candelario's body was found in Churchville? Three Cs? That's an odd coincidence isn't it? The girl had double initials and her body was left in a town with the same initial?"

Detective Sullivan stood speechless as he squinted off into the distance, his face hardened with concentration. His partner could almost see the wheels turning in his mind as the pieces started to come together.

"What is it? What are you thinking, boss?" Williams inquired.

"I'm just thinking that if this girl is identified as that missing girl Whitney Walkowski and since we are here in Webster . . ."

"Damn Sully, are you thinking the same killer?" Williams asked, pointing in the direction of the body.

Sullivan's expression conveyed a sense of seriousness. "I think there is a very good possibility of that, Dave."

"Detective!" One of the officers shouted out. "Over here! We found something!" With a rubber glove on his hand, the officer carefully carried over his discovery. It was a small pink jacket. "Found this about three hundred feet from the body." He said as he pointed in the direction of where it was located.

"Close to the road. Killer probably threw it out of the car window as he pulled away." Sullivan said as he flipped open his small memo pad and jotted down a few notes.

Later that afternoon, the young girl's body was positively identified to be that of ten-year-old Whitney Walkowski. It didn't take long for authorities to link the two crimes that soon became known as *The Double Initial Murders*.

CHAPTER 2

ROCHESTER, N.Y.
AUGUST 1988

Rina Rosello was beginning what would be the next chapter in her life. She had just returned from a much-needed vacation to London after graduating from law school. It had been a long road, one fraught with many difficulties and setbacks. One might say that she had been to hell and back again, several times. But no one sitting in the Old Toad British Pub on that summer evening would have been able to figure out based on the way she was dressed, the way she looked or the way she was carrying herself—exuding the type of confidence that was reserved for only a select few—that she had come from nothing. Rina sat with her girlfriend, her spirited sky-blue eyes, framed by long thick eyelashes, were captivating as they sparkled under the overhead lamp. She was wearing a flowing red dress that was low-cut, her long sun-kissed blonde hair perfectly coiffed and lifted in '80s splendor. She looked more like a Hollywood actress than someone who had just landed a job as an assistant district attorney. Yes, there were many parts of her that her attire and her makeup could cover up nicely, however, the truth was that she was only one miscue away from revealing a partially broken spirit.

Rina's good friend and former college roommate, Cheryl, had called her earlier that evening in hopes of going out for a drink so she could learn more about Rina's recent trip to England. Cheryl was an exotic-looking brunette with brown eyes and a dark complexion that made her appear to be from a Hawaiian island instead of upstate N.Y. Cheryl's looks were a complete contrast to Rina's, and the two beauties were used to attracting scores of unwanted men during their college years together. Cheryl, herself a successful accountant, was tackling a big audit at Xerox, one of Rochester's largest employers, second only to Kodak. Taking the time to go out for a drink where the cares of corporate life could be washed away, would be good for both of them, Cheryl proclaimed. That was what convinced Rina to go out with her when she phoned that night.

"Hey there, welcome home, world-traveler!" Cheryl said with enthusiasm when Rina answered the call.

"Hello!" Rina replied as she pulled up the antenna and walked back out to the front porch with the cordless phone in her hand.

"How was your trip?"

"Oh, Cheryl, London was *fabulous*! I wish you could've been there with me, I mean it wasn't like our trip to Virginia Beach when we met those sailors, and, you know," Rina laughed out loud at the memory of them on the beach with the guys. "But regardless, you would have loved it. I cannot believe there is a whole other world out there outside of this crappy little city. I honestly did not want to come back but, unfortunately, here I am," Rina said with a heavy sigh. "So, how are you?"

"Well, I've been working on that audit, you know, and I've been putting in a lot of extra hours. It's exhausting but, other than that boring accounting stuff, I'm good," Cheryl chuckled. "Hey, why don't we go out and grab a drink?"

"Ugh, I don't know, I'm still a bit jet lagged. Can I have a rain check?"

"Come on, I really want to hear about your trip. I'll even buy you dinner!" Cheryl said. She knew just what to say to get Rina out of her stupor. It was part of the reason they had become such good friends. Later that night they sat in a booth in the bar, moving in time to the sound of "Take My Breath Away" playing overhead.

"Oh, if only," Rina said with a dreamy sigh.

"If only what?" Cheryl replied with a curious look.

"If only I could meet a handsome and sexy Navy fighter pilot like 'Maverick.' What do you think my chances of finding a guy like that in Rochester are?"

"How about 'slim to none' or 'a snowball's chance in hell?'" Cheryl said sarcastically as they both burst out in laughter at the unrealistic romantic fantasy portrayed in their favorite movie, "Top Gun."

Rina was starting to feel more comfortable and with Cheryl there to keep her from feeling down or insecure, she sipped her drink and flashed a wide smile.

She glanced across the dining area and observed a gentleman sitting at the bar all by himself. When their eyes locked, she froze for a second. The drink she was holding froze along with her as if it also was suspended. The man, who was clearly enthralled by Rina, smiled. He stroked his chin slightly and shifted in his seat. Just then a bartender filled the space between the man and Rina, partially blocking their views.

"Can I grab you another beer?" the young woman asked.

"I . . ." the man began, "I think I'm all set for now." He stroked his chin once more as the bartender politely excused herself, resolving to come back in due time.

By that time, Cheryl had caught wind of Rina's distraction. After craning her neck in the direction of the man, whose arm and chest muscles strained against his white golf shirt, she leaned in and gave Rina a curious look, raising her eyebrows. It was one of the many nonverbal signals that the two of them used when out on the town. This one seemed to suggest to Rina that perhaps Cheryl might have the hots for this strange but undeniably sexy, dark-haired man.

"What's that look for?" Rina inquired as if she didn't already know. Cheryl didn't say anything but continued to look at Rina in a knowing way. Rina looked away from Cheryl, in the direction of the strange man, and noticed him getting up from his seat. *Oh, God*, she thought.

Rina covered her mouth partially and in an almost whisper she said to Cheryl, "Oh God! I think he's coming over here! Oh God!"

Cheryl cracked a half smile and then turned away from Rina. There were no words exchanged between the two ladies.

Then the man walked up to the table. He cleared his throat and showed a confident smile.

"How's your roast beef and Yorkshire pudding?" the man asked, looking directly at Rina.

"Um, it's good," Rina said, rudely refusing to look at him. Her nervousness was beginning to morph into annoyance, and she wished that he would simply return to his spot at the bar and let the two of them go back to their girl talk. When that didn't work, she looked at Cheryl and continued with her conversation.

"Sorry, I don't mean to interrupt you two," the man said assertively. "My name is Steve Amalfi, by the way."

Rina rolled her eyes and went back to playing with her food.

Cheryl was starting to feel uncomfortable. She knew she had to break the ice for Rina because Rina was getting into one of those moods. Cheryl knew that Rina's past had caused her to be very mistrusting of men, and she also had just gotten out of a serious relationship with Richard, who was not at all good for her. At least Cheryl could tell Richard was not right for her friend, even though it took Rina some time to get to that point. Cheryl also knew that for Rina, the pain of the breakup still stung.

"This is Rina," Cheryl said, pointing in her friend's direction. "I'm Cheryl."

"I see," Steve said. He politely acknowledged Cheryl but then went right back to talking to Rina. "Are you from Europe?" Steve asked. Rina didn't think that her time in London was long enough for her speech to transform into the local dialect.

"No, why do you ask?" Rina said, intrigued by his question.

"I saw the way you are using your utensils, you hold them like a European." Rina looked down at her hands and sure enough, her fork was turned upside down in her left hand. She had been scooping her food onto the backside of the fork with her knife that was held in her right hand.

Only slightly impressed, she said, "I'm not European but I've just returned from London."

"That's great! I love to travel. I was just in China for work recently."

Hmm, a handsome man who is also a world traveler, Rina thought. *And he has a job—also a plus. But no! No, No, No! Shake it off. You are not impressed or interested in him!* She told herself.

"Would you ladies mind if I buy you a drink and join you?"

Please tell him no! Rina said to Cheryl with her eyes. *I don't need some slick muscle- headed guido messing with my life*, she thought. A slight frown appeared on her face.

Cheryl understood but paid no mind. "Sure," she said and then slid over, making room for Steve to join them.

CHAPTER 3

MONROE COUNTY DISTRICT ATTORNEY'S OFFICE
JULY 1991

That night at the Old Toad Pub in 1988 was truly the start of a new life for Rina. She had been dating Steve for three years now, and their relationship was serious. They shared an apartment together in the trendy Park Avenue area that was close to downtown and Rina's office. Steve was handsome with thick dark curly hair, a deep voice, and smoldering brown eyes. His face was strong and defined with a rugged stubble, his body toned and tan. What made him even more attractive was what came from deep within him. It was his great spirit, his honesty, his nobility, that eventually won Rina over. But even though Steve gave Rina every reason to feel safe and secure with him, she was still somewhat cautious. Her life experiences had taught her that, and it was especially important in her job as an assistant district attorney that she be very vigilant.

It was a lucky thing that Rina had left the table to go to the restroom that night at The Old Toad, as it allowed Cheryl and Steve to have a quick talk, during which Steve expressed his interest in Rina to her friend.

"You know she's not in the best place right now," Cheryl said to Steve.

"I could not tell that," he replied.

"She is just getting over a bad relationship, plus she is stressed out about starting her new job as an ADA next week."

Steve paused briefly, rubbing his chin with his index finger and thumb before flagging down a passing waitress. "Excuse me, do you have a pen I can borrow?"

"Sure," the waitress said, pulling out one of the several pens she had in her black apron, and placing it on the table.

"I don't want to pressure her," he explained to Cheryl, "I was already a bit bold coming over here to begin with, and I don't want her to think I'm pushy," Steve said after writing down his phone number on a cocktail napkin and sliding it across the table to Cheryl. "Will you please just give this to her when you think she may be ready to date again?"

"Okay, I will do that," Cheryl said as she folded up the napkin and shoved it in her purse. "But you're just going to have to give her some time."

"I understand. And I'll wait for her," Steve said with conviction.

When Cheryl eventually told Rina that she had obtained Steve's number, Rina was un-wrapping a note attached to some roses that had shown up at her office on her first day of work. The roses were, of course, from Steve, wishing her luck in her new job. That night after an in-depth encouraging phone call with Cheryl, Rina mustered up the courage to call Steve.

Now, the vase in which those fragrant roses were once housed was home to a new set of fresh flowers. Three years of flowers to replace the first dozen, and it was like the originals had never died. The same could be said about Rina's feelings toward Steve. The fire that was first ignited on that summer evening back in 1988 had never ceased to glow. In fact, it only seemed to grow brighter as time went on.

With Steve in her life, it seemed as if everything was going very well for Rina. That was until today, the day everything caught up with her in one fell swoop when she heard a commotion outside of her office and went out to investigate what was going on.

"Oh, Rina," Lynn Price, her legal assistant, said as she took a tissue off her desk and dabbed at the tears in the corner of her eyes.

Rina looked beyond Lynn toward the congregation of office workers that had gathered. She couldn't help but notice the covered mouths, sad faces and tears in the eyes of some of the women. "Lynn, what on earth is going on?"

"It's awful. We all just heard that Jeff Palmer from the Major Felony Bureau had a major heart attack last night."

"I'm so sorry to hear that," Rina said. She knew who Jeff was, but she didn't know him well as he worked in another division located on a different floor. He was an older guy, balding and a bit overweight. He was a veteran in the DA's office and Rina believed he was close to retirement. She recalled him from the office holiday party this past year and remembered laughing, along with everyone else, at his karaoke rendition of "Funky Cold Medina." "Is Mr. Palmer going to be alright?" she said with genuine concern.

"They don't know. He is undergoing quadruple bypass surgery as we speak." Just then, the phone on Lynn's desk rang. She quickly composed herself before she answered it. "ADA Rosello's office, how can I assist you?" After a brief silence she replied, "Of course, I'll let her know right away." Lynn apprehensively looked up from her desk at Rina, her eyes wide, like a deer caught in the headlights. "Um, that was Mr. Allen's executive secretary. Mr. Allen wants to see you in his office at 9 o'clock sharp this morning."

"*The* Mr. Allen? District Attorney Allen wants to see me? Really?"

In the three years that Rina had worked there she had never been called into the DA's office for a one-on-one meeting. In fact, most of her interaction with him had been in groups with the other ADA's at their monthly meetings or at other various outings. Being a female in a traditionally male field, Rina tended to keep a low profile. The other ADA's would try extra hard to be seen and heard by the big boss, but she preferred to sit quietly in the back of the room, trying not to bring any more attention to herself than she already did as a female.

"Yes, the one and only. Wow Rina . . . this sounds important," Lynn replied with trepidation.

"Okay, well then, I guess I better get ready for my meeting." Rina tried hard to not sound rattled. She tried to project confidence in front of her assistant even though on the inside she was a nervous wreck.

Thirty minutes later, Rina found herself sitting in the office of the Monroe County District Attorney, Richard Allen. She focused on sitting up straight as she held her sweaty hands together firmly on her lap. *Breathe!* She told herself. *Just breathe!*

"Ms. Rosello, thank you for making yourself available to see me on such short notice," the DA said to her as he hastily rushed in and sat behind his desk.

"Of course," she replied, secretly thinking to herself, *as if he didn't realize that anyone would immediately drop what they were doing and obey when the big boss called them into his office.*

"I hope you will understand that I'm going to make this quick as I have some urgent matters to attend to this morning," he said abruptly.

"I understand," Rina replied with a nod.

"Great! I'm sure you have heard what has happened to ADA Palmer?"

"Yes sir, I am aware and very sad to hear that."

"I know, terrible and completely unexpected. We're all keeping him and his family in our thoughts and prayers. With that said, the reason I have called you in here this morning is that I am redistributing his workload. He has one active case and one that was just indicted by a grand jury yesterday. I have reassigned the active case to another ADA, and it is my understanding that with your current workload you might be able to help us out with the new case?"

"Yes, certainly. Whatever you need, Mr. Allen."

"Great. I'll give you a short briefing on the case. It's a cold case from the early 1970s. No solid evidence, and unfortunately, the lead investigator passed away. You'll also be up against defense attorney Thomas Cugino."

Rina's eyes grew wide. Although she had never met him she knew the name of the legendary Thomas Cugino, often referred to as "Cuz" by his colleagues. He was a very prominent defense attorney who was one of the toughest and most successful in the state. He was most notably known for representing Aric Shawcroft, a local serial killer who was responsible for the rapes and murders of prostitutes in the area. Rina nodded at Mr. Allen, hoping her face was not giving away the anxiety she was feeling.

"Look, honestly I think this case is a long shot. But I guess the grand jury, and Jeff, I mean ADA Palmer, saw enough evidence to feel it was worth prosecuting. Actually, I think Jeff might have even been working here when the murders happened and he witnessed the interrogation of a suspect at the time. Anyway, he's been doing this a long time and is a great attorney, so respectfully, we need to trust his judgment. The arraignment is later this afternoon."

Rina swallowed hard. "This afternoon? As in today, sir?"

"Yes. I apologize for the short notice, but it should be rather quick since, as you know, it is just the identification of the defendant and attorneys, the ascertaining of the charges and the judge's decision on bail."

"Okay," she said nervously.

"Oh, and I've already spoken to Mr. Cugino's office and he is aware of the change. Also, he is tied up finishing another trial today so his law partner will be at the arraignment in his place. I'll have the files delivered to your office within the hour." Mr. Allen stood abruptly as an unspoken official ending to the meeting. "Please excuse me as I have a few more fires to put out this morning," he said as he escorted Rina to the door and hastily opened it. "Mrs. Coppini, can you please reschedule my meeting with Mr. Robinson for this morning to next week?" He said to his executive secretary as Rina walked away.

An hour later, Lynn entered Rina's office holding the handles of a white corrugated storage box, fighting to keep the stack of folders on top of it from falling onto the floor. Rina looked up from what she had been reading on her desk. She gasped slightly when she realized what Lynn was carrying.

"Is that what I think it is?"

"Yup. Your new case," Lynn replied.

"Good grief! That is more than I was expecting it to be!" Rina said with wide eyes as Lynn tossed the box down on her desk with a thud.

"I guess I'll leave you to it. Let me know if you need anything else," Lynn said with a hint of sarcasm.

"I will, thanks," Rina said with a heavy sigh as she reached for the first folder on the top of the box and opened it. The case dossier read *"The State of New York versus—"* she quickly skimmed over the document and let out a tiny shriek when she came to the names of three young victims. It was enough to grab the attention of Lynn, who was headed back to her desk.

"Rina?" Lynn asked as she stepped backward and tipped her head back in through the doorway while the rest of her body remained outside of the office. "Rina, are you okay? Can I get you a glass of water or something?"

"Oh no . . ." Rina uttered, but could say no more. She put her hands to her face and shook her head.

Lynn turned the paper around and read the dossier for herself. "This looks like it is about three rapes and murders from the early 1970s," she said.

"It is. I remember those murders," Rina disclosed.

"You remember them?"

"Yes, I was a little girl living here in the city of Rochester, in a bad neighborhood at the time. I am familiar with the names of those girls and was fearful myself as I thought I was going to be next."

"That must have been terrifying," Lynn said.

"Believe me, it was. It was not a good time in my life," she said softly, tears beginning to form in her eyes.

"I don't understand," Lynn said, surprised by the emotion her boss was displaying. She imagined someone as successful as Rina having grown up living a privileged life in a sprawling house in an affluent suburb without a care in the world—at least that was the impression she got from her boss.

"Maybe I should go get some air," Rina said as she mustered enough strength to rise from her desk chair.

CHAPTER 4

MONROE COUNTY JAIL
JULY 1991

Thomas Cugino strolled past the guards at the Monroe County Jail unfazed by the dingy featureless building with its darkened windows and the smell of stale urine. The sophisticated attorney possessed a dignified power as he walked with purpose and authority. He looked as if he were a leading man on a movie set, with distinguished salt and pepper hair, lightly slicked back and styled to perfection. He straightened his red tie, buttoned his expensive double-breasted suit jacket, and with his shined Italian loafers making a distinct clicking sound on the concrete floor, he made his way to the interview room.

There sat the man he would be defending, waiting to meet with him. It wasn't often that someone was charged with such horrific crimes in Monroe County and the crimes this man allegedly committed had occurred nearly two decades ago. Thomas knew it would be an uphill battle for the DA's office to make a strong case against his client. Time was on his side, he thought. Science was on his side. He knew that people could forget certain details of events, like what a suspect had been wearing on that day or what kind of car he was said to have been driving. That worked to his advantage. Additionally, one of the main witnesses that the prosecution had come up with thus far was a child at the time. These were just some of the chips Thomas would inevitably stack into the "win" pile. But he also had confidence in his ability to sway a jury as there was always someone among them, someone whose heartstrings could be tugged on or someone whose brain was fuzzy enough to produce a hung jury. These and other things were on his side, like the fact that he just learned that the veteran prosecutor originally assigned to the case was deathly ill, and the case was re-assigned to a young and inexperienced female ADA. This made him feel certain he would emerge victorious.

"Mr. Burns," Thomas said as he entered the room. There sat the man, with a fringe of gray hair around his balding head and gray stubble on his chin. The deep wrinkles on his wide forehead depicted worry as he sat there forlorn. His wrists were bound in handcuffs and fixed to the table that stood between the two of them. "You have retained my services through the recommendation of one of my close friends and I'm going to be representing you at the trial. I just have a few questions for you today."

The man hardly looked up at him. Instead, he concentrated on the wood grain in the table, tapping his foot occasionally, suggesting that he was slightly nervous. It was three days ago that he had arrived at the jail and as the officer walked him to his protective custody cell past the other inmates, they glared and spit at him, shouting out the names "Chomo" and "Diaper Sniper." His eyes were bloodshot as though he had spent countless hours sitting wide awake. In fact, he had spent a considerable amount of time alone, huddled in the fetal position, unable to move or think or breathe. Frozen. Shell-shocked.

"Now, Mr. Burns, I would like to start off with how you got here. It is my understanding that you were arrested in Los Angeles after being pulled over by the California Highway Patrol for swerving on interstate 5. After a failed sobriety test, you were arrested and brought to the station where your fingerprints came up in the database as a match to the one found on the button of the sweater worn by Carmella Candelario, a young rape and murder victim from 1971. Is that correct Mr. Burns?"

The man looked up at the attorney. He nodded then went back to focusing on the table.

"I'm going to need you to trust me. I'm going to need you to talk to me and realize that I am here to help you," Thomas said as he slid out the metal chair and sat down across from his client.

"They tried to get me to confess to raping her." The man blurted out.

"Are you referring to Carmella Candelario?" Thomas asked.

"No, that girl in California. They said I looked like the guy that did it."

"I'm aware of that, Mr. Burns. But the girl could not positively identify you in the lineup, so they could not charge you with that crime. I don't want you to worry about that though, we need to focus on the current charges that caused you to be extradited back here to Rochester. Let's talk about this one," the attorney said, sliding a school picture of a young girl across the table. The man studied the picture and then looked away. It was a posed picture of a nine-year-old girl, her dark brunette locks hung just below her shoulders, her smile wide and unencumbered.

"Do you know who this is?"

The man didn't say anything.

"This is Carmella Candelario. She went missing in November 1971 and was then discovered on the outskirts of town. There's evidence that she was sexually assaulted and strangled to death. And there were two others, Whitney Walkowski and Maria Mancuso. All girls with the same type of background, all murdered the same way."

Again, the man was unresponsive. Thomas studied his client's expressions and attempted to phrase his questions and statements in such a way that he could convince him to start speaking.

"All three of them were Catholic." Thomas thought for another minute, recalling his own religious affiliation and attending Mass when he was a young boy. "I'm Catholic myself. A lot of people are. You're also Catholic, aren't you, Mr. Burns?"

The man heard organ music in his head. He smelled the incense that the priest would use to bless the faithful who had come to church to partake in the sacraments.

"Yes. I am," the man said. He had known no other way of being. It had been a part of his life since birth, since the day he was baptized.

Thomas sat up straight in his chair before he asked the next question. He wanted to make sure that he framed it the right way so that the man would answer it truthfully. "Tell me about your own childhood, Mr. Burns."

The man's eyebrows sunk lower over his cold and emotionless gunmetal-blue eyes. His brow furrowed. His cheeks drooped. "I went to a Catholic orphanage when I was ten."

"How did you wind up there Mr. Burns?" The muscle in his jaw twitched as he stared intently at his client.

"My mother wasn't able to take care of me, so that's where I ended up."

"You mean your mom left you there?"

"You might say that. She said . . . I thought she was going to come back for me," was all he could say at the moment.

In Thomas's mind, he felt like he was picking away at a granite façade and that he was just now getting to the veins of gold. "That must have been hard for you, losing your mother at such a young age. I can't imagine what it must have been like. Is that why you've been so nice to children? Perhaps you wanted to help so that they didn't have the same experiences as you?"

Burns looked up. He thought Cugino was a genius as he stared into the astute attorney's eyes. "Yes," he said with confidence. "I wanted to do God's work. I wanted to help them. I didn't want those children to go through the same things that I went through."

Thomas nodded in agreement. Burns thought that Thomas was agreeing with his statement, but Thomas was agreeing with his own thoughts about how he was going to win this case. He had struck gold!

"Listen, Mr. Burns, I'm going to let you in on a little secret," Thomas said, beckoning so the man would lean in closer. "I just heard this morning that this case was re-assigned to a young *female* prosecutor. That, combined with the lack of evidence against you and my experience in cases such as this, I'd say you should rest assured that this is going to be a slam dunk!"

"Really?" The man straightened up, suddenly optimistic, with thoughts of going back to his life in sunny California.

"Oh, and one more thing. I will not be able to be at the arraignment this afternoon as I am finishing up with another commitment, but my partner, Jason Housel, will be there. I have full confidence in him, so do not worry as it will be quick."

"Thank you Mr. Cugino," the man said with a half-smile.

CHAPTER 5

MONROE COUNTY COURTHOUSE
JULY 1991

Typically, the prosecuting attorney is part of the proceedings prior to the arraignment and would have witnessed the interrogation, worked with the investigators and met the defense attorney already, but since Rina wasn't the initial ADA assigned the case she was coming into the process after it had already begun. She was concerned about this being a disadvantage for her especially due to her colleague's illness, as he was not going to be available to bring her up to speed.

Rina sat in the wood-paneled courtroom with its marble floor and modest wooden benches. The air was humid and the room smelled musty, a stark contrast to the more elaborate courtrooms that were reserved for the actual trials. She was deep in thought while the hustle and bustle and the hushed conversations between attorneys and clients surrounded her. There had been a non-stop parade of lawyers and their clients, some in orange jumpsuits, making their way to the stand, when Rina's case was called out. She stood and approached the prosecution podium in front of the judge's bench. She set her briefcase down on the floor next to her and nervously dug through it for a file as the judge asked the attorneys to identify themselves.

"Ms. Rosello, representing the people, Your Honor." Rina's voice cracked as she spoke.

"Mr. Housel, on behalf of Mr. Cugino. I am representing the defendant Mr. Burns, just for the purpose of this arraignment, Your Honor."

"Very well," Judge Crandall said matter-of-factly, his jet-black hair a perfect match to the robe he wore. "Mr. Burns, you are hereby formally notified that you are charged with the murders and rapes in the 1st degree of Carmella Candelario, Whitney Walkowski and Maria Mancuso. How do you plead?"

"Not guilty!" Mr. Housel replied on behalf of the defendant.

No surprise there Rina thought to herself, still distracted with sifting through a few pieces of paper in her file folder. "Your Honor, due to the seriousness of the charges, the time that has passed and the potential for a flight risk, the people of the state of New York request that Mr. Burns be denied bail," Rina recommended.

"I object, Your Honor, the defendant is not a flight risk," Mr. Housel declared.

"Mr. Housel, I agree with Ms. Rosello. Due to the nature of the crimes committed in this case, and quite honestly, after all these years, I don't want to risk it." Judge Crandall turned and directed his attention to the defendant. "Mr. Burns, I order you remanded into custody in the Monroe County Jail pending trial, which is set to be held in six weeks on September 2nd," Judge Crandall said.

"Thank you, Your Honor," Rina responded, happy with the Judge's decision. Finally, after the whirlwind of the last hours, Rina, whose focus had been solely on the girls, casually glanced over, catching a brief glimpse of the man accused of these shocking crimes. *Just another dirtbag!* She thought. She was used to focusing on the crime and victims, not the defendant. She turned back to gathering her papers together and shoved her folder into her briefcase as the next case was called up. As she turned to leave, she could feel the defendant staring at her. She glanced over at him and he winked at her. *How creepy.* She gave him a dirty look and looked away. Curiously, she pulled her head back to look over at him again, this time allowing her eyes to focus in on him. That's when she felt a spine-chilling sensation and it hit her. *Wait a minute, he looks familiar. I think I know him!*

"Oh my God!" she said out loud as she felt her face flush and she began to sweat.

The defendant, who had been staring at her the entire time, realized he had just been recognized and a condescending smile slowly came across his face. He could clearly see how uncomfortable Rina became and he felt smug in knowing that he had that effect on her.

Like a slideshow, Rina's past encounters with the defendant began flashing through her mind. He looked a lot different than she remembered and it appeared as though he hadn't aged very well. She was only eight-years-old when she met him and it was around the time when the first murder happened. Suddenly her heart began to race as the realization that she may have been a potential target hit her. She looked down at her briefcase that held her files on the brutal rapes and murders of Carmella, Whitney and Maria. *Those poor defenseless little girls, what a monster!* She had to pull herself together for them. That was when her panic turned into anger and, like an enraged tiger defending its territory, her eyes narrowed, and she felt a surge of strength as the adrenaline rushed through her body.

It is said that in the wild the female species are the fiercest, and as Rina lifted her head she stared right into the eyes of this horrendous criminal. A hauntingly self-assured smile slowly crossed her face as she stared at him with an intense gaze. He shifted on his feet uncomfortably and turned his head away from her. His smile slowly disappeared. *That's right you piece of shit, you better wipe that smile off your face because you are going down!* Rina thought as he was escorted off to his cell.

Once back in her office building, Rina rushed through the

department scooting quickly past her assistant. Clearly, on a mission, she paused briefly in the doorway, "hold my calls!" she instructed Lynn.

"Of course," Lynn replied. "Um, I don't mean to pry, Rina, but are you feeling alright?"

"I'm fine," Rina said abruptly closing the door behind her. She leaned up against the wall for support as she took in several deep breaths in an attempt to calm down. She tossed her briefcase up on her desk and frantically took out the files. She sat down in the chair behind her desk, wheeled it closer and peered at the stack in front of her. Anxious to get started she reached over and picked up the file that was on the top of the pile. The tab was labeled with the defendant's name.

Rina buzzed her assistant. "Lynn, please come in here for a moment."

As Lynn entered Rina handed her the defendant's rap sheet which wasn't very long. "Reach out to our investigator, pull every resource we have. I want everything and anything you can get on this guy, starting with the day he was born. Overturn every rock he ever crawled out from underneath!"

"I'm on it, Rina," her assistant dutifully replied.

"Oh, and Lynn . . . I cannot stress enough that this is a *top* priority!" Rina emphasized.

CHAPTER 6

RINA'S OFFICE
JULY 1991

Not much about these cases was unfamiliar to Rina, but in the memories of her younger self, many of the details had compacted into a single period, a single event, as though the three girls had been snatched up at the same time on some schoolyard playground. The most palpable part of it, the hysteria that forced mothers to clutch their daughters tighter and warn them about talking to strangers, was something that she carried with her into adulthood. But for the most part, she wanted only to store that information in some secret compartment in her mind with the hope that she would never have to face it again. *How easy it would have been for me to also have been snatched up by some creepy pedophile*, Rina now thought, so many years later, as she began to read the details of the case in front her.

Collectively, they had been known as The Double Initial Murders, based on the fact that all three victims had the same initial in their first and last names. Additionally, the places where their bodies were discovered also started with the same letter as the victims' names. After interviewing a few suspects after the murders occurred in 1971 and 1973, authorities were unable to determine who the perpetrator was. The cases remained cold until this week when a suspect was indicted for all three murders based on a single fingerprint. It was now Rina's job to convict him.

An energetic, cheerful, and dark-eyed brunette, ten-year-old Carmella Candelario disappeared on November 16, 1971. Lauren Candelario, the girl's mother, had told police that she had just come home from taking Carmella's baby brother to the doctors and that she needed to go to the corner drugstore to pick up a prescription. Carmella had overheard the conversation Lauren was having with her parents, with whom they were living at the time, and volunteered to go to the drug store to pick up the medicine for her mother. After several minutes of Carmella's relentless pleading to go alone, against her better judgment Lauren gave in, citing that it was only a few short blocks away. Sadly, Carmella never returned home that night, and her bloodied and badly beaten body was found, wearing only a sweater, in the town of Churchville two days later.

Whitney Walkowski, a freckle-faced redhead, was eleven years old when she disappeared on April 2, 1973. Whitney's mother had asked her to run to the corner store, only three blocks away from their house, for groceries. Niki, one of Whitney's friends, had witnessed Whitney struggling with her bag of heavy groceries on that rainy afternoon. Niki also recalled a newer model car inching down the street near where Whitney was. Later, she explained how the car was gone and Whitney was nowhere to be found. Whitney's body was found the next day in the town of Webster. There were signs of strangulation and evidence that she had been sexually assaulted.

The third victim was Maria Mancuso. It was two years after Carmella Candelario was killed and nearly eight months after the murder of Whitney Walkowski when Maria, a quiet girl who was teased at school because she was overweight, turned up missing on November 26, 1973. A neighbor girl had told Maria's mother that Maria had to stay after school. Her mother assumed that Maria would make her way home the same way she had done many times before. Her body was found two days later in the town of Macedon, about seventeen miles from Rochester. The cause of death, as in the previous cases, was asphyxiation from strangulation with a smooth object. She too, was raped.

Apart from the things that connected the three murders—the fact that they had double initials and were found in towns bearing that same initial—there were also other commonalities among the three. All were about the same age. All three were living in low-income, single-parent homes and their mothers were on public assistance. They were all Catholic, and all three were found with the same white cat hair on them.

Rina sat in her office and continued to pore over the details. The more she had read about the three cases, the more she came to understand just how similar their circumstances were to her own. Like Carmella, Whitney and Maria, she was raised Catholic. She was raised by a single mother who was living on public assistance. And, most notably, she also had double initials, Rina Rosello. She thought about where her lifeless body may have been discovered by some detective in the mid-1970s and counted her blessings. She could have been one of those victims, one of those young, impressionable girls who had died a horrific death and was left to rot in a ditch.

But she wasn't. She was still alive, and she wanted desperately to put this dark chapter in Rochester's history to rest. In the process, she might be able to come to terms with her own childhood. Even though she hadn't been strangled to death, even though she had not been beaten and raped, the emotional scars from how she came to be, and the anger she felt towards her mother for how she was brought up, were starting to resurface. In the process of solving this case and locking up a cold-blooded pedophile, she would also have the chance to release herself from years of resentment. It was something she would need to do whether she was ready or not.

The fact that she recognized the defendant in the case made her wonder if it was a divine intervention and the hand of God himself that had saved her. Perhaps she was led to this point in her life so that she would have the opportunity to put the man responsible for all of this behind bars and see to it that justice would finally be carried out after so much time had passed. She thought about her grandfather, whom she affectionately called Hun, and thought he might be watching over her. In her mind's eye, she could picture an old porcelain music box. It was her most treasured possession, a gift from Hun. She had it with her all these years and imagined what he might say to her. She envisioned him holding her chin up and staring adoringly into her eyes. "I know you'll make me proud, sweetheart," he might say.

Rina closed the folders and placed them on her desk. "I don't know if I am strong enough to do this," she said to the air hanging in her office. "Hun, I'm worried, please help me. I really need you now more than ever."

CHAPTER 7

STEVE AND RINA'S APARTMENT
JULY 1991

S teve was sitting on the tan leather couch with his feet up on the coffee table laughing loudly at the television as he watched the latest episode of Seinfeld. He pressed the nearly-empty bottle of Heineken to his lips and was enjoying the opportunity to wind down after a long day at work when he heard Rina entering through the front door. She sighed heavily as she tossed her car keys and purse on the entryway table.

"Hi honey! You're home late tonight, everything okay at work?" Steve called out from the living room.

Rina was still silent. She carefully took off her pumps, dropped them on the floor and walked toward the kitchen.

"Rina?" Steve inquired.

"I'll be there in a minute. I just really need a drink right now."

"Would you mind grabbing me another beer from the fridge while you're in there?" Steve asked.

After pouring herself a full glass of wine, Rina took a bottle of beer from the refrigerator and walked into the living room with it.

Steve looked up at Rina as she handed him the bottle and he sensed immediately that something was bothering her. "Damn Rina, you look like you've just seen a ghost," Steve said as he reached for the television remote. He turned the volume down and then moved to a more upright position in the chair, waiting for Rina to come to life and respond.

"In a manner of speaking, yes, I have," Rina stated plainly, still trying to wrap her head around what had happened at work. *It's a ghost from my past* she thought.

Steve turned off the television and rose from his seat to give Rina a hug. The warmth of his embrace seemed to melt Rina's worries, but only slightly. Rina looked up at his tall muscular frame and sighed. She realized that she was lucky to have found someone as sympathetic and caring as Steve. It was something she had only dreamt about when she was growing up, but she had assumed she would never cross paths with a bright, well-put-together, devoted partner. Oftentimes, she thought that she must be dreaming and she feared that she would someday wake up from that dream. She assumed that one day even Steve would break her heart, much like all the other men in her past did.

"What's going on?" Steve responded with concern.

"I got a new case today and it's a very big one."

"Isn't that good news?" Steve asked. "I thought that was what you have been waiting for, a big case to prove what you're made of?"

"Yes, I have, but this one is—is different."

"I'm perplexed, what do you mean by *different?*" Steve knew that Rina had been waiting for something to come along at work that would put her in the driver's seat—a time for her to show that she was confident and capable, not just a pretty blonde in a power suit and high heels. Most of the time when she talked about her job it was to say that she was rather bored. The cases she had been working on in the DWI bureau were the same, monotonous, day in, day out, someone drank too much and stupidly got behind the

32

wheel of a car. Although she was receiving credit for her work, Steve knew that she was unfulfilled. He had hoped, just as much as Rina did, that something would come along, something that was worthy of her talent. That's why it was surprising that Rina seemed to be overwhelmed with today's news.

"This case is different because it is bringing back a time in my life that I've tried desperately to forget," she said as she looked away from him. Steve reached for her open hand which seemed colder than usual. Her usually rosy cheeks had a pallid hue.

Steve wasn't sure what Rina meant. He knew her mother lived in Texas and they weren't close. She had no siblings and her grandparents passed away a long time ago. As for her father, all she ever said about him was that he died when she was young, so she never really knew him. It occurred to Steve that he didn't really know very much about his girlfriend's childhood, even though he realized that her young life was not as good as his own. He had tried on many occasions to get Rina to open up more about her past, but he could tell when he was digging too deep, as the more he asked, the tighter her lips got.

"Hey, I have an idea. It's a beautiful night. Why don't we go out? We can go to the Brook House and have dinner on the outdoor patio, then perhaps go for a drive afterwards. What do you say?"

"I don't know. I'm not sure I'm up for going out tonight."

"Come on, I want to take my beautiful girl out on the town. Besides, it might just take your mind off things for a bit."

"Okay. You're right. Just give me a few minutes to freshen up," Rina said as she turned towards their bedroom.

About an hour later, Steve and Rina walked into Red Fedele's Brook House, a very popular Italian restaurant and their personal favorite dinner spot. The Brook House was best known for its family atmosphere, authentic recipes, large portions, and a special visit to your table from Red Fedele himself, which often included a kiss for the ladies. They left their name with the hostess and strolled towards the bar, passing the family portraits that lined the walls, along with autographed photos of celebrity guests of the restaurant, the likes of Thurman Thomas of the Buffalo Bills, Michael Richards, also known as Kramer on Seinfeld, and Steve Gadd, one of the most highly regarded drummers in the world, to name a few.

"Come Fly with Me" by Frank Sinatra, played softly on the audio system above as Steve and Rina found stools at the busy bar and squeezed in to order a drink. Steve waved across the bar to Billy Fedele, the owner's son, who was also his best friend from high school.

"Hi sweetie!" Billy said enthusiastically as he came over and greeted Rina with a hug. "How have you been?" he asked.

"Busy Billy, very busy, but I'm doing good. It's so great to see you too," Rina replied. "Please tell Eileen I said hi, and that we need to get together soon."

"Will do. Hey, Laurie, their next drinks are on me!" Billy said to the bartender as he pointed at Steve and Rina.

"Thanks, Bud!" Steve said as he patted Billy on the back and the bartender put an upside-down shot glass as a bubble on the bar in front of them.

After an unusually quiet dinner, they said their goodbyes to their friend Billy and got into the car to go for a ride. Rina asked Steve if they could take a drive down by the lake as she had someplace she wanted to show him. Along the way, she looked out the passenger window wondering if Steve was going to understand what she was about to tell him. She had done a much better job of getting through all of Steve's many layers than he had hers. He was fortunate enough to have grown up in Greece, a thriving suburb of Rochester, which benefited greatly from its close proximity to photography giant Eastman Kodak. Steve was the third generation at Kodak. His father was an engineer there and his grandfather made precision parts during World War II. Steve once told Rina that his grandfather used to see the two great inventors

George Eastman and Thomas Edison walking through the plant together. Steve seemed to have everything a boy could want. Unlike Rina's own experience, Steve had a wonderful childhood. He had two parents that loved him, he had lived in a big house and had a brother and a sister with whom he was still very close.

As far as Steve knew, Rina's mother was her only living relative and, out of respect, he never asked her to share anything more about her family than she was willing to, but tonight that was about to change. Triggered by her new case, Rina was about to reveal to him more than she ever had with anyone before, and in doing so, she feared it could be the demise of their relationship.

CHAPTER 8

DURAND EASTMAN PARK
AND LAKE ONTARIO BEACH
JULY 1991

As they drove along the Great Lakes Seaway Trail, which was a two-mile-long beachfront trail along the shores of Lake Ontario, they passed Durand Eastman Park. The park, founded in the early 1900s by prominent businessman George Eastman and his good friend Doctor Henry Durand, was well-known in the Rochester area. They were driving along Lakeshore Boulevard, a scenic drive, and the main road that divided the beautiful hilly landscape of the sprawling forest-like park, with the overlook to the beachfront on the other side.

Durand Eastman Park was a very popular recreational spot for the Rochester area in all seasons: in autumn for its colorful array of fall foliage, in the winter time for the thrill of sledding on its snow-covered hills, and in the spring for the pink flowering blossoms of the dogwood trees. But Durand Eastman Park was especially popular in the summertime, with picnic pavilions, small lakes for fishing, hiking trails, a classic eighteen-hole golf course, and a lakeside beach haven to escape the summer heat.

"Boy, this place sure brings back memories," Steve said to Rina with a wink as they drove down Lakeshore Blvd. He was alluding to a moment early on in their relationship that he believed to be their first turning point, the moment that convinced him that he had found a special girl and that she felt the same way about him.

"It sure does," Rina said although in that moment she wasn't referring to the same memory that Steve was.

"I think it was right over there, wasn't it?" Steve inquired, pointing to the beach side of the street near a parking area referred to as Lovers Lane. "Although I couldn't see much more than your boobs in my face," Steve admitted with a smirk.

Rina wasn't quite herself tonight but the memory of them early in their relationship brought her out of her sullen mood for a brief moment as she thought back to that night.

It was after they had gone to Concerts by the Shore, an opportunity for them to enjoy the best summer had to offer where they enjoyed the fresh lake air while listening to the band and dancing the night away. The Skycoasters, a local cover band, was playing that night, and their performance set Rina's spirits soaring.

"Oh my God, I LOVE this song!" Rina had said as she jumped up, grabbing Steve and pulling him toward the packed dance floor.

"Ba de ya, say do you remember . . ." Rina sang out to Steve as she danced happily around him. "Ba de ya, never was a cloudy dayyyyyyy!" she waved her arms back and forth above her head to the familiar "Earth Wind and Fire" tune to which she, along with everyone else, knew all the words.

The band slowed the music down giving Rina and Steve an opportunity to take a break. They went back to their folding chairs and as Rina took a sip of her beer, she sat back and looked around at the crowd of people. Never had she ever seen such a wide variety of people in one place at the same time in her life. Young, old, black, white, rich, poor, misfits, lost souls, homeless and lonely, all were smiling, happy and enjoying the music together.

Some were waving their arms in the air while others were bouncing and singing along.

She was especially drawn to a hunchbacked old woman who danced to every song with an enviable energy. It was a beautiful sight for Rina and she thought about how amazing it was that no matter what everyone had going on in their lives, in that moment in time, everything was perfect. She wanted to bottle up some of that euphoria and save it for times when she was feeling less inspired.

Rina looked over at Steve's profile. A gentle breeze blew her blonde hair away from her face and, in that very moment, she felt truly blessed for the first time in her life. This was her heaven on Earth, and all the bad that had ever happened in her life, was forgotten.

After the concert, Steve and Rina found themselves at Lovers Lane. They parked the car and walked down the embankment to the sandy beach where they found a secluded spot, a little nook surrounded by trees from the overhang above. Steve had brought a blanket which he shook out so it landed flush on the sand. Rina hopped on and sat with her arms around her knees facing the water as Steve lay down on his side, propping his upper body with his elbow so he could look at her.

Rina was looking out toward the water smiling. Even with the scenic view that surrounded him, Steve could not take his eyes off her silhouette against the backdrop of the lake. He shook his head in disbelief. "You know, I have never met anyone like you before," he whispered.

"I've never met anyone like you before either," she said as she turned her gaze toward him.

"I'm just an average guy, but you—you are just so amazing."

"Believe me, I'm nothing special," she said self-consciously.

"All I have to say is that you truly amaze me and every time I am with you I want more. I can't seem to get enough of you!"

"So does that mean you're not going to dump me?" Rina said seriously. At the time they had only been dating for a month, but Rina had convinced herself that Steve was growing tired of her.

"Dump you? Why would you say something like that?" Steve said, surprised by her question.

"I guess I just can't imagine a guy like you wanting to be with a girl like me."

"A girl like you?" Steve had a confused look on his face. "You mean a beautiful, smart and sweet girl who has an amazing job as an assistant district attorney? What more on Earth do you think I would want?"

"I—I don't know," she turned away unable to look him in the eye. She didn't want to get into any details of her indigent past. She didn't want to scare him away.

"Tell me what you mean."

"Nothing, really. It just seems that it's around this time in a relationship that guys are ready to move on to the next girl, that's all," she said sadly.

He reached over, cupped her face in his hand and turned her head to face him. The moonlight was reflecting in her eyes and he was feeling completely infatuated with her. He held her gaze for a moment before he said, "Actually Rina, I have to say just the opposite. In fact, the truth is that I am falling in love with you."

Her heart skipped a beat, but she looked at him in disbelief. She continued to stare at him silently, and her eyes began to well up with tears. Her eyes were telling him she felt the same way and he leaned in with a gentle kiss.

His lips were so soft on hers, and she could feel her stomach fluttering, a feeling she never had before, especially not from just a kiss. She opened her mouth slightly to allow his tongue between her lips, eagerly responding with her tongue softly playing with his. His hands moved from cupping the side of her face, down to her neck where he stopped for a moment. The last thing he wanted was for her to think his feelings were insincere.

Rina sensed his hesitation and reached up to his face pulling him into her, showing him with her actions that she wanted him too. Encouraged by her response, Steve continued, and he made love to her passionately for the first time that night right there on the beach, under the stars. Rina smiled at the thought of that night and she recalled the beautiful sky. It was ablaze with color as they watched the sun fall behind the horizon. The shades of crimson, pale pink and magenta were so vibrant it reminded her of a Monet painting. Durand Eastman Park was very sentimental to her, but sadly, this place didn't hold all good memories for Rina.

"That was quite a night, and I'm so glad the White Lady didn't come after me," Steve said with a laugh, as he jokingly referred to the legend often told locally of a ghost known as the White Lady.

The story of the White Lady, who haunted Durand Eastman Park, had been told for generations. It was said that the woman had a teenage daughter who went out for a walk along the shore one night and never returned. Every night after her daughter disappeared, the woman obsessively searched the park and would be seen walking along the shore, wearing a white dress and calling her daughter's name. The woman believed that her daughter had been raped and murdered, and it is suspected that she eventually became so distraught and overwhelmed with grief that one night she drowned herself in Lake Ontario, committing suicide. Now, nearly two centuries later, her ghost still haunted the beach and park where on foggy nights people claimed to see have her, wearing white, gliding over the water and rattling cars looking for her daughter.

"If only . . ." Rina said with a heavy sigh.

"If only what?" Steve asked with confusion.

"Oh nothing. Just thinking out loud," Rina said. *If only the White Lady had been there to scare off those boys on THAT night.*

CHAPTER 9

DURAND EASTMAN PARK
JULY 1991 | JUNE 1962

It was evident as they drove by the beach on this night that Steve was basking in the afterglow of the moment that had solidified their relationship three years ago. It was something that was special to Rina too, however, she was struggling with what she was about to confess. Rina looked over at Steve's profile as he drove. He looked back at her lovingly and smiled. She relied on his strength and was thankful for her friend, Cheryl, the one who had seen something in this man and believed that he was a perfect match for Rina. Now, years later, as they drove through Durand Eastman Park past "their spot" and made their way toward the other side of the lakefront, Rina looked out the window in silence, fearful that everything was about to change.

"Rina, where are you taking us? You know if you wanted to go on the roller coaster you should have let me know sooner," Steve said jokingly as they approached Seabreeze Amusement Park.

Rina looked over at him with a scowl. "Turn left here," she said at a street directly across from the carousel and the main entrance to the park. It was a short street with bungalow-style houses on it except for the one at the end. There, up on a hill, was a big white farmhouse that took up the entire corner. It had green shutters and a wraparound porch in the front with a wooden swing. Around the back there were three fruit trees along with a screened-in porch that had a view of the lake.

"Stop here," Rina said with a heavy sigh as she looked sadly at the house. The trees seemed much smaller, and the house was slightly unkempt compared to how she remembered it.

"That's a nice house, who lives here?" Steve asked, thinking there might be a purpose to visiting the house and considering what it might be like to live in a house like that. Perhaps it was for sale. In that moment he allowed himself to think about a future with Rina, maybe a few kids playing in the backyard or walking together as a family toward the beachfront. He imagined that Rina might be heading up the driveway after a long day at the office and glowing at the sight of her babies, who would run out excitedly to greet her.

"I don't know who lives there now, but this is my grandparents' old house. I used to live there with them when I was a little girl, and it was the only real home I ever knew." Rina closed her eyes. She could almost smell her grandmother's homemade sauce cooking on the white, claw-foot stove, the big pot filled to the brim with meatballs, sausage and pork. The dining room table was covered with rolled out dough, where the homemade pasta was spread out to dry, and the ravioli, stuffed with meat, were being sealed along the edges with a fork. Rina's grandmother wasn't Italian, her family was from Stockholm, Sweden, which explained her fair complexion and features. Regardless, Phyllis did her best to appease her northern Italian husband in the kitchen.

Rina reached for Steve's hand, and he reciprocated her desire for connection. She could see her grandfather and grandmother. In her mind's eye, instead of Steve's warm and oversized hand, it was her grandpa's. Warm, strong and rough from work. The hand of a hard worker, he used to tell her, when she would touch the raised veins on the back of his hand with her small fingertips. That hand had been the epitome of strength for young Rina. It had symbolized the embodiment of love and safety in a world that was so full of dangers, known and unknown. She choked back the lump in her throat as she pictured her grandfather, all five feet six of him, with his full head of wavy gray hair, a farmer's tan from being outdoors in his garden, and the deep smile lines around his eyes. He was small in stature but what he lacked in size he made up for in integrity, passion, and character.

Rina let out a heavy sigh. "My life started out here and those were definitely the happiest days of my childhood, but unfortunately I lived here for only a short time."

"I see," Steve said after Rina opened her eyes again. The evening breeze through the open car window had begun to waft strands of her blonde hair into her face. There was something very vulnerable about how Rina looked in that moment. Steve had the urge to ask her a bit more about what life was like for the love of his life before they met, but then he remembered something about how she had been embarrassed to tell him anything. He had been curious, wanting her to open up a bit more about these more secretive parts of her life, but he didn't want to push her too much.

"I guess I should start at the beginning." Rina said, after feeling as comfortable and safe as she had felt in a very long time, "It's about my mother. What I didn't tell you about her is that she was a tortured soul. It wasn't easy for her to raise me. It wasn't easy for her to even love me, I think. But I believe that could be due to how I came to be."

"What do you mean? Like how you were born?" Steve asked.

"Yes. Let's just say I wasn't planned. And the fact that I was born at all meant that my mother had to give up her plans."

"Okay," Steve said, cautious about what he might ask her next. "But lots of people's lives are interrupted by a pregnancy, right? After all, there are lots of women who become pregnant and then have to deal with—"

"My mother was raped," Rina interrupted. Steve was still holding her hand but her pulse was starting to escalate at the thought that he might recoil at what she had just said. Surprisingly, there was no sudden jolt from Steve, no flinch, not even a raised eyebrow.

Instead, he remained calm. He did so because he knew instinctively that he needed to do that for Rina, he needed to be her rock. After taking a moment to process what Rina had just confided in him, he merely squeezed her hand tighter.

"So, what you're saying is . . ." Steve began while Rina nodded in silence as a tear escaped her eye and streaked down her cheek. "Honey, I'm so sorry," he continued. "How old were you when you found this out?"

"I was about eight years old when I first found out but I was too young to understand at the time. Then, when I was sixteen, my aunt Linda came from Arizona to visit me, which is when she told me what happened. I guess she was worried about me since I was in high school and was going to be going off to college. She wanted me to know so I would be careful. She wanted me to know that bad things can happen and easily get out of control when . . . well . . . when boys are under the influence of alcohol."

* * *

It was an unseasonably warm Saturday afternoon in early June 1962, just a few weeks before Dorothy, Rina's mother was about to graduate from high school. Dorothy and her sister Linda decided to enjoy the day by taking a walk to the beach through Durand Eastman Park, which was just a mile away from their house. It seemed everyone was out enjoying the nice weather that day after a long, cold and snowy winter followed by a wet spring.

Dorothy, at nineteen, was a petite blonde beauty with blue eyes and an innocent smile. Linda, a fifteen-year-old brunette with big dark brown eyes, was opposite in features compared to her sister but equally attractive. The girls had just hiked through the wooded trails in Durand Eastman Park when, on their way home, they came across a group of high school boys having a party in one of the shelters that was tucked back in the trees and camouflaged from the park road. The boys spotted Dorothy, her long blonde hair pulled back from her face with a white cloth headband, and Linda, wearing a tight sundress that accentuated her ample bosom. They whistled at the girls, calling out for them to join the party. Dorothy recognized a few of them from her high school and she convinced her reluctant sister to go over. As the girls walked towards the shelter the excited guys began to clap, hoot and holler in celebration. Dorothy was not part of the popular groups at school so she was flattered by the attention. She blatantly ignored Linda's obvious apprehension.

A while later, after much drinking, the boys got a bit rambunctious and flirtatious with the girls, especially Linda, causing them to feel very uncomfortable. But when the sisters wanted to leave, the boys would not allow it. They started to get aggressive and belligerent. Dorothy stood up to the one that was manhandling her sister. She pushed him away from her and things escalated from there. Linda escaped the grip of one of the boys and Dorothy yelled for her to *"Run home and get dad!"*

Unfortunately, by the time Dorothy's father Louie pulled up to the shelter in the park with Linda, it was vacant except for the empty beer cans scattered all around, and Dorothy lying in the fetal position on top of one of the picnic tables. Louie was heartbroken to see his daughter like that, her t-shirt ripped, her cut off jean shorts in a heap on the cement floor of the shelter. He wrapped a blanket around her and carried her back to his pickup truck placing her gently in the passenger seat. Linda sat in the middle and held her sister's hand as they drove away in silence. No one uttered a word as Dorothy, with her forehead pressed up against the window on the passenger door, watched the trees whiz by in a blur.

* * *

After Rina finished telling Steve the story as she had heard it from her aunt, they sat there silently, staring out the windshield in the direction of her grandparents' old house. After a few minutes had passed Rina looked over at Steve and could tell from the look on his face that he was shocked by her revelation. He shook his head in disbelief and his eyes welled up with tears. "You?" Steve said, dismayed. "You are the product of that rape?"

She nodded her head sadly. "Yes." Rina looked down shamefully, feeling certain that with this knowledge Steve would feel differently about her now. He reached over and put his hand over hers that were resting in her lap.

"I don't even know what to say except for that it's—it's just so hard to believe," he said in disbelief. "What happened to the guys?"

"Apparently nothing."

"They didn't press charges against them?" Steve asked with surprise.

"No. I guess my grandparents wanted to spare my mother and the family the trauma of all that. Maybe it was their strong Catholic beliefs or maybe because my mother was flirting and drinking with them. Perhaps they felt it would be hard to prove, so they just let it go. I'm sure they had their reasons. But sadly, my mother was so embarrassed and afraid to see any of them again that she didn't even attend her High School graduation. It wasn't until several months later that they realized she was pregnant."

"How awful," Steve said sympathetically.

"Thanks," Rina whispered. "You are the only person I have ever told this to. Everyone else I know thinks my father is dead. That was what my mother always told me. She said as far as she was concerned he was dead. I continued to believe that he was until my aunt told me the truth." Rina looked out the passenger window so Steve could not see the tears rolling down her face.

"Listen to me!" he said as he put his hand under her chin, turning her face towards him. He wiped a tear from her cheek and looked into her eyes when he said, "I mean this when I say it, please don't you think for a minute that this changes how I feel about you or anything between us."

"Honestly, I understand if this makes you feel uneasy about me and if—"

"Stop! Don't even say it." He interrupted her mid-sentence, putting his hand up.

"But what if we have children someday? What if we have a boy and well, he could grow up to be a rapist you know."

"Listen, I'm pretty sure there is no such thing as a rape gene, and quite honestly, I believe that who you are morally is stronger than your father's DNA."

"I'm terrified, Steve. I don't want to lose you."

"You're not going to. I think you are amazing, and in fact, knowing this about you makes me love you even more."

She smiled halfheartedly and, although she had hoped he meant what he said, she worried that he didn't. As they drove off, she glanced out the window at the house in the rear-view mirror. As her grandparents' old house slowly disappeared in the distance, she wiped the tears from her face.

It was a quiet ride home as Rina thought back to her childhood and the tumultuous relationship that she had with her mother while growing up. Rina had come a long way and had overcome so much since then. But now as she recalled those painful memories, the abuse she suffered and the feelings of being unloved, she was overwhelmed with emotion.

CHAPTER 10

GENESEE HOSPITAL
FEBRUARY 1963

It was three months after her rape when Dorothy discovered she was pregnant. She wanted to have an abortion but her parents, Louie and Phyllis, were devout Catholics and abortion was not only illegal, but out of the question. They did have several discussions with the priest from their church and had planned to give Dorothy's baby up for adoption.

On the day that Rina was born, Louie was working in his workshop and Phyllis was in the kitchen cooking dinner when they heard a blood-curdling scream coming from the bathroom. It was Dorothy, and even though her due date wasn't for another month yet, the fear in her voice could be heard as she shouted, "Mom! Dad! Oh my God! Please come quick, something is really wrong!"

Louie immediately dropped what he was doing to run to the aid of his daughter. He burst through the bathroom door to find Dorothy in hysterics, sitting in a puddle of blood on the floor. He called for Phyllis to, *"grab the car keys!"* as he swiftly picked up his daughter and rushed her out to the car.

At the hospital, Louie and Phyllis had been waiting for several hours when finally the automatic metal doors opened and the emergency room doctor emerged. "Is my daughter all right?" Louie asked with concern.

The doctor wore a stoic expression from years of hiding his feelings behind his white lab coat. He knew that whatever was happening he had to be an unfaltering source of support for the family. "I have to tell you that your daughter has lost a lot of blood and we had to give her an emergency transfusion." Phyllis gasped at the doctor's words. "We almost lost her but, thankfully, your daughter pulled through." The doctor noted the wide-eyed distress on their faces and he put his hand on Louie's shoulder as he said reassuringly, "Don't worry Mr. Rosello, your daughter is going to be all right."

Several long seconds had passed when Louie remembered there was someone else. "What about . . . the baby?" he blurted out.

"Oh yes, I apologize, the baby," The doctor cleared his throat as he continued. "Mr. Rosello, unfortunately the baby was breech, and to further complicate matters, the umbilical cord was wrapped around her neck," the doctor explained.

Phyllis's held her breath, hand over her mouth and eyes filled with worry.

"We lost her heartbeat several times and quite honestly it was touch and go for a while. We performed an emergency caesarian section and were able to save her." The doctor smiled relieving them of their worst fears.

"Her?" Louie asked.

"Yes, a baby girl," the doctor answered.

"Is she . . . um, is she okay?"

"She's fine and perfectly healthy," he said patting Louie on the back. "She may be small but that is one tough and determined little girl you have there sir! Congratulations, Grandma and Grandpa. Now if you'll excuse me, I have some other patients to attend to."

"Yes, of course, doctor, thank you!" Phyllis said as she hugged him. She turned to her husband and excitedly told him she was going to find a pay phone to call home and let their other three children know that Dorothy was okay.

Louie watched as Phyllis walked down the hall to the pay phone. Once she disappeared from sight he sat down, letting his heavy head fall into his hands. He had been strong for his wife during the entire ordeal, and as he sat there by himself, he broke down at the thought of almost losing his daughter. His body shook from his silent sobbing and it took him several moments before he could compose himself. He sat up, wiped his face, and decided to take a walk around the hospital to calm his nerves. He turned down a corridor and, unbeknownst to him, he walked in the direction of the nursery.

He was carrying a heavy burden and was in deep thought when he came up to an area of windows with happy spectators smiling, pointing and peering in through the glass as the pediatric nurse lifted the various babies for viewing. He was planning to walk past but instead he stopped to look and was drawn to a tiny little baby in a clear plastic bassinette in the corner. She was swaddled in a pink and blue blanket with a pink knitted hat on her tiny head. The postcard sign above her head read *"Girl Rosello, 5lbs, 9oz, 17in."* He stood there and stared at the baby for a moment. No one paid any attention to him or the tiny baby girl in the corner.

Eventually everyone dispersed and Louie was standing there alone when the nurse behind the glass spotted him peering in. She motioned for him to come in through the side doorway. Louie looked around and pointed to himself as if to say, "Who, me?" She smiled at him and nodded. Hesitantly, he walked through the doorway into an area with a sofa and a couple of rocking chairs. The nurse came in from the other room to greet him. Her name tag read Danielle.

"I've been doing this for a very long time and I can tell you are a new grandfather. Baby Rosello? Am I right?" Danielle said with a cheerful smile.

"Yes, but—"

"Wait right here!" she interrupted as she rushed back into the area where the babies were.

After a few minutes she came back into the baby visiting area with a little bundle in her arms. "Now don't be nervous," Danielle said reassuringly to Louie, as she transferred the tiny baby to his arms and he awkwardly fumbled with the handoff. "I'd like you to meet your new granddaughter," she happily announced with a wink before quietly leaving the room to give them some privacy.

It had been many years since Louie had held a baby in his arms, and he had almost forgotten how fragile they were. He was looking down at the sleeping baby when all of a sudden she squirmed. He loosened and opened the receiving blanket, allowing her to stretch out her legs and arms. He reached down to touch her tiny hand with the tip of his finger and in an instant she wrapped her entire hand around it with a strong grip. Her eyes fluttered a few times before she opened them completely and looked up at him with the biggest and roundest blue eyes he had ever seen.

Louie got choked up as he looked down at this precious little baby. As a tear escaped from his eye, it landed on the cheek of the baby, and he fell instantly in love with her. It was in that moment that he knew he could never give up this precious baby, his first grandchild, his granddaughter, for adoption. He leaned in closer and kissed her forehead. In his mind he already had the perfect name picked out for her, Rina, named after his mother who had passed away a few years previously.

Fortunately, they were able to back out of the adoption, much to the disappointment of the childless couple who were anxiously awaiting this opportunity.

So it was settled and with their four children fully grown, Louie and Phyllis were thrilled to have another little one around the house. They took care of Rina as if she were their own and they planned on helping Dorothy in raising her as long as it took, or at least until she was married or mature enough to take care of Rina on her own.

CHAPTER 11

RINA'S GRANDPARENTS HOUSE
APRIL 1966

Rina was three years old when Dorothy's best friend Nancy asked if she wanted to go to Boston with her. Nancy had just graduated from Monroe Community College and was moving to Boston for a job opportunity. Dorothy thought going to Boston might give her a chance to move forward or at least to move in a different direction. Her parents were on board, willing to take little Rina under their wide, protective wings.

Rina had become especially attached to Louie, who had, by that time, become her de facto father figure. Louie was given the nickname "Hun," Rina's name for him when she was learning how to talk.

"No, that's *paah-paah*," Phyllis said slowly, as she heavily emphasized the words.

"Hun!" Rina said as she shook her head back and forth as if saying no. "Hun! Hun!" she said again in her little voice. No matter how many times they repeated "Papa" Rina would say, "Hun."

At first Louie had scoffed at the notion of a little girl calling him that, however, they then realized that Rina was merely repeating what Phyllis had been calling him all this time, Hun, which was short for Honey. So Hun it became.

Whenever Hun was outside in his garden or tinkering in his workshop, Rina would always be there by his side, eager to learn and assist. Hun was an engineer for the water authority, and he recognized early on that Rina was a very bright and inquisitive child. She would ask intelligent questions, and he could almost see her analyzing the answers. If something didn't make sense to her, she was quick to question it.

At home, Rina and Hun loved listening to music together. There was one song in particular that was their favorite, Bing Crosby's "Let Me Call You Sweetheart." Rina would sit on Hun's lap and he would put his head down right next to hers as he sung the words. They swayed back and forth together, and when he sang, "In your eyes so blue," Hun would accentuate the word "blue" by singing it louder and more drawn out and Rina would giggle. Just the sound of Hun singing to her was soothing. It was a very happy place for the both of them.

One day Dorothy called to announce that she would be returning to Rochester to introduce her parents to her fiancé, a young soldier named Robert, whom she had met in Boston. Phyllis was in the kitchen when she heard the crunching sound of the gravel driveway as the car pulled in. She wiped her hands on her apron and called out for Hun and Rina.

As they rushed out of house, the wooden screen door slammed behind them. "Mom! Dad!" Dorothy squealed with excitement as she jumped out of the car that had barely come to a full stop. "Oh mom, I missed you so much!" Dorothy cried as she ran to her parents and into a wholehearted embrace with Phyllis.

Phyllis commented on how good Dorothy looked. Her blonde hair was casually styled in a high, teased beehive with a sweep of bangs and side spit curls. She was wearing a stylish belted, drop-waist dress and tan t-strap pumps. She looked happy and mature. Phyllis joyfully noted that Dorothy's time living in Boston obviously agreed with her.

A quiet Rina stood nervously, hiding behind Hun's legs when the drivers-side door of the car opened and a tall man with dark hair in a fancy Army uniform stepped out. "Come see mama, Rina," Dorothy said with her arms outstretched. Rina backed up, hiding further behind Hun. "It's okay sweetheart, go see your mommy," Hun said reassuringly as he gently pushed Rina toward her mother.

Dorothy was sure in that moment that she had done the right thing by leaving her young daughter in the care of her mother and father. She wondered if Rina would be able to understand that she had returned for good, and that everything was going to be right with them now that she had a good man in her life to help her. She pointed at the tall soldier, who bore an uncanny resemblance to Elvis, and said, "Rina, say hello to your new daddy!"

Robert reached down to greet his soon-to-be daughter. Most new fathers hold their daughters for the first time in the hospital and pass out cigars. But Dorothy's dark past would not allow her to dwell too much on that moment. She assumed the biological father was probably a few semesters shy from graduating from college by now and would loathe to admit his wrongdoing. At least with Robert, she could promise some stability to her confused little daughter, in hopes of making a happy new home.

Dorothy picked Rina up, and as she doted on her in an exaggerated fashion, Rina peeked beyond her mother with one eye. She couldn't take her gaze off the impressive soldier. Dorothy saw Rina staring at Robert and she handed the little girl to him stating, "Rina, this is your Daddy!"

"Take it easy, Dorothy, I think she is a bit overwhelmed with all the excitement at the moment," Robert said as he gently took Rina in his arms. "Hi Rina, I'm so happy to meet you," he said as he kissed the top of her head covered with fine blonde hair.

Rina was instantly comfortable in Robert's arms and she was entranced by the shiny medals, colorful ribbons and badges on Robert's uniform. She reached out to touch one of them but then hesitated. "It's okay, you can touch it," Robert said to her reassuringly.

Rina gently felt a shiny badge that looked like a silver cross with a bulls-eye in the middle and a wreath around the bottom of it. Rina looked up to him questioningly as she placed her hand underneath the shiny medal dangling from his jacket.

"That is my Expert Sharpshooter badge," Robert said. "It's for my accomplishment of the highest achievement in marksmanship . . . or I should say for my aim in shooting guns," he clarified with a laugh, in his attempt to explain it so that Rina could understand. Her eyes widened with interest and, as she was a curious child, a conversation ensued. "What's this one?" she questioned as she pointed at each of his various badges, and he patiently answered all her questions.

Dorothy had her head resting on Roberts' arm and she was blissfully looking up at the two of them. They looked like a natural family and Dorothy's parents were delighted that after everything Dorothy had been through she had finally found a wonderful man. Hun really liked Robert and had already given his blessing for him to marry his daughter and adopt Rina. Hun looked over at the three of them together and smiled. He was very pleased in knowing that his little sweetheart was going to have a father and a wonderful new life.

Robert had orders to head to Vietnam in a few days. The plan was for Dorothy to stay with her parents for the six months he was going to be overseas, giving her time not only to plan the wedding, but also to have some time to reconnect with Rina as they all agreed the change might be a bit traumatic for her.

Dorothy and Robert kept in contact faithfully through letters over the next several months, and Robert always included a short note to Rina also. Rina was too young to read but she would bring her notes to Hun and he would read them to her. They all did very well at preparing Rina for her new family life and she was adapting to her mother and the idea of having Robert as her father.

"Mommy! Daddy said he is sending me a surprise!" Rina exclaimed happily as she ran to Dorothy, in her hand the letter from Robert that Hun had just read to her.

"That is very exciting Rina, we'll be sure to look out for the package, but please be patient as it is coming from Vietnam, which is far away, so it may take a while," Dorothy explained to Rina. She laughed to herself as she thought that Robert was going to be home in five weeks and that he might make it back home before the package did.

On a Sunday afternoon three weeks later, the phone rang and Hun answered it. "Dorothy, it's for you!" he yelled to Dorothy from the kitchen. It was Virginia, Dorothy's soon to be mother-in-law, calling from Boston.

With the wedding so close, Dorothy was expecting Ginny to call to confirm all the arrangements and their hotel accommodations. "Hi Mom!" Dorothy said into the phone with excitement. "You are all set with your reservations at the . . ." Dorothy paused, "Mom, what is wrong? Why are you crying?" There was a brief pause followed by a deafening scream. Dorothy dropped the phone. She fell against the wall and slowly slid down until she reached the floor where she buried her head in her knees and let out an agonizing wail.

Louie and Phyllis heard the commotion and went running into the kitchen with Rina just a few steps behind them. Rina was frightened at the sight as she stood frozen in the doorway staring wide-eyed at her mother on the floor in hysterics.

"Dorothy, what is it? What's wrong?" Louie asked, and after he was unable to get a response from his distraught daughter, he picked up the receiver that was dangling by its cord from the wall mounted phone. "Ginny? Ginny are you there? It's Louie. What on earth is going on?" he said, his voice quavering.

Louie stood there silently listening for a few seconds when sadness filled his eyes and he raised his hand up to his forehead. "Dear Lord, no!" Louie said when he spoke. "I am so very sorry Ginny. Please give our condolences to Joe as well." He paused as he listened before he spoke again. "Yes . . . okay . . . we'll be in touch." He said as he softly hung up the phone and shook his head as he covered his eyes with his hands.

Dorothy, overcome by emotion, was unable to speak, and Hun was clearly anguished. "What is it, Louie? What has happened?" a worried Phyllis asked.

"It's Robert," he said as he hung his head. "The plane he was on was shot down over the jungle in Vietnam." Phyllis gasped as she covered her mouth in disbelief. "It went down in hostile territory with his entire platoon aboard, and they don't think there are any survivors," Hun said as tears fell from his eyes. Dorothy cried out again in utter pain as she heard her father repeat the horrifying news they had just received.

Rina looked intently at them and everything that was happening without truly understanding what it all meant. She didn't know yet that her daddy wasn't going to be coming home after all.

Three days later a package arrived from Vietnam addressed to Rina from Sergeant Robert Karasinski. Inside was a note that read;

> *Dear Rina,*
>
> *I think of you every day. I'll be home soon and I can't wait to see you and your mommy. I love you both so much and I am looking forward to the happy life we are going to have together. I have a picture of you both in my pocket at all times and it is the only thing that keeps me going over here. You are a very special little girl. I could see it in your eyes the moment I met you and I am so happy and proud to be your daddy. I had this gift made especially for you, my little girl, and I hope you will cherish it forever.*
>
> *Love,*
> *Daddy*

Inside the box was a handmade porcelain doll, a young Vietnamese girl. Its face was expertly hand painted and it was dressed in a traditional Vietnamese Áo dài made of red and gold silk. The card at the bottom of the box read: "This porcelain collectible doll has been carefully handmade for Rina by Vietnamese Doll Master, Hoang Kim."

* * *

At the full military service in honor of Robert, Rina, her mother and grandparents sat in the front pew of the church as the priest delivered the eulogy. Rina glanced over at the American flag-draped coffin on which was a large wood-framed photograph of Robert in his uniform. Her eyes were drawn to the shiny object that was hanging from the corner of the frame. It was a wide purple ribbon with white stripes down both sides. Dangling from the ribbon was a purple heart with a gold border and in the center it had the profile of General George Washington.

The congregation sang "Amazing Grace" in unison as the coffin was being led out of the church by eight soldier pallbearers in full army dress uniforms. Directly following the coffin were Robert's parents and Dorothy. Robert's mother Virginia was so devastated by the loss of her only son that she had to be held up with interlocked arms by her husband on one side and Dorothy on the other. Behind them were Rina and her grandparents. Rina was despondent as she held tightly onto Hun's hand and they walked slowly down the aisle of the church. She looked up with wide eyes at all the sad people standing in the pews looking down at her. She had never seen so much sadness, and as the coffin passed, people bowed their heads, many in tears. Without knowing the true dynamics of their family most people directed sympathetic eyes towards Rina as they looked at this little girl who would grow up without a father.

At the gravesite Rina sat next to her mother with Hun on the other side. Seated next to Dorothy was Robert's mother Virginia. Virginia was dressed in all black with a black hat that had a short-netted veil covering her face. The priest asked everyone to bow their heads as he said the final prayer, "O God, by whose mercy the faithful departed finds rest, look kindly on your departed soldier Robert who gave his life in the service of his country."

Once the prayer was finished, two soldiers lifted the flag off the coffin and began the flag folding ceremony. Wearing pure white gloves they meticulously and solemnly made the folds of the flag, each one with its own special meaning. After the thirteenth and final fold was neatly tucked in and smoothed out, one of the soldiers approached Virginia and bent down. "On behalf of the President of the United States, we thank your son for his service," he said as he handed her the triangular shaped flag with the stars uppermost.

The Army Commanding Officer in charge of the military service stepped up and asked everyone to rise as he initiated the rifle volley. The seven soldiers lined up with their rifles taking aim over the casket and they fired into the sky. The blast startled Rina, causing her to jump. She held her hands over her ears as the second and third rounds were fired. She flinched with every blast until the soldiers completed their three rounds for the twenty-one-gun salute. They lowered their rifles and stood there in silence as another soldier with a trumpet lifted his instrument and began to play "Taps," the traditional military last call of the day.

CHAPTER 12

RINA'S GRANDPARENT'S HOUSE MAY 1971

L ife went on and throughout those years Rina and Dorothy continued to live with Louie and Phyllis as Dorothy tried to move on with her life. Dorothy was very attractive and there was no shortage of young male suitors. Sadly, though, it seemed that any time she would meet a guy she liked, as soon as she let him know about Rina, he would become distant and eventually stop calling her. Dorothy already harbored resentment towards Rina for the way she was conceived and, with Rina putting a damper on her love life, her resentment continued to grow. It was obvious that Dorothy felt burdened by her daughter and now this was just another reason why Dorothy couldn't seem to show real love or affection towards Rina. Luckily, living with Louie and Phyllis helped keep Dorothy in check where Rina was concerned.

As the years passed, Dorothy's sister and her two older brothers had all married and moved away to Arizona. It was just before Rina was going into 4th grade when her grandparents retired, announcing that they were moving to Arizona to escape the winters and to be with the rest of their children. They wanted Rina and her mother to come with them too, but Dorothy had become friends with a couple of other single mothers and she wouldn't even consider leaving.

One night while Rina was in bed she overheard her grandparents and her mother arguing downstairs. She climbed out of bed and cracked open the door, putting her ear up to it so she could better hear what was being said.

"Dorothy, if you don't want to come with us, that is fine, but please, you have to let us take Rina!" she heard Hun say.

"No, she's my daughter and she's staying with me!" Dorothy responded firmly

"Don't you want her to be able to grow up surrounded by her family and her cousins?" Hun said, trying to appeal to her nobler motives.

"I am her family and no, you can't take her! She is staying with me. She is my daughter and there is nothing you can say or do to change my mind!" Dorothy stubbornly insisted.

"But you don't even have a job. How will you support yourself and take care of her?" Hun argued.

"I'll get on welfare. My girlfriends are on it and everything is taken care of. They even give you food stamps if you have children." Dorothy said, sarcastically adding, "Don't worry about your precious little Rina, Dad, she will be just fine."

Knowing he was fighting a losing battle at this point, Hun let it go for the moment, but he planned to hire a lawyer and fight Dorothy for custody once they got to Arizona.

The day Rina's grandparents packed up the van and left for Arizona was the worst day of her young life. They were loading in the last of the boxes when Rina looked over at Hun. She had never before seen him look so sad. Hun sensed Rina looking his way and he quickly wiped away a tear.

"Come here my sweetheart," he said as he held her little hand in his and walked her over to the front porch swing. They both sat silently for a moment as Hun slowly swung them back and forth with one foot. "Rina," Hun said gently when he spoke, "I want you to know that I really want to take you with us, but I can't right now."

"Why?" she said as the tears began to roll down her face.

"I don't know how to explain it, but you must know that I won't give up. I will fight to get you back with us someday."

"Hun, please don't leave me!" Rina said as she began to cry harder.

Hun was struggling to hold back his own tears and his overwhelming heartache. He rubbed his thumb across her cheek, wiping away a tear. "I don't want to leave you Rina," Hun said as he felt a huge lump in his throat.

"Then why do you have to go?"

"I know you don't understand any of this right now but someday you will. Look, I have a little gift for you," he said as he reached into his jacket and pulled out a small round jewelry box with little pink roses on it. "I want you to have this as a reminder of me. I also want you to know that I will always be thinking of you." He gently lifted the gold-rimmed lid of the fine porcelain piece. The underneath was lined in pink velvet and it had a gold turnkey. Hun carefully wound the key, and as the soothing sound of the familiar melody played, Hun set it on the seat in between them and he began to hum along.

She knew the melody very well, it was their favorite song, "Let Me Call You Sweetheart." As the music played it began fast and then slowed down, slower and slower until it eventually stopped. Rina looked down at the tiny little music box and then up to Hun. She was still sobbing as Hun pulled her into him and held her close to his chest. "Any time you need me, just turn the key to this and, as it plays our song, know that I love you and you will always be my little sweetheart," he said as he kissed her on the forehead.

"I love you Hun," Rina said, trying to catch her breath.

"I love you too. Please be good for your mom," he said softly, his voice cracking, as he stood up and turned to walk away.

Phyllis had already said her goodbyes and was waiting patiently in the moving van as Hun walked over and hopped up into the cab. He turned the key in the ignition and the truck revved up. Hun kept his eyes on Rina as he carefully backed the truck out of the driveway. There she stood on the step, frozen, with her little music box in her hand. Rina stared at Hun the entire time, her big eyes red and puffy from flowing tears. Hun stopped in the street and rolled down the window. "I will be back for you!" he said as he blew her a kiss.

He pulled away from the house and was driving slowly down the street when he looked in the rear-view mirror and saw Rina chasing after the van. Her little legs were running as fast as they could, and she was crying hysterically as she called out, "No! Hun! Noooooo!!!!!! Please don't go, come back! Come baaaaack!!!!!!" she bawled. It was in that moment that Louie could feel his heart break into a million pieces.

Rina ran after the van for several blocks until she couldn't run anymore and she collapsed in a heap on the street.

CHAPTER 13

RINA'S OFFICE
JULY 1991

After a sleepless night, Rina arrived at work early, anxious to get busy on her new case. She was at the coffee maker in the small kitchen area of the office when Lynn came in and grabbed a Styrofoam cup from the counter.

"Good morning Rina, are you feeling better today?" Lynn asked politely as she shook the sugar packet before she tore it open and poured it into her cup.

Rina was absently twirling the stir stick in her coffee cup as she thought back to the whirlwind events of the day before. She was deep in thought about her new case and her memory of the young victims, her recognition of the defendant, and worst of all, her disclosure about her past to Steve. "I'm okay, Lynn," she replied simply, without looking up.

Not wanting to talk about anything more, Rina was appreciative of Lynn knowing her well enough to not engage in a conversation or question her any further. With coffee in hand, the ladies quietly headed towards their desks to begin their workday.

"Here's your mail, Rina," Lynn said, switching into work mode as she passed a handful of envelopes to Rina. Rina sifted through her mail before picking up her coffee cup and turning towards her office. Once inside she set her coffee and mail down on her large wooden desk before walking over to the window. She opened the vertical blinds letting the natural, albeit gloomy, light in before she went back to her desk and sat down. She took a sip of her coffee and looked over the edge of the cup at the manila folders relating to her new case stacked up in front of her. She picked up the file on Carmella Candelario and shuddered at the thought that she knew the man responsible for killing her all those years ago. She thought back and wished she could have done something, anything at all that might have led to his capture and spared those girls a gruesome death. But what could she have done? After all, she was just a young girl at the time when Carmella was killed.

Rina carefully turned the page in the report and began to read the specifics. It was eerie as she noted all the similarities that her own life had to Carmella's. Their mothers were on welfare, they were Catholic, and even more coincidental was the fact that they both had double initials. The unnerving thought crossed Rina's mind again that she could have been a potential target.

She turned her thoughts back to reading the file. It was around 5:00 pm on November 16, 1971, when Carmella hadn't returned home yet from going to the drug store a couple of blocks away. About two hours had passed when the Rochester Police Department recorded receiving a call regarding a missing girl. A large-scale search ensued and police officers conducted a door-to-door search of the entire neighborhood. Unfortunately, the police found only one witness who reported seeing a young girl who looked like Carmella climb into a car near the drugstore.

Rina shook her head as she read the report. She knew that while the police were searching for Carmella, it was already too late. Rina knew how this story ended before she even read it. She knew that an hour earlier, during rush hour traffic on Interstate 490, as cars were traveling from downtown Rochester, a girl matching Carmella's description was seen near the Churchville exit attempting to escape from her killer.

As Rina continued scanning the file she couldn't help but feel sad that people were so consumed with their own thoughts and agendas that they would pass by a young girl and her desperate need for help. The newspaper headlines across the nation were brutally critical of the incident and of those individuals that saw Carmella but did nothing. Some even had excuses, citing that they thought it was none of their business, a family squabble or maybe a father letting his daughter out to relieve herself.

Although Rina had a hard time comprehending how something like this could happen in broad daylight, especially during the busiest time of the afternoon, she recalled a thesis she wrote in law school about a case from 1964 in which a twenty-nine-year-old woman was raped and stabbed to death in front of her apartment. What was unique about that case was that it was believed that more than thirty people had either seen or heard the attack, yet no one stepped in to help or call the police. It was very hard for Rina to imagine how anyone could not help another person in desperate need, however, she was aware that it was far more common than most people knew.

Rina remembered from her research that psychologists believe there are two contributing factors to crowd apathy, also known as the bystander effect. One is a perceived distribution of the responsibility and the other is social influence, wherein people in a group act as those around them do. This was the most common, especially in gang rapes or when a rape happens with only one person committing the crime, while others watch. It was what she imagined happened to her mother. How could it be that not one of those boys stepped in and stopped it from happening? Maybe they felt they had to act in a socially acceptable way in front of their friends, or perhaps they just felt the situation was ambiguous and Dorothy wanted to have sex.

Unfortunately for Carmella, no one stopped that day or got off at the nearest exit and called for help and sadly, two days after she went missing, her brutally battered body was discovered by a couple of teenage boys who were out riding their bikes.

The final document in the case file was the autopsy report that stated Carmella was raped and strangled to death with what appeared to have been a smooth object, believed to be a belt. She had eaten within two hours of her death and the report also noted that white cat hair was found on her clothing. In addition, it was also determined that she was beaten severely, evidenced by the bruises and scratches that covered her little body along with a fracture to her skull.

Rina finished reading the details on the abduction, rape, and murder of Carmella Candelario and it disturbed her to think that someone could do that to another person let alone a small defenseless young girl who weighted barely sixty-five pounds. Somberly, she moved aside the papers exposing the gruesome crime scene photos, and she spread them out as if she were trying to put the pieces of a puzzle together. In the center was the photo of Carmella's body in the brown foliage up against a boulder wearing nothing but a sweater.

The sweater. The one and only piece of solid evidence that tied the defendant to the crime. It was a single fingerprint on the button of Carmella's sweater that came up when the defendant was arrested for an unrelated crime he committed in California, a driving while intoxicated charge.

But Rina knew that Thomas Cugino was a legend and he would be shrewd in his defense. She recalled a notorious case from the previous year where a prominent local doctor was accused of giving his wife a fatal dose of morphine. Even though the dosage given was four times the amount the doctor claimed, Thomas Cugino was able to get the one key piece of evidence, the blood test, thrown out, citing that it was not properly protected at the hospital and therefore could have been tampered with. The doctor never went to trial, and when he married the woman he was having an affair with and moved away, the community was outraged, believing that he got away with murder.

Rina was very aware of Thomas Cugino's triumphs in the courtroom and especially for him winning cases with far more evidence against his clients. However, she could not allow that to get inside her head, she needed to focus. She put the photos aside and reached for another folder that held the records that were part of the police investigation. The first page was the list of suspects, and Rina noted that the police focused their investigation on acquaintances of Carmella's. This was not surprising as it was the typical procedure since most child molesters are either related or known to their victims.

Early in the investigation, the report showed that since the only witness who came forward was a woman who said it appeared that Carmella got into the car willingly, the police believed that Carmella knew her killer.

Exhausted, Rina stood up, put her hands on her hips and leaned backwards for a stretch. The rain had stopped and the sun was shining now. She walked over to the window, peered out and tried to put her thoughts together. She looked down at the street below and noticed all sorts of people walking around. It made her wonder if any of them witnessed a crime happening right now in front of them, would they do anything? Or would they be so caught up in their own worlds and concern for themselves that they would ignore someone's obvious cries for help? Perhaps they would assume that someone else would step in to assist.

Rina looked away, and as she turned back to her desk, out of the corner of her eye she caught the movement of some workers on scaffolding across the street. They were smoothing out the creases of the new billboard sign they had just changed. She swung back around to watch them for a moment as they were putting up what was recognizably a popular cigarette advertisement that used a handsome man with a mustache, in a cowboy hat and with a cigarette in his hand. This triggered a memory of when she had seen a much different billboard a long time ago. It was the billboard that the police used to offer a reward in an attempt to get the public to contact them regarding any information on the murder of Carmella Candelario.

CHAPTER 14

CITY OF ROCHESTER
DECEMBER 1971

Rina was only eight years old at the time, but she remembered the day that she first saw the name, Carmella Candelario. It was a typical day just like any other, but a day when Rina's life would be forever changed in more ways than one.

It was soon after her grandparents left for Arizona in 1971 when Rina and her mother moved to the city. With the help of her mother's new friends and their children who were close to Rina's age, she adjusted to her new life. Rina was especially happy that her mother allowed her to keep a stray cat that followed her home from school one day, with the strict understanding that Rina was to take care of it, feed it and clean out the litter box. The city streets were fairly safe in the early 70s and it wasn't uncommon for parents to allow their children to walk the streets alone. As an only child, Rina often walked the short distance to school, to the corner store to pick up groceries for her mother or to Laura's, her mother's friend's house, which was only a few blocks away.

Dorothy sometimes worked part-time at a bar, and when she wasn't at work, she would often be at Laura's. Rina was instructed that if she came home from school and her mother wasn't there, then she was to walk over to Laura's house. It was a cold day in early December 1971, on her walk to Laura's, when Rina saw a billboard that read, *"Who killed Carmella Candelario? Be a secret witness, no clue is too small."* Her young mind was just starting to grapple with what that had meant, but she knew that it had something to do with a young girl about her age who had disappeared and was later found raped and murdered.

That past weekend, Laura had just moved into a new house and Lisa, another one of Dorothy's friends, and their kids, were all there helping Laura move in. The kids did the best they could by carrying some of the furnishings, boxes and smaller furniture pieces from the U-Haul moving van into the house. Rina was mystified by the house when she compared it to the small apartment she and her mother had been living in. It had a fenced-in yard, an enclosed front porch, two bathrooms, four bedrooms and a walk-in closet—something unique that the kids were all excited about. The closet connected the rooms of Laura's two boys, Bobby and Alex.

Laura was inside unpacking when Bobby and Alex greeted Rina at the gate on the side of the house. "Hi, Rina! My mom wants us to stay outside and wait for Uncle Frank to get here."

"Uncle Frank?" Rina questioned as this was the first she had heard of him.

"Yes, he is coming over to see the new house and help my mom move around some furniture."

Rina shrugged and went off to play in the yard. A short time later, Uncle Frank, a man of average height and slightly overweight in his midsection, appeared. The man held a plant in one hand and a box of ice cream sandwiches in the other as the boys ran up to the fence gate to greet him.

"Uncle Frank! Uncle Frank is here!" they chimed together. It didn't take long for them to notice the ice cream in his one hand. They threw open the gate to let him in.

"Hi boys!" Uncle Frank said as he gave Alex a pat on the back. His long yellowish-gray hair was receding, somewhat greasy, and it hung all to one side as if he were trying to cover up the thinning on the top of his head. His face was partially hidden behind a mustache and beard. He was a hairy man with thick eyebrows and long hairs coming out of his nose and up from his chest over his unbuttoned collared shirt. He looked over at Rina out of the corner of his eye as he made his way past the excited boys. "Who do we have here? Is this little cutie a friend of yours, boys?" The man asked.

"That's Rina, she's Dorothy's daughter," Bobby said, waving his hand as if to say no big deal. "Come on in, my mom is in the kitchen." Bobby continued. He gripped Uncle Frank's arm and led him into the kitchen where Laura was still unpacking.

"Hi Frank. So happy to see you," Laura said as she put a plate in the sink and went over to him give him a hug. He handed her the plant and ice cream sandwiches as the boys eyed the box as it moved, like dogs following a bone.

"Thank you, Frank. That is very nice of you. The kids can have these after dinner."

"You're welcome, and I tried to get here sooner but I had to take care of something at work."

"Don't mention it. I'm just thankful you are here as I really need some help moving around some of the furniture."

Bobby and Alex were anxious to give the man a tour of their new house and Rina was quick to jump on board in calling him Uncle Frank and sharing in the excitement along with the boys.

"Hey, Uncle Frank, you've got to see the upstairs!" Bobby shouted out as he ran toward the stairs with Alex in tow.

"Come on Uncle Frank," Rina said. She grabbed his hand and tugged him toward the stairs. "We'll give you a tour."

"I'd love to see the rest of the house." Uncle Frank said as he took her hand and followed Rina, who was behind the boys as they all stomped up the stairs in single file.

They had toured the oversized bathroom which had enough floor space to conduct a small concert. Frank thought that it was unnecessary to have so much space, but raising two young boys and a teenage girl was not something that he had ever tried to do. Then they viewed the master bedroom where the boys' mother would sleep. "Look, Uncle Frank, Laura lets us jump on the beds. It's so much fun! Wheeeeee!!" Rina squealed in delight.

Uncle Frank's eyes became glazed over as he watched her as if he were in a trance. He stared as, with every movement, her flowy skirt lifted exposing her little pink panties. *Tuesday. It's Tuesday and her panties say Tuesday on them,* he thought as his head bobbed up and down with her every move.

When the boys tried to usher Uncle Frank onward, he shook off the spell he was under and turned to leave. Rina jumped off the bed and pushed her way through them, not wanting to be left behind. She practically ran down the hallway to Alex's room trying to beat them there. Once in Alex's room, Uncle Frank complimented him on his choice of paint color—a stark electric blue.

Rina was feeling a bit jealous and left out. She knew there was no way she would have the opportunity to invite Uncle Frank or anybody else over to her apartment and give them a tour. There wasn't enough room for that. Here, at Laura's house, she wanted to be a part of all the excitement, so she blurted out, "Uncle Frank, there is one more thing to show you, it is the coolest part of the whole house. You've got to see it!"

"That sounds great Rina. Why don't you lead the way?" Uncle Frank said.

The closet was like a dark cave, and Rina and the boys found it to be a fun hiding spot. Rina was the first to go into the closet. "Come in, Uncle Frank, you have to see how cool this is," she exclaimed.

Uncle Frank followed her in while Alex stood in the doorway.

Rina quickly realized that it wasn't quite as big as she thought with an adult in there. Uncle Frank bent down and whispered in Rina's ear that this was the coolest closet he had ever seen and that she was the best tour guide. She looked up at him with her big eyes shining and feeling proud, she smiled sweetly at him.

Uncle Frank was breathing heavily, as though he had just finished a race. He was unusually close to her. She could feel the heat emanating from his sweaty body, which made her uncomfortable. Something frightened Rina, and in a panic, she tried to push past him, but he was blocking the doorway. She found herself helplessly pinned against the corner in the closet when Uncle Frank bent down and roughly pressed his lips against hers. She was defenseless. She couldn't move or even breathe.

His wet, heavy body was crushing her and his skin smelled stale and sour. She felt sick to her stomach. She couldn't understand why a grown man was being so rough with her. He pried open her lips with his repulsive wet tongue and stuck it into her mouth. His foul breath filled the air between them and she felt like she was about to faint when he reached up under her skirt for her Tuesday panties. She tried to wiggle free. She tried to kick him off her, but she couldn't move or even scream. Suddenly, Alex yelled out, "Ewwww, gross! They're *kissing!*"

Then, just as quickly as it began, it stopped. It was as if he was spooked back into reality by the sound of Alex's voice. As soon as he released his hold on her, Rina scooted as fast as she could past him and bolted down the stairs to safety. She sat quietly in the kitchen, and the look on her face was one of utter shock. Even after Frank left and Laura asked if she was okay, she just nodded and sat there silently until her mother came to pick her up.

Back at home, Rina told her mom that she had met Uncle Frank earlier and she didn't like him. All Dorothy said was that she had better be nice to him because he was a good friend to them. Rina didn't want to get into trouble with her mother, so she dropped it. Ever since Rina's grandparents had moved to Arizona, Dorothy was impatient and angry. Most of it was aimed at her young daughter who just seemed unable to do anything to please her.

Sometimes it wasn't what her mother said but more the look of disappointment and annoyance that was clearly visible on her face.

CHAPTER 15

CITY OF ROCHESTER
JANUARY 1972

Bert was Dorothy's boyfriend who she had been dating for several months. He was a middle-aged man, and although he was several years older than Dorothy, he was charming, physically fit and energetic. Of all the boyfriends Rina's mother had in the past, Bert was by far the nicest and most attentive. It was Saturday morning and Rina was watching cartoons while eating a bowl of cereal when her mother came bursting out of her bedroom.

"Rina!" Dorothy yelled, "Turn down that TV!" Startled by the sudden outburst, Rina jumped, spilling her cereal bowl filled with milk all over the couch.

"What the hell is wrong with you? You are so clumsy!" Her mother said as she grabbed Rina by the hair and dragged her into the kitchen. She roughly shoved her face into the paper towels that were hanging between the arms of the plastic holder under the cabinet, "Now grab those and clean up the mess you've made before Bert wakes up!" she hissed between her clenched teeth.

Awakened by the commotion, Bert emerged from the bedroom wearing only jeans and an unbuckled belt, "Dotty, what is going on?" he asked.

Dorothy quickly changed her tune as she replied to Bert lovingly, "I'm so sorry darling. Rina didn't mean to wake you!" Dorothy had released her hold from Rina's hair before he could see and stroked her head like she would that of a dog's. She tore off a few paper towels from the holder and handed them to Rina, "here you are, now please be a good girl and go clean up your mess for mommy," she said sweetly.

In fear of her mother's tirade after Bert left, Rina took the paper towels and held back her tears. However, her head was throbbing where a large clump of hair was pulled from her scalp, and she unconsciously rubbed the spot as she walked past Bert on her way to the living room.

Bert bent down and lifted her chin, "Are you okay?"

"Yes, I'm okay and I'm sorry I woke you up," she replied nervously.

"It's okay, you didn't wake me," he said as he reached into the pocket of his dungarees and pulled out a quarter. "Here, why don't you go get yourself some candy at the corner store?"

With her head held low, she peeked over at her mother looking for a sign of approval.

"It's okay, take it," Bert insisted.

She reached out and reluctantly took the coin. "Thank you," she said softly.

A short time later, a quarter in hand, Rina entered the store and put the coin on the counter and greeted the store owner. "Hi, Mr. Jim, I've got money for candy!" she said with excitement.

"Wow, you sure do!" he said as he picked it up and inspected it as if it were a gemstone. "Hmmm," he said as he looked closely at the back then over to the front "1971, that's a nice shiny new quarter that you have here Rina!" he said and smiled down at her. "What's it going to be for you, Miss Moneybags?"

Rina giggled. She wanted to get the most for her money, so she chose twenty-five Tootsie Rolls that were a penny each.

"Twenty-Five Tootsie Rolls coming right up! "One, two, three . . ." he slowly and dramatically counted them before placing them in a small brown paper bag as Rina bounced up and down in anticipation. "Twenty-four, twenty-five . . . and one more for good luck!" he said as he put the twenty-sixth Tootsie Roll in the bag.

"Wow, thanks!" she said. Jim waved to Rina as the bell on the door jingled.

On her way home from the store, Rina reached into the bag to eat one of her Tootsie Rolls. She was skipping along and didn't notice a car on the opposite side of the street that was driving slowly as it passed. The car drove down a couple of blocks and turned around to come back. It stopped next to her and an older man inside waved at her to come over. She looked from side to side to see if he was waving to someone else but she realized it was her.

"Excuse me, little girl," he said. "I'm looking for my lost kitten. Do you think you could help me find her?"

"Geez mister, I don't know," she said with hesitation.

"I'm very worried. She's never been outside by herself and she must be really scared," he said with seemingly genuine concern.

"Oh no, poor kitty! Okay, I'll help you find your cat," she said as she stepped off the curb and towards the car. "What does she look like?" she asked as she reached for the door handle. Just as she was about to open the door, she looked up and saw her mother down the street waving for her.

"I'm sorry sir, but that's my mom and I gotta go. Good luck finding your cat," she said as she ran off towards home.

Rina hurried home and dashed up the five steps leading to the apartment door where her mother greeted her. "Bert went to Carrols to get us all some lunch and he'll be back any minute now so you better get washed up."

"Carrols? Really!" Rina said with excitement, and with the thought of cheeseburgers, french fries and soda in mind, she happily sprinted towards the bathroom. She was overjoyed as they never ate at fast food places since their food stamps would not pay for it, and they couldn't afford such an extravagance otherwise.

An hour later as Rina, Dorothy and Bert were eating their cheeseburgers at the kitchen table, Dorothy asked Rina about the stranger she was talking to earlier. "Who were you talking to in that car today?" Dorothy blurted out.

Rina shoved a french fry in her mouth and took a sip of her soda from the yellow and red striped straw. Bert stopped chewing and looked up from his burger as Rina shrugged her shoulders.

"Rina, answer your mother!"

"Huh?" Rina replied with a mouth full of food.

"Who were you talking to?" Bert asked firmly.

"Just a man who was looking for his lost kitten."

"Rina! You should *never* talk to strangers!" Bert scolded.

"But—but he just seemed really worried about his kitten, that's all," she said apologetically.

"Don't you ever do that again! Do you hear me?"

She nodded fearfully, her eyes wide.

"Now promise me that you will not talk to strangers!" Bert demanded.

"Okay, I promise."

Later that night, Rikki, Laura's older daughter, came over to babysit. Rina really liked when Rikki babysat because she would always let Rina stay up late to watch TV. Rikki was a lively sixteen-year-old with straight dark hair cut in a popular shag style. She also liked to babysit Rina because she had a crush on Eric, the good-looking fireman who lived in the small studio apartment behind Dorothy's. Rina knew Eric the fireman as he not only lived in her building but often visited the school in uniform to talk to the class about fire safety and what to do if there was a fire.

Rikki always hoped for an opportunity to talk to Eric and tonight she got it. Eric was standing at the mailbox sorting through his mail when Rikki came through the gate and up the sidewalk. He had just finished work and still had on his uniform with his suspenders hanging down to his knees.

"Oh, hello there, Eric," she said, trying to sound surprised to see him.

"Hi, um . . ." he paused.

"Rikki!" She blurted out.

"Hi Rikki," Eric replied nonchalantly as he looked up, his head cocked and one eye closed.

"I'm babysitting Rina tonight. The exciting life of a single girl these days." Rikki said with a laugh and a heavy emphasis on the word single in her attempt to make sure that Eric knew she was available.

Sounding distracted, Eric replied, "That's nice, how is Rina doing?"

"She's good. I think we're going to make Jiffy Pop popcorn and stay up to watch TV tonight. 'Three Dog Night' is performing on Don Kirshner's Rock Concert show, you know."

"That sounds like fun. Well, I'd better get going." Eric said. "Tell Rina I said hello."

"Right on," Rikki said as she waved goodbye to him.

She floated through the front door, fanning herself with her hands. "What a hunk, I think I am in love," she said to Rina with a wink and a smile from ear to ear.

"Gross!" Rina said as she scrunched her nose.

Dorothy came out of the bathroom all dressed up, her long blonde hair feathered back in the latest style and her makeup nicely done. She was in a good mood when she greeted Rikki. "Rikki, I didn't hear you come in. I just want to say thank you, I really appreciate you watching Rina tonight. There's some macaroni and cheese for dinner, soda in the fridge and popcorn. Please help yourself to whatever else you want."

"Thanks, Dorothy, and no problem. Is it okay if Rina stays up a little later tonight to watch a show with me?"

"I guess that is okay as long as it isn't too late," she said just as she heard the toot of a horn out front. "That must be Bert, I'd better go. Thanks again Rikki, I'll see you later."

"No problem, have fun!" Rikki said as Dorothy pulled her purse strap over her shoulder and walked out the door.

Later, Rina was settled down in front of the TV as Rikki, at the stove, shook the pan back and forth over the flame, waiting for the heat to cause the foil on the top to rise. Once the popcorn had inflated the foil, Rikki turned off the stove and ripped open the top, exposing the kernels.

"Perfect timing!" Rikki said as she set the popcorn in the middle of the coffee table just as the show began. They dove right in as they watched the brief introduction, a cartoon character resembling the host who was holding a sign with the show name on it. The camera panned the audience of mostly females who were screaming and jumping up and down in excitement. The host announced the popular band and they ran out onto the stage, picked up their guitars and as they began to play one of their current hit songs, the crowd exploded with loud applause and squeals. Rikki jumped off the couch and got right up to the TV and kissed the screen. "Oh Rina! Isn't Cory just dreamy?" she said of the lead singer, falling back on the couch with her hand over her heart.

"Yuck!" Rina looked at her with disgust.

"Someday you'll be interested in boys," Rikki replied with a wink.

"No way! Boys are nasty!"

"That'll change, you'll see."

After a brief commercial break, the show came back on and the host announced that this next song was an overnight sensation and at the top of the Billboard charts. As soon as the guitarist began to strum the start of the familiar song, Rikki knew instantly it was "Shambala."

"Ahhhhhh!!! This is my *favorite* song, Rina!" Rikki yelled out as she lept up and fixed her gaze on the television screen, swaying back and forth to the music.

The beginning of the song began with a guitar intro before the lead singer sang out, *"Wash away my troubles, wash away my pain, wi-ith the rain in Sham-ba-la!"*

"Come on Rina," Rikki said, grasping Rina's hands and pulling her off the couch. "Dance with me."

As she sang along to the song, Rikki swung Rina's arms back and forth and they danced around the room.

Rina had heard the song on the radio, so she was familiar with it and she took Rikki by surprise when she lifted up her chin like a dog howling at the moon and sung out the chorus, "Ah, ooo, ooo, ooo, ooo, ooo!!! Yeah, yeah, yeah, yeah, yeah, yeah!"

Rikki burst out laughing at Rina's dramatic rendition. She was laughing so hard that she held her stomach and fell backward onto the couch.

Rina didn't know what was so funny, but she also chimed in with laughter. Rikki composed herself so that she could enjoy the rest of the song and they both continued to dance and sing along through the entire song. The band played a few more songs and, before they knew it, the show ended and the local news came on. "Okay my dear, all good things must come to an end."

"Awww man, it's over already?"

"Yes, I'm afraid so, and it's time for a little girl I know to go to bed," Rikki said.

Rina was heading towards her bedroom when she heard the newscaster on the television say, *"People across the nation are shocked tonight as more information is released regarding the rape and murder of ten-year-old Carmella Candelario."* Rina stopped in her tracks in front of the TV.

"Come on Rina, it's late, you'd better get going," Rikki said sternly.

"Wait, can I please watch this first?"

"Why on earth would you want to watch this? It's just the news, silly."

"Please, please, please?" Rina begged.

"Okay but only for a few more minutes," Rikki gave in, thinking Rina was just stalling.

The newscaster continued with the story, *"Authorities are still looking for help in finding the killer of Carmella Candelario whose body was found strangled and sexually assaulted in a ravine in the town of Churchville,"* the reporter said somberly. Behind him in the corner of the screen was a photo of a young girl with long dark hair, bangs and a big smile. It was a photo of Carmella Candelario, and it was the same photo that Rina had seen on the billboard.

"Oh my, that poor little girl, who could do something like that?" Rikki said sadly.

"What does sexually assaulted mean?" Rina asked.

"Rina, I don't know if you will understand this, but it means she was raped."

"Oh raped? You mean like my mom was raped?"

"Good Heavens, child, where on earth did you hear that from?" a shocked Rikki exclaimed.

"Your mom and Lisa. I heard them talking once and they said that they couldn't believe Dorothy was raped."

"You must have dreamt that from hearing all of this news coverage that has been on about Carmella Candelario," Rikki said, trying to lighten the conversation. "Speaking of dreaming, it's time for you to get to bed. Your mother will kill me if she comes home and you are still up. Now scoot along, missy." Rikki said as she playfully tapped Rina's bottom.

CHAPTER 16

RINA'S OFFICE &
HOME OF TRIAL WITNESS
AUGUST 1991

Rina had zoned out in front of her computer when the phone rang. She snapped out of her fog. It was Lynn.

"Rina, I've got Mr. Cugino on line two for you," she said.

"Thank you, please put him through," she put down the file and answered the call. "ADA Rosello speaking," she said as she pushed back her chair and spun around to look towards the window.

Rina's conversation with Thomas Cugino was cordial and professional. He had apologized for not being at the arraignment, and Rina explained that everything had gone off without a hitch and that they were out of the courtroom in fifteen minutes.

Before they discussed anything further, Rina began with her imminent disclosure. "Mr. Cugino, I'd like to inform you that the defendant is familiar to me from when I was a little girl. It was a brief acquaintance and a long time ago. I assure you that this in no way affects my ability to try this case," Rina stated.

"I am aware of this Ms. Rosello, as my client mentioned to me that he recognized you at the arraignment," Tom replied. "I am not concerned about it and I have no objection," he stated. He was not about to protest and risk getting a more seasoned ADA who would make him have to work harder. He was confident that Rina's age and inexperience was a better bet for him. Besides, her knowing the defendant as a child couldn't possibly implicate his client in any way in these crimes. In fact, Tom believed the fact that she knew him would more likely be to his advantage.

In closing, Thomas told her he was looking forward to meeting her in person at the pre-trial meeting with the judge that was scheduled for the following week and then he ended the call. *He sure is a smooth talker. I think I just may be in way over my head on this one.*

Rina went back to reviewing the case file of Whitney Walkowski before she left to interview Niki Gaezzer, the prosecution witness and childhood friend of Whitney Walkowski.

The rape and murder details in the case file for Whitney Walkowski were sadly like those in the file for Carmella Candelario. It was a cold and rainy April day in 1973 when Whitney's mother asked her to go to the corner store to pick up some groceries. The store was only three blocks away from her home, and it was a familiar path that Whitney walked often. The records noted that the store cashier told investigators that Whitney left around 5:15 pm with a heavy bag filled with milk, bread and tuna fish.

The next morning, the body of Whitney Walkowski was discovered by a dog at a rest area in Webster. She had been sexually assaulted before being strangled to death just as Carmella was. Rina pulled out the autopsy report, which revealed that Whitney was also strangled to death with a smooth object, again, presumed to be a belt. The report also revealed that the contents of Whitney's stomach showed that she had eaten custard within two hours of her death.

As Rina continued reading through the files, she noted that the lead investigator, Michael Sullivan, who was now deceased, had spent the days following the murder bringing in several men for questioning including a known sex offender living in the area. He was convinced that it was someone Whitney knew. In addition, Whitney's mother insisted that she would never accept a ride from someone she didn't know unless it was an authority figure, like a police officer or a fireman. With that in mind, investigator Sullivan focused on the possibility that the killer could have been someone that children felt they could trust. Hundreds of tips were received by the police, but unfortunately, none of them were useful in catching the killer at the time.

There was one piece of evidence that stood out to Rina, which she didn't think much of the first time she read it: The same white cat hair found on Whitney was also found on Carmella, so it was believed that the killer had a cat.

One of the witness accounts was from Niki. She was a friend of Whitney's who was walking with another friend just ahead of Whitney the day she disappeared. It was believed that Niki was the last person to see Whitney alive.

It was a twenty-minute ride from Rina's office downtown to the home of Niki Gaezzer in Henrietta, a suburb of Rochester. Rina arrived at the newly built colonial-style house right on time and flashed a wide smile as the door opened. She tried to project a warm, affable demeanor as she introduced herself to the thin woman with long brown wavy hair who was around Rina's own age. Niki's hazel eyes appeared apprehensive as she invited Rina in and waved her in the direction of the living room.

"Is this your baby?" Rina asked, instantly captivated by a framed picture that was positioned over the fireplace mantel, in which Niki and her husband, Chad, sat proudly with their baby daughter against a solid blue backdrop.

"Yes, she was only six months old in that picture." Niki perked up at the mention of her daughter.

"She is adorable! How old is she now?"

"Two." Worry replaced the joyful look on her face. "Well, and now, now that I have a little girl . . . you know . . . after what happened to Whitney."

"Why don't we take a seat so we can talk about it," Rina said. She knew that even though so much time had passed, painful memories could still be as fresh as the day they happened in one's mind.

After a few minutes of questions that were meant to put Niki at ease, Rina became more focused.

"I believe my assistant explained to you why I am here, is that correct?" Rina asked, her demeanor turning serious.

"She mentioned that the police caught the guy who killed Whitney after all these years, is that true?"

"Yes, it is, and I need you to be a witness at his trial."

"I have to be honest, I'm not really sure how I can help or how I feel about doing that," Niki replied, the reluctance evident in her voice.

"Listen, I truly understand how difficult it is to bring back these unpleasant memories."

"I don't think you truly understand how it was for us back then," Niki bowed her head in embarrassment over her impoverished childhood.

Rina paused for a moment contemplating whether she should divulge the details of her own life. "I understand more than you know. I grew up in the city too."

"You did?" Niki looked at her in disbelief.

"Yes. My mother was single and on welfare too. I was the same age as Whitney, and I remember hearing about what happened to her. I lived in fear of becoming a victim myself. I also have double initials."

"Really?" Niki said. She couldn't imagine that someone in Rina's position could have ever been poor. Niki had come a long way since living in the city. She had a husband, a baby, and a nice home, but she wasn't as polished and as successful as Rina. Still, knowing Rina could relate seemed to give her a sense of comfort in confiding in her.

"Yes, and I understand exactly how you feel. Now, I know it was a long time ago, but do you think you can tell me about that day?" Rina asked, hoping that Niki would want justice for her friend Whitney.

"I'll tell you that it was a day I'll never forget as long as I live," Niki said with an unblinking stare.

"Please, go on." Rina encouraged, gently touching the young woman's knee.

"Whitney and I were friends. We lived in the same neighborhood, went to the same school, and we attended the same church. I wouldn't say we were the best of friends but we got along pretty well." Niki recalled several times when she would see Whitney at the park near their houses.

"Do you remember the last time you saw her?" Rina asked.

"I do. It was in April 1973," Niki said with certainty.

"It was raining that day, wasn't it?"

"Yes. I believe it was."

"Tell me what else you remember."

"I remember seeing Whitney leaning up against a fence and I thought she must have just come from the store because she was trying to balance a couple bags of groceries. There was no one else with her. I thought about going to see if she needed help but it was raining, you know, so we just kept walking fast to get home," Niki said, seemingly ashamed.

"I understand," Rina said, sensing Niki's inner turmoil.

"That was the last time I saw her. I turned around again and she was gone."

"The police report stated that a minute or so later you saw what looked like Whitney in a Lincoln Continental near the place where you had just seen her walking?" Rina asked.

"That's right."

"Are you sure Whitney was the girl you saw in the car?"

"It was rainy, but yes, I believe it was her," Niki explained that she was about thirty yards from the car, and she could see a small figure that looked like Whitney in the front seat as the car drove away from her at a slower-than-normal pace.

"Do you remember what Whitney was wearing that day?"

Niki paused for a moment and looked up at the ceiling. "I want to say that it was a light pink raincoat? Yeah, I think that it was pink."

"Was the girl in the car wearing a pink jacket?"

"I believe so."

"Okay," Rina said as she pulled a photo out of her briefcase and slid it across the coffee table towards Niki. It was a photo of the pink jacket found at the scene where Whitney's body was found. It had a yellow numbered photo evidence maker next to it. "Does this look like the jacket you saw Whitney wearing that day?'

"Oh my God," Niki said with a gasp. "Yes, that's it! I remember now. Oh God, we should have waited for her to catch up," she said as she buried her face in her hands and cried.

"Mrs. Gaezzer, it isn't your fault. You were only ten years old and you had no way of knowing what was going to happen," Rina said as she slipped out of her professional persona for a moment. "Niki, is it okay if I call you that?"

Niki answered with a nod.

"Listen, I'm going to share something very personal with you," Rina said with a slight pause as Niki looked up, intrigued. "I too used to go to the corner store in my neighborhood all the time, all by myself. I remember hearing about Whitney's murder and I must tell you that I've often thought that what happened to her could have happened to me. That's why I need to make sure this guy spends the rest of his life in prison," Rina said. "But I am going to need your help to do that."

"Okay, what can I do?"

"I know it will be very difficult for you but I'm going to need you to testify in court about what you saw that day. It's very important that you're specific and confident, especially about the car you saw drive by."

"I will do whatever I can," she said with renewed strength and conviction. "I have carried so much guilt all these years over not going back to help Whitney that day. I've never been able to forgive myself."

"I understand," Rina said. "I just want to prepare you by letting you know that you will be receiving a subpoena to appear in court. It is standard procedure so please don't be alarmed by that. Also, my secretary will be in touch to set up a time with you to come to my office to go over your testimony. We will visit the courtroom to familiarize you with the atmosphere, and we can use that time to practice for the trial so it will be less intimidating on that day. Would that be okay?"

"Sure."

"Honestly, Niki, I want to thank you. I believe your testimony, in this case, will be instrumental in bringing this cold-hearted killer to justice. It is also my hope that it ultimately helps relieve you of all the guilt you are carrying inside as well."

"I hope so," Niki replied with a sad nod.

The interview with the witness was successful. Rina felt that her age and ability to relate to the fear young girls felt back then would be helpful in her direct examination of Niki on the witness stand. As Rina drove back to her office, her mind drifted back to when, like Whitney, she was often sent to the corner store to pick up groceries for her mother.

CHAPTER 17

CITY OF ROCHESTER
APRIL 1973

Dorothy had been having a bad day. If she had to count the number of good days versus bad in any given week, she would struggle to get to the third finger. Her life didn't seem to be going anywhere, and she felt overwhelmed with the responsibly of raising a ten-year-old girl virtually on her own. Yes, there was the assistance she was getting with food stamps and housing vouchers, but that was barely enough to keep food on the table and a roof over their heads. She was working at a bar part-time, but that meant hiring a babysitter for the evenings and weekends or relying on her friends to pick up the babysitting tab pro bono. She thought that she would be able to live a simpler life. That is what had convinced her to move to the city after her parents moved to Arizona. However, she clearly was not ready for all the duties that came with being a single parent, especially to a child she did not want to begin with. It was a constant reminder of the worst day of her life.

"Rina!" her mother shouted from the living room. Rina instantly dropped her dolls and ran to her mother's side. "I need you to run to the store. We are out of milk and we need a loaf of bread too."

"Sure, mommy," Rina said. She knew what to do as she had done it several times before. She took the food stamps from her mother and ran out the door.

On the way to the store, she saw Jessica, Lisa's daughter, walking toward her. As the two met, an exuberant Jessica gushed with excitement, "Hey Rina, check this out!" Jessica said as she opened her hand exposing several coins.

"Wow, thirty cents!" a wide-eyed Rina said.

"I know, isn't it cool? I can get candy or whatever else I want because it's real money, not those plastic food stamp coins we get."

"Where did you get that from?" Rina asked.

"The man who lives above the store."

"The man above the store? He just *gave* it to you?"

"Yup! All I had to do was visit him," Jessica said proudly.

"For real?" Rina asked suspiciously.

"I'm serious, that's it. I just keep him company for a little while."

"Nothing else? Are you sure?" Rina said skeptically. Her eyes narrowed at Jessica as she thought it sounded too good to be true.

"Positive!" Jessica replied. "Come on. I'll show you." With that, Jessica retreated in the direction she had come from with Rina in tow.

They approached the store but instead of entering at the front, they went around to the side of the brick building where they came upon a glass door leading into a small vestibule. Inside the entryway, there were several silver metal mailbox slots with small keyholes in them and above each one was a speaker with a button on it. Jessica pushed a button and after about thirty seconds they heard a man's voice say, "Who's there?"

"It's me. Jessica. I brought a friend with me."

The second door inside the entryway buzzed and Jessica opened it quickly. Once inside, Jessica led the way towards the stairs to the second floor to an apartment located in the very back of the building.

Jessica knocked and the man opened the door. Jessica slipped through, but Rina hesitated for a moment in the hallway.

"Come on, Rina. It's okay," Jessica assured her.

The man took an instant liking to Rina. There was something in her eyes, an innocence that he liked. "Yes, my little darling, please come in," the man said.

Rina hesitantly entered, and as the door closed behind them, she instantly felt uncomfortable when the strange man began to turn the several locks he had on his door, especially a deadbolt that was too high for her to reach. A distrustful Rina held strong in her position as she didn't want to be too far from the only escape she could imagine there was in the apartment. She looked at the man intently. He looked familiar to her, but she couldn't figure out why. Perhaps she had seen him in the store? After all, he did live right above it and she was there often.

"My goodness, you certainly are a pretty little girl, please come in and sit with me," the man said to her, his voice calm. Jessica was already sitting comfortably on the sofa.

"I'm okay here," Rina said refusing to leave her post close to the door.

"Would you like some ice cream? I just bought some. It's chocolate," he said.

"No thank you," Rina said. Then, just as the words came out of her mouth, she saw a cat slowly emerge from the kitchen. The cat leaped up onto Jessica's lap, and as she began to pet it, Rina instantly remembered where she had seen the man before.

It was one day about a year ago that this same man was asking her to help him find his lost kitten. Apparently, he found her, or perhaps she was never "lost," Rina thought. Her heart was thumping in her chest. She recalled the incident with Uncle Frank and felt trapped.

"I'd like to leave, sir. Please open the door," Rina said abruptly.

"What's the rush?" The man asked, smiling. "I just want you to tell me more about yourself. Please, just sit with me for a while and tell me about school and your friends and . . . whatever you like. Then you can have some money. You can spend it on whatever you like." he urged. Jessica was giddy with excitement, it was her favorite part of the deal. Not to mention that of all the adults who had invited her to sit down and talk about her young life, he was by far the kindest. And he rewarded her for it.

Although Rina was eager to put a bit of real money in her pocket, maybe save it up to help her mother not feel so stressed all the time, she feared another Uncle Frank encounter. "I'd like to leave now," she said, raising her voice. "Please open the door!" she looked at the locks, realizing she was too short to reach all the deadbolts.

"Now let's not be hasty, darling. I'm not going to hurt you."

"Rina, chill out!" Jessica interjected, fearful that if Rina upset the man too much he might get angry and not fork over the change in his pocket.

"Open this door *right now* or I am going to scream!" Rina threatened when the man did not do as she had asked.

The man hesitated at first but then, with an agitated look, he unlocked the deadbolts on the door. As soon as the last one was unlocked, Rina pushed past him. She urgently grasped the door handle, pulled open the door and rushed out into the hallway. "Come on, Jessica," she called back.

"I'm going to stay," Jessica said.

"I don't think that's a good idea. You should come with me!" Rina shouted.

"Oh, stop being a baby, Rina," Jessica said, rolling her eyes. At least with her gone, the attention will be all on me again, Jessica thought.

"Fine!" Rina said. She turned on her heel and walked hastily down the hall towards the stairs. Once safely outdoors she ran around the corner to the storefront and barged into the store. The bell on the door jingled as she entered, and she let out a sigh of relief, when she saw Jim, the store owner, talking to Eric, the fireman who lived in her building. She leaned her hand against the wall briefly, gasping for air.

"My goodness, Rina, you are out of breath. Did you run here today?" Jim asked.

"Yeah, that's it. I—I ran here because we are out of milk and bread," she said as she proceeded to the dairy section in the back of the store.

Jim looked at Eric, he seemed a bit concerned. There was a serial killer on the loose grabbing up little girls, he thought. Perhaps she was just doing what she needed to make sure she got here safely. But he wasn't so sure that she was going to be able to run as fast on the way home with a bag of groceries in her arms.

As Rina left the store with both arms around the heavy brown paper bag, she noticed through the glass of the newspaper box a headline that read, *"Can You Help Find Whitney's Killer? $2,500 Reward!"*

Thinking that $2,500 would certainly make her and her mother rich, she occupied her thoughts with the notion that the creepy man above the store was the killer and she would be the one that helped the police catch him. She dreamed of collecting the reward money. She imagined that her mother would be proud of her, never angry again, and grateful to her.

As she was making her way home, struggling to keep the bag in her arms, she heard a voice calling her name. It was Jessica. Jessica caught up and, without missing a beat, began bragging to Rina about how the man had given her another fifty cents, almost double what he normally gave her.

"Gosh, Jessica, you're crazy!" Rina said. They saw clouds forming above their heads and knew that they would have to get home soon.

"I don't see what the big deal is, Rina. He's nice to me!" Jessica retorted.

"The big deal is that girls our age are getting taken away by bad men. They are getting raped and murdered. For all you know that man could be the one who killed that girl," she said, referring to the newspaper headline she had just read.

"Him? That is stupid! Bad men are mean, right? They're scary, but he's nice."

"He could be the killer! He's creepy and I really don't think you should go back there!"

"Oh, you are such a drag, Rina. He just loves children." Jessica said. She grabbed the bread in an attempt to help her friend walk a little faster. "Come on, we better get going or my mother is going to give me the belt across my behind when I get home."

"Yeah, mine too," Rina responded. She had known the feeling of that belt across her bottom a little too well. As the raindrops began to fall, the girls ran the remaining block to their building.

CHAPTER 18

CITY OF ROCHESTER
APRIL 1973

Rina burst into her apartment with newfound energy. She had done what her mother had asked her to do, and she had escaped the wrath of the creepiest of creepy men. "Hi, Bert!" she said cheerfully. Bert and Dorothy had been dating for quite a while now. Their relationship was something that gave Dorothy more stability, something that took a bit of the pressure of single motherhood off her shoulders. For Rina, it was nice to have a father figure around, even if it only was on occasion. It meant that she didn't have to fear upsetting her mother too much. Bert would be there to rescue her.

Bert was sitting in the recliner with his feet propped up by the chair. He was reading the newspaper while he sipped from a can of beer. Bert had the newspaper opened wide, eyeing it curiously. That's when Rina saw the headline again about Whitney Walkowski and the picture of the freckle-faced redhead. She thought about the creepy man. She thought about the big reward she would get if she helped the police arrest him. Then, resigning herself to the fact that no one would listen to a ten-year-old, she brought the milk and bread into the kitchen. She put the milk in the refrigerator, and just as she opened the breadbox to put the bread inside, her mother yelled out at her.

"What on earth happened to the bread, Rina?" Dorothy shouted.

Afraid to answer, Rina looked down at the crushed loaf that she was holding in her hand by the twist tie.

"I'm waiting for an explanation," Dorothy said, standing firm, her arms crossed across her chest, her lips pursed, and her right foot tapping on the linoleum floor.

"I—I guess it got crushed," Rina said nervously.

"I can clearly see that!" Dorothy yelled. "I asked you to do a simple thing and you can't even do that right! This bread is useless now!" Her mother said, raising her hand up.

In anticipation of a blow, Rina ducked her head, closed her eyes, and covered her delicate face with her hands.

"Dorothy, calm down! It's just a twenty-seven-cent loaf of bread!" An irritated Bert spoke from the living room.

"Just twenty-seven cents?" she shot back at him sarcastically. "I'm glad that with your nice cushy job twenty-seven cents isn't much money to you, but as you know, with what I get on food stamps, I can't afford to throw away food like that."

"Just relax! I'll get you another loaf of bread, for Christ's sake!" He shook his head and went back to reading his newspaper.

Upset, Dorothy stormed into the bedroom and slammed the door. Rina walked into the living room and sat down on the floor, unsure of what to do next. She had upset her mother, even after she had done what her mother had wanted her to do. She felt like she could do nothing right and it seemed there was no way of knowing when her mother would lose her temper.

"Don't mind her, she is just having a bad day," Bert said reassuringly to Rina as he took a sip of his beer. He patted his lap for her to come over and sit with him.

"I think I should go feed the cat," she said as she turned away from Bert and silently went back into the kitchen.

CHAPTER 19

CITY OF ROCHESTER
JULY 1973

It was just a few weeks after Rina's last day of school when Dorothy told her daughter that they were going to a Fourth of July picnic at Laura's house. After that, they were all going to watch the fireworks downtown. Lisa and her kids, along with some others, were also going to be there and Rina was very excited about it. It was a nice warm day as they walked up the driveway toward the gate leading to the backyard.

"Rina's here!" Alex called out as he ran to the gate to greet Rina and her mom. "Guess what?"

"Hi Alex," Rina replied. "What's up?"

"We're going to have hot dogs, cheeseburgers, macaroni salad, and a surprise for dessert!" He was brimming with excitement.

"That sounds great." She echoed his contagious enthusiasm.

All the kids were out in the backyard and the adults were in the house so as Dorothy went inside, Rina followed Alex out back where Bobby and Jessica invited her to play a game of "Mother May I."

It was Alex's turn. "Mother, may I take one giant step forward?"

Just then Uncle Frank approached the young children at play. He was wearing a white undershirt that showed his hairy back and chest. His eyes were specifically on Rina who was in the prime position as the mother with her back turned to the group and completely unaware of his presence. Uncle Frank tapped Alex on the shoulder and put his index finger to his lips to silence him. He motioned for Alex to step out of the game so that he could take his place. Thinking this was funny, Alex covered his mouth with his hand to stifle his giggle, and he gladly let Uncle Frank step in for him.

"Yes, you may," Rina said. Then Uncle Frank stood within arm's length of Rina, catching up to her with his giant step.

"Gotcha!" He said as he grabbed her from behind. Rina nearly jumped out of her skin when she realized who it was.

All the other kids were laughing so hard they didn't notice the look of shock on her face and sheer terror in her eyes.

Uncle Frank swung Rina around the yard as the children were teeming with excitement. All except for Rina, who was by that time horrified and screaming, "Put me down! Let me go!"

Frank laughed. "Okay, take it easy. Geez, I was just having some fun with you."

All the other kids really liked Uncle Frank and they gathered around him. "Uncle Frank, swing me around the yard too!" one of them squealed.

"Uncle Frank, I really like your belt," Bobby said, intrigued by the shiny belt buckle with a turquoise eagle on it.

Uncle Frank unhooked his belt and whipped it off in a single motion. "Want to try it on?" he asked a captivated Bobby.

"Yeah, can I?" Bobby said eagerly.

Frank folded the belt in half and pulled hard at the ends, causing the belt to make a loud snapping sound, like a cowboy cracking a whip. He did this a few times and laughed as the kids jumped at the sound. They were all laughing, except for Rina. Then, as Frank put the belt around Bobby's stomach, he looked at Rina and winked.

"Time to eat, everyone!" Laura yelled from the back door, carrying out a tray of food with Dorothy and Lisa right behind her, their arms also full.

Rina sat with the kids as far away as she could from Frank. The images of her frightening encounter filled her head, and it was enough to make her fingers grow cold on such a warm summer day. She thought about telling her mom what happened that day, but then she recalled what her mom had said to her before, that he was a nice man who was good to them and that Rina should be nice to him. She feared that her mother wouldn't believe her if she told her that Uncle Frank had tried to do things that felt wrong, to touch her in places that no one was allowed to touch.

Just then Dorothy's boyfriend Bert unexpectedly showed up. He stayed long enough to have a beer, and then he whisked Dorothy and Rina away for an adventure of their own.

"What about the fireworks?" Rina said, worried she would miss seeing them.

"We're going to see fireworks, don't worry," Bert assured her.

They said their goodbyes and walked out to the street where Bert's car was parked. It was a big shiny new car, and it was by far the nicest car that Rina had ever seen. It looked like a rich person's car, and Rina was so excited that she happily hopped into the back seat.

"Where are we going?" Rina heard her mother ask as she was in the back seat playing with the power windows.

"It's a surprise." Bert winked at Dorothy. They both looked back and laughed at Rina as she pushed the power window button up, then down, then up again. After a while, Rina stopped playing with the window and focused on the soft seats as she rubbed her hand over them. As they drove along, she gazed up toward Bert and Dorothy in the front seat and saw her mom looking lovingly at Bert. In that moment she envisioned them as a happy family.

"We're here!" Bert announced after a short drive. He pulled off the road and into a parking lot. Rina hopped up from the back seat to look out the windshield to see where they were. She could make out a beach and a carousel in the distance as they passed a sign that said, "Welcome to Charlotte Beach."

They got out of the car and began walking in the direction of the pier. Bert was holding Dorothy's hand. It was a beautiful night. Waves were lapping along the sides of the pier, leaving small puddles of water along the path. They walked out to the red and white striped lighthouse at the end and stopped there.

"You have to touch the lighthouse to make it count," Bert said jokingly. Rina obediently smacked the lighthouse with her hand as they all laughed together. After sitting there for a few moments, they strolled back to shore. As they got closer to the carousel, Rina grew hopeful. But then disappointment set in. She knew that her mother didn't have any money for a carousel ride. She knew the difference between the money she had used to buy groceries at the corner store, and the money that other kids from nicer homes got from their parents to have fun. Even though Bert obviously had money, she also knew it was impolite to ask, so she walked alongside them, wishing.

Then, the moment she had been waiting for arrived. "How about a ride on the merry-go-round?" Bert asked.

Rina, eyes wide with excitement, nodded her head eagerly. The three of them entered the corral to get on the ride. Once on the carousel, Rina walked around, carefully inspecting all the horses, until she found the perfect one, making sure not only that it went up and down but also that it had her favorite color on it, pink. Bert lifted Rina up, helping her so she could swing her leg over the horse. Once Rina was on, Bert stood beside her with his arm around her waist for safety. Dorothy hopped up on the horse next to Rina's and sat side-saddle on it as the ride began.

When it was over, they walked to the beach to watch the fireworks as they shot up over the water. The red-white-and-blue-themed display was captivating, with plenty of pops and booms to excite the crowd.

After the fireworks show ended, Bert decided to make a stop at Abbott's, a popular local establishment best known for its chocolate almond frozen custard.

"Do you like frozen custard, Rina?" Bert asked.

"I don't know. I've never had it before," she replied. She wanted to say that they never had money for such things, but she thought it would upset her mother.

"I think you'll like it. It's like ice cream, only better." He let out a laugh.

They pulled up in front of Abbott's and Rina was peering out the backseat window when she saw a girl from her class in the crowd. The girl looked over at them. She waved. It was a defining moment for young Rina. She had never had very many nice things in her life, and now she was driving around in a fancy car, about to have a frozen treat that she would not otherwise have had. She felt proud. She held her shoulders back and puffed up her chest, and then she waved back at the girl, thrilled that someone could see her living like a princess. If her other classmates found out, they might be jealous, Rina thought. It was enough to give her a feeling of superiority.

After a delicious cone, they hopped back into the car and drove home. Rina peered out the window and noticed they were passing several big, beautiful houses with sprawling front yards and the lake as a backdrop behind them. Her eyes were heavy, and she had just enough alertness left to notice the soft glow of lights coming from the houses. She felt envious of the fortunate children whose parents could afford to live there. She imagined happy families—

playful children without a care in the world—dressed in the best clothes and running around the yard. She imagined happy mommies and daddies, holding hands and laughing with delight as their children played. Maybe that life wasn't very far off for her, if this day with Bert and her mom was any indication.

Bert looked in the rear-view mirror and whispered to Dorothy, "She's out like a light."

Rina had lost her fight against sleep, and she dreamt that her mom married Bert and that they were rich. In her dream, the three of them moved into one of those big houses on the lake and she had everything she had always wanted. Enough toys to fill up two bedrooms, both painted pink, white bedroom furniture, a canopy bed, a fluffy pink comforter and lots of pillows.

But it was just a dream, and when she woke up in the middle of the night, she found herself back in her cramped bedroom in their shabby inner-city apartment.

CHAPTER 20

JUDGE CRANDALL'S CHAMBERS
AUGUST 1991

The trial was just a few weeks away when Rina made her way, walking the short distance, from the DA's office to the County Courthouse for the pretrial meeting with the Judge and Thomas Cugino. She approached the front of the three-story curved glass entryway of the brick building with its two large, dark gray cement pillars on each side and the American flag flying high above. Over the facade, in large letters, it read, Monroe County Civic Center – Hall of Justice. Rina reached for the brass handle on the large glass door and caught a glimpse of a plaque bearing the words TRUTH, JUSTICE, and LIBERTY.

Finally, she would meet Thomas Cugino. Although Rina was aware of his local legend status and reputation as a very tough defense attorney, she wasn't about to let herself get caught up in all that. She was fully invested in this case, and she realized he was the one person that she would be fighting against at the upcoming trial. She knew she had to focus on one thing and one thing only— convicting a despicable murderer.

Rina arrived a few minutes early at Judge Crandall's office. She checked in with the secretary at the desk who instructed her to have a seat in the waiting area. Deciding to make good use of the time, she pulled out her file folder and began to study its contents. After several minutes, the door opened and in walked a middle-aged man with movie-star good looks. He was polished and sophisticated, his eyes captivating, his smile contagious.

An earthy cologne aroma filled the room, and the secretary lit up as she greeted him. "Good afternoon Mr. Cugino," she said with an exuberant smile. "It's so nice to see you."

Rina peered over the top of her folder to get a peek at her rival and caught the secretary gawking at him like a star-struck teenager. *Geez, you'd think Michael Douglas himself just walked in,* she thought as she rolled her eyes.

"Ms. Rosello is here already, Mr. Cugino," the secretary said as she extended her hand in Rina's direction.

Rina stood up with an outstretched hand. "Mr. Cugino, it is my pleasure to have the opportunity to meet you," she said with a friendly smile.

"Nice to meet you in person as well," he said as he returned her firm handshake. "And please, call me Tom."

He hesitated slightly. He was expecting someone young, but he wasn't prepared for his opponent to be so attractive. Or maybe it was the way that she gripped his hand with such confidence. Whatever it was, he was intrigued, and he felt certain there was something familiar about her.

Tom squinted his eyes. "Have we met before?" he asked.

"I don't think so. You look familiar to me also, but then again, I saw you on TV during the court proceedings for Aric Shawcroft." Rina said, trying to act nonchalant.

"Perhaps I've seen you in passing at the courthouse?"

"That is definitely a possibility. After all, I am there often," Rina answered.

"Judge Crandall is ready for you, Mr. Cugino and Ms. Rosello," the secretary announced as she stood and directed them towards the Judge's chambers. As Tom led the way, Rina caught the secretary giving him one last flirtatious smile.

"Cuz!" Judge Crandall shouted as he jumped up from his chair. He greeted Tom with a friendly handshake. "How's the family?"

"Doug, so great to see you. Everyone is doing great. Angela is back from visiting her parents in Lake Placid, TJ just got his driver's license, and Alisa, she is doing typical thirteen-year-old girl things, sometimes bratty, you know what I mean?" Tom said with a wink.

"Oh yeah, don't I know it," Judge Crandall said recalling when his own daughter, now in college, was a young teenager.

"And how about you, my friend?" Tom asked.

"Busy, you know. Mikayla is headed back to med school next week and Ann enjoyed having an active house over the summer."

"Fabulous! Glad to hear that things are well in the Crandall household," Tom said as he patted his friend on the shoulder.

Tom and Judge Crandall had quite a long history together. They met playing softball back in the day, when they were just beginning their careers, and became fast friends. The two of them were also active members of the prestigious Oak Hill Country Club, where they often played golf together and had attended many exclusive parties with their wives over the years.

Rina knew that it was not uncommon for those in the legal community to have close relationships with each other. After all, she knew that it was a very difficult profession that only those in it could relate to. Regardless of Tom's friendship with the Judge, Rina hoped that in the courtroom it would be strictly professional.

"*Ahem!*" Rina, who was quietly standing behind Tom, cleared her throat to make her presence known, breaking up the comrades' friendly reunion.

"Ah, Ms. Rosello, I apologize. Please come in and have a seat," Judge Crandall said, as he waved his hand towards one of the two brown leather armchairs in front of his oversized oak desk.

Tom considerately pulled out her chair for her and waited for her to sit before he did himself. *Well, he certainly is charming,* Rina admitted to herself.

The hour-long pretrial conference went as expected. The defense and prosecution could not agree on a plea for the defendant, but the meeting with Judge Crandall was productive in terms of the agreements between Tom and Rina regarding the undisputed facts and points of law that didn't need to be proven during the trial.

Now, with the trial date set, Tom and Rina left the Judge's office. They conversed briefly in the hallway before saying their professional goodbyes and going their separate ways. As Rina turned and walked away, Tom paused. He held his right hand up to his mouth and tapped his lip with his index finger. He was struck by that eerie feeling again, that there was something more familiar about her than just a casual encounter. As he watched her walk to the end of the hallway, she stopped and bent down to wipe something off her shoe. That is when the memory of a young girl he met once a long time ago came to him. But certainly, this couldn't possibly be the same girl.

Several hours later, Rina was back at her office reading the case files. She was about to close her eyes from sheer exhaustion. It was Friday and most of the office had cleared out two hours prior to start the weekend, yet she sat in her chair. Her eyes focused on the words and images on paper while her mind would occasionally drift elsewhere. It was all a bit too much, she thought. The circumstances. The fact that she had lived through the events.

Regardless of the challenges, Rina knew she had one thing in her favor and that was that she knew the defendant, and she could remember things about him, things that others did not know.

It was embarrassing for Rina to think of how much like the three girls she was. Aside from the obvious double initial connection, they were all from Catholic backgrounds and living in low-income neighborhoods with single mothers who were receiving public assistance.

Rina shuddered at the memory of her mother paying for groceries with food stamps, especially the time when she spotted a young girl in the grocery store shopping with her parents. Rina had guessed the girl was about her age and she couldn't help but feel jealous of the nice clothes she was wearing and their shopping cart full of food. Rina looked down with humiliation at her own clothes, secondhand from the Salvation Army, and at the boxes of macaroni and cheese and TV dinners in their cart. It wasn't until they were checking out that she saw the young girl again in the checkout line next to them. This was when she prayed that the girl would not look over. Unfortunately, to her mortification, just as Rina's mother handed the cashier the food stamps the girl looked over and sneered at Rina.

Rina tried to clear the embarrassing moment from her memory, but she kept thinking about the fact that all the girls were on public assistance, just as she was.

Rina was focusing on the evidence, one point of which was the description of the car that was seen in the area on the days when Carmella and Whitney were abducted. It was also the same car described by a witness who had an encounter in Macedon with a man fitting the description of the defendant. The witness not only described the car and the defendant but also the young, dark-haired chubby girl that was with him. Another interesting detail was the time of day the girls disappeared. They all were abducted late in the afternoon, perhaps after the man got out of work.

Rina looked at the clock. 7:17 pm. She decided to call it a day and closed the file. She knew that Steve was going to be out with his buddies for happy hour, so on her way home she made a quick stop at the liquor store and treated herself to her favorite bottle of wine. She was juggling her briefcase, the bottle of wine and their mail as she struggled to unlock the apartment door.

She was anxious for a glass of wine. As she poured herself a glass, she noted her hand was shaking. She closed her eyes, took a deep breath and went out onto the balcony while she waited for Steve to come home. Her mind was on overdrive, and she was so deep in thought that she didn't even hear him come up behind her.

"Hi honey, how was your day?" Steve said happily, slightly buzzed from a few drinks with the guys.

"Geez!" Rina jumped, spilling some wine in her lap. "You nearly gave me a heart attack," she said as she covered her heart with her hand.

"Sorry about that." Steve was oblivious to her mood as he continued talking loudly about how many laughs he had out with his friends. It wasn't until after a few moments of her unresponsiveness that he finally asked her if she was okay.

"I'm okay," she answered. "I am just very nervous about this case."

"That is normal, isn't it? Being nervous, right?" Steve said matter-of-factly.

"Yes, it is, but today I met Tom Cugino, the defense attorney," she explained.

"Hmmmm, sounds familiar, why do I know that name?" Steve asked.

"Probably because he was the defense attorney for Aric Shawcroft. You know that serial killer who killed those prostitutes in the 1980s."

"Ah yes, now I remember. That attorney is a local superstar. I've even heard people say that if you're guilty, hire Cugino. Isn't he known for getting criminals off on minor technicalities?"

"Ugh! I am well aware of his celebrity status and thank you very much for the reminder of how he helps put guilty pieces of shit back on the streets. You know that really doesn't make me feel any better," she snapped.

"Rina, you just have to do the best you can."

"Are you serious right now? You don't understand," she said as she folded her arms, and turned away from him.

"I guess I don't," a defeated Steve replied.

"This is my first big trial, and not only is there very little evidence and few witness accounts, but I am up against the toughest defense attorney in the state. Clearly, I'm doomed."

"Please try not to obsess over this."

"That is easier said than done," she said as she got up and went inside to refill her glass.

CHAPTER 21

STEVE AND RINA'S APARTMENT
AUGUST 1991

Tony and Joanne were Steve and Rina's closest friends. They had met at a going-away party for Cheryl before she moved to Atlanta a couple of years back and they became friends instantly. It all began when Steve, always sociable, struck up a conversation about football with Tony who was wearing a Buffalo Bills T-shirt. Rina turned to Joanne, who was a few years older, and shrugged. Rina was drawn to the cheery smile of the ash-blonde Joanne who was high-spirited, and whose lively caramel-colored eyes reflected her enthusiasm. Joanne possessed a genuine, compassionate heart and it wasn't long before she became Rina's most trusted friend. She was someone whom Rina could always depend on to offer honest, beneficial advice.

The couples tried to get together as often as they could, but it wasn't always easy to coordinate their busy work schedules, especially for Joanne who was an airline stewardess. This was to be the first Saturday in a long time that they were getting together for dinner, and Rina was looking forward to taking a break from the trial to catch up with her best friend.

Rina was in the bathroom checking her makeup when the doorbell rang. It was 6:03. Right on time, as usual, she thought to herself with a smile. One last dab of her light pink lipstick. She pressed her lips together to spread it evenly and went into the living room to greet their guests. Steve had already let Joanne and Tony in and he was taking their jackets when Rina welcomed them both.

"So great to see you guys, it's been too long," Rina said cheerfully as she hugged her friends.

They gathered around the kitchen peninsula, making small talk while Steve got out four wine glasses and opened the cabernet sauvignon that Tony and Joanne had brought. He poured from the bottle and handed everyone a glass, then lifted his for a toast. "Cheers to great friends!" Steve said as the others lifted their glasses and clinked them together in their traditional toast. Conversations quickly ensued, and it wasn't long before the guys got right into talking about how they hoped the Buffalo Bills training camp and the upcoming season would amount to a better outcome than in this past Super Bowl. The guys were passionate about how they had the best offense in the league, yet they lost the Super Bowl with a missed field goal in the last minute of the game. Joanne and Rina rolled their eyes at the boring sports talk and retired to the living room to talk about more interesting subjects.

"Tell me about all the exotic and exciting places you've been to recently," Rina asked, looking forward to a distraction from her own work.

"Oh gosh Rina, this last trip was amazing. For a month my schedule had me going from New York City to Paris."

"Paris? Wow, that is incredible! I'm so jealous!"

Joanne laughed, "I get that a lot. It was amazing, but the eight-hour flight is not much fun."

"Ugh, I feel sick just thinking of such a long flight."

"It really isn't that bad as the plane is very comfortable and, it's Paris you know, definitely worth the trip. Oh, that reminds me, I have a gift for you."

"A gift for me?"

"It's nothing big, just a little something for your collection," Joanne said as she jumped up and bolted to the kitchen. It took just a few seconds for her to come back with her purse in hand. She reached in and pulled out a small paper bag. Inside was a magnet of the most recognizable structure in the world with the word Paris inscribed below it.

"It's the Eiffel Tower!" Rina squealed. "This is so amazing!"

"I'm glad you like it. Honestly, it's one of the coolest things I ever saw, especially at night when it lights up and sparkles every hour from sunset until 1:00 am."

"That sounds incredible!"

"It truly is. Did you know that the Eiffel Tower was built in 1889 by Alexandre-Gustave Eiffel for the World Fair, which was a celebration to mark the 100th year anniversary of the French Revolution?" Joanne explained. "And, would you believe the French people hated it because they thought it was an eyesore?"

"Really? I didn't know that."

"Actually, it was only meant to be temporary, for the entrance to the fair, and it was almost torn down in 1909. But visitors to Paris during and after the World Fair were so infatuated with it that the French recognized its value and decided to keep it. And now, the Eiffel Tower is considered an architectural marvel. It's the city's most beloved symbol, and one of the world's most visited iconic monuments."

"Wow! That is incredible, Joanne! This is so beautiful. Thank you, I will cherish it forever." Rina said with genuine appreciation.

"You're welcome. So, tell me, what's going on with you? How's work going?"

"Ha. That sure is a loaded question," Rina laughed sarcastically.

"What do you mean?" Joanne asked.

"Monday is the start of my trial. It's my first big one."

"That is great!"

"Well, yes and no."

"Okay, I'm confused."

"Do you remember the three little girls with double initials that were killed in the early 1970s?"

"Do you mean the murders of . . . wait, don't tell me," Joanne said as she snapped her fingers. "I know exactly who you are talking about. It's Carmella Candelario, Whitney Walkowski and Maria. Maria—"

"Mancuso."

"Yes, Mancuso! Sure, I remember, The Double Initial Murders. How could I forget? Gosh, my parents wouldn't let me out of their sight for years and I didn't even have double initials," she said with a laugh. "But seriously, they never caught the killer, right?"

"They didn't, in all those years, but they have him now."

"Get the hell out of here! That was such a long time ago, are you joking?"

"No joke. Police in California got a hit on the database for a partial fingerprint found on one of the victims."

"Seriously, Rina? I heard something on the news about it, but I had no idea that was your case. I thought you handled DWI cases?"

"I typically do but I guess I must have drawn the short straw for this one," Rina said, looking pained. "Unfortunately, as you know, I can't tell you about it, but I imagine you'll be hearing more soon. I'm sure the media will be all over it."

"I can't believe that after all this time has passed they finally caught him. What's it been like fifteen, twenty years?"

"Seventeen years, ten months and twenty-six days since he killed Maria, to be exact."

"Geez, that is crazy. Good luck, Rina. I have a busy travel schedule coming up, but I would love to sit in on it one day if I am here."

"Thanks. I appreciate that, and I'm really going to need all the luck I can get because this is not going to be easy."

The guys had given up their sports talk and decided to join their girlfriends. "Can we join you two beautiful ladies?" Tony said as he and Steve entered the living room.

CHAPTER 22

STEVE AND RINA'S APARTMENT
SEPTEMBER 1991

Rina looked over at the clock on the nightstand. It was 3:07 am and she couldn't sleep. She glanced at the other side of the bed and saw Steve sleeping soundly. She just couldn't seem to turn off her thoughts of this case. Giving up on the idea of falling back to sleep, she leaned over and kissed Steve softly on the cheek. He stirred slightly as she quietly slipped out from under the covers and went downstairs. Her briefcase was leaning up against the wall near the door. She went over to it and pulled out the folder on Maria Mancuso.

It was two years after Carmella Candelario was brutally murdered, and only ten months after the body of Whitney Walkowski was found, when Maria Mancuso went missing. Maria's parents were divorced, and she lived with her single mother in the city. It was a November day in 1973 when Maria's mother went to pick up Maria from school and was told by a schoolmate that Maria had to stay after. Assuming that Maria would be fine walking home alone, as she had done it so many times before, she returned home.

The records showed that at 5:40 that afternoon the Rochester Police Department received a call about another missing girl. Authorities quickly launched a massive countywide search. This time, police received several reports of young girls in cars but nothing had panned out.

Sadly, just two days after Maria Mancuso had disappeared, her badly bruised body was found dumped in a ditch in Macedon, about twenty miles from home. The autopsy report confirmed the official cause of death to be "asphyxiation by strangulation." Again, as in the other cases, Maria had also been brutally beaten and raped before being murdered. Additionally, the medical examiner reported that Maria had eaten a cheeseburger within an hour and a half of her death.

Rina shook her head knowingly. After this third killing, it was obvious that these murders were committed by a serial killer. He clearly was servicing a sick psychological gratification. His murders were all committed with the same distinct pattern and his victims all had similar characteristics.

Steve awoke around 8:00 that Sunday morning to find Rina asleep in the living room chair, the folder still in her hand. "Rina?" he said, trying not to startle her as he gently shook her shoulder.

Her eyes opened slowly. "Oh, was I sleeping?" she asked as she rubbed her eyes.

"Yes, is everything alright?" Steve asked, with concern over the unusual behavior his girlfriend was displaying.

"I'm okay, I just couldn't sleep," Rina replied with a yawn.

"You sure?"

"Yeah, I'll be fine."

"It seems that you are really struggling with this case."

"Honestly, I am. I know this despicable monster is guilty and I'm afraid that I won't be able to prove it as there really isn't any hard evidence against him. It just turns my stomach."

"Getting a conviction, in this case, is really important to you, isn't it?"

"Yes, it is. I really want to bring justice to those girls and closure to their families. I've never wanted anything more in my life."

"You'll do it."

"I hope so, but if I can't figure out a way to get the jury to convict him soon, he's going to get away with it."

"I understand," Steve said sympathetically. "You know, with everything going on with you and this case, I think we should go to church this morning," Steve recommended.

"You're right, that is probably a good idea. I sure could use some prayers right now, especially with the trial beginning tomorrow," Rina agreed. "We'll have to pray that God sends me some good choices for the jury pool in the morning."

Steve and Rina arrived at church and said their hellos to their fellow parishioners before they took their seats in the pew and waited for the sermon to begin. Steve was reading the church bulletin as Rina looked around and up towards the altar where she saw the figure of Jesus on a wooden cross, reminding her of another day of worship a long time ago when she first heard the name Maria Mancuso.

CHAPTER 23

CITY OF ROCHESTER
DECEMBER 1973

It wasn't uncommon for Rina to walk by herself the four blocks to church on Sunday. Even though she was born and raised Catholic, Dorothy didn't go to church. Rina was baptized as a baby, at the insistence of her grandparents, but once they left for Arizona her mother stopped going. Something drew Rina to the church, and even though her mother didn't go, at ten years old, she chose to go alone.

Rina hadn't been taught much about religion, but she would listen carefully to the Bible readings and mimic what everyone else did. She would watch as people entered the pews, noticing that they would kneel and make the sign of the cross with their hands, so she would do the same. She now knew that this gesture showed reverence and respect and that it symbolically represented the Holy Trinity: The Father, Son and Holy Spirit. She was careful to follow along within seconds of others kneeling during the service, as if she knew all along what she was doing.

On this Sunday in December 1973, Mass began as it usually did until the priest made a special request during the service for everyone to pray for Maria Mancuso, who was the latest little girl that was found raped and murdered. Additionally, he asked for the

123

congregation to pray for the other little angels, Carmella Candelario and Whitney Walkowski. All three girls were Catholic and appeared to have been killed by the same person. Rina put her hands together, closed her eyes, bowed her head and prayed, "Dear Lord, I Pray for Carmella, Whitney, and Maria. Please help the police find the killer so that he can be put in jail. Amen!"

After accepting communion, Rina went back to her pew and was kneeling when she saw a familiar figure walking back from communion with his hands folded as if in prayer. It was the creepy man who lived in the apartment above the corner store. He smiled at Rina as he walked by, giving her a chill.

Walking home from church, Rina saw Jessica walking towards her. "Hey Jessica, where are you going?"

"My mom wants me to go to the corner store to buy her some cigarettes," Jessica answered. "I'm going to stop by to visit my friend and his cat, and to get some money too. Do you want to come with me?" she asked Rina.

"No way! That man gives me the creeps and I don't like him." Rina said shaking her head, "You really should be careful Jessica, there is a killer out there raping and murdering girls our age."

"Don't be a spaz, Rina, he's a cool dude. He just works all day and is lonely."

"Suit yourself, but I gotta go."

Later that afternoon, Dorothy and Rina were at Laura's house when Uncle Frank showed up. He had a clever way of doing that, Rina thought. She wasn't sure why he happened to appear every time she was there. Whatever the reason, he joined Laura and Dorothy in the kitchen while Rina played with the boys in the next room. Rina studied Uncle Frank, pretending to be playing while she kept a careful eye on him. He had his arm around Rina's mother and had apparently told her a joke as she was laughing very loudly. Rina felt her stomach turn at the sight.

Uncle Frank bent over to whisper in Dorothy's ear when he caught Rina scowling at him. Her mother was still laughing when Uncle Frank turned his gaze toward Rina. His eyes narrowed as he looked at her. She didn't stop staring at him. Unfazed, he let out a fake laugh and turned away. He went back to entertaining the ladies with his bogus charm.

Just then Bobby got Rina's attention. "Wanna make some dough?"

"Yeah!" she said eagerly, but then she got suspicious. "Wait a minute. What do I have to do?" She wasn't keen on sitting at some creepy man's house. She didn't want to put herself in a situation like that ever again.

"Alex and I are going to go to the bar to shine shoes!" Bobby said excitedly. "We made three dollars and fifty cents last week!"

"Wow, that's a lot of money. Okay, I'll go!" She said, thinking that she could certainly use the money. Anything to get away from Uncle Frank sounded very appealing to her.

"Cool! I have an extra shoe shine kit you can borrow."

The kids arrived at the crowded bar. It was a Sunday afternoon and the Buffalo Bills game was on TV. The kids got right to work. Rina went up to a man at the bar who looked to be in his 30s, his dark hair stylishly parted in the middle and feathered back. He was in jeans and a leather jacket.

"Hello, sir, would you like your shoes shined?" Rina said shyly.

The man looked down toward the unlikely sound of a little girl's voice in a bar. He stared at her for a minute, noticing her worn clothing and torn sneakers. "You know," he began, "your timing is perfect. I was just thinking that my shoes sure could use a nice shine."

Smiling, Rina set down her box and opened the lid to grab her supplies. She took out a can of shoe polish and a rag and then closed the lid. She sat on the top of the box using it as a stool as her customer placed his foot on the edge. She gently dabbed her rag in the can of polish and began the process of spreading the polish on the expensive-looking shoes. She carefully rubbed the polish in a circular direction all around the top and sides of the shoe until it was completely covered. Then she used the clean cloth to slide back and forth on the shoe to rub off the polish leaving a clean shine. Impressed by her hard work and dedication, the man took his attention off the football game for a minute and addressed the little girl. "What is your name?"

"My name is Rina, sir," she replied.

"That is a very pretty name. And wow, my shoes look brand new," he said, moving his foot from side to side so he could view the shine on them. "You do very nice work, Rina."

"Thank you, sir."

"You can call me Tom," the man said with a broad smile, showing perfectly white, straight teeth.

"Yes sir, Mister Tom."

Tom let out a chuckle, and then his conversation became serious. "What are you doing here, Rina?"

"I'm here with my friends and we're trying to make some money." She pointed over in the direction of Bobby and Alex, who had found customers of their own and were working diligently.

"I'm glad you are with your friends," Tom said, "but you know, you really should be careful. Haven't you heard that there is a bad man on the loose, killing young girls?"

"Yes, I know. He killed Carmella Candelario, Whitney Walkowski, and Maria Mancuso," she said, easily rattling off the names.

"I guess you do know about the killings."

"Yes, I do. I prayed for them in church today."

"That is very nice of you, Rina, but I want to tell you that you need to be very careful. I am a lawyer and I come across a lot of bad people that do horrible things to other people."

"I'll be careful," Rina said.

"Good girl!" Tom said as he reached in front of him toward the pile of bills on the bar, took a five-dollar bill and handed it to her.

Her eyes were wide with disbelief. "Wow, thank you very much!" she said as she took the bill and ran over to show it to Bobby, who was working on a shoe-shine himself.

"Rina! Where'd you get that from?" Bobby said enviously when he saw what Rina had in her hand.

"Mister Tom over there gave it to me for shining his shoes. He's a very nice man."

A begrudging Bobby looked away as he finished with his customer. A short time later, Bobby, Alex, and Rina began their walk home, stopping briefly to count their earnings. Bobby had made two dollars and ninety-five cents, Alex had made a mere seventy-five cents and Rina had made five dollars and thirty cents. The boys couldn't contain their resentment and jealousy of her.

"That's not fair," Alex said with his hands on his hips.

"Yes, it is. I worked for it!" Rina snapped back.

"It's only because you're a girl!" Bobby chimed in.

"And that man just felt sorry for you," Alex said.

"Yeah, he feels sorry for you because he knows you are the next girl that is going to get raped and murdered!" Bobby said.

"What? Don't say that, Bobby!" Rina cried.

"It's true, you have double initials, Rina Rosello, and *you are next!* He'll probably leave your body in Rochester too," Bobby said with a sneer.

"Shut up, Bobby!"

"The killer was probably in the bar today watching you. I think it is that Tom guy. That's why he gave you five dollars, 'cause he knows he's going to kill you next."

"No, he's not!" Rina said, defending the man who had been so nice to her.

"Rina Rosello is ne-ext! Rina Rosello has double initials! Rina Rosello is going to get raped and di-ie!" Bobby chanted.

"Stop it!!!! You're dumb," Rina said, hitting him on the head.

"Tom is a rapist and he's going to get you, Rina!" Bobby said.

"Nice knowing you, Rina Rosello," Alex said as he joined in on his brother's cruelty and continued to torment her.

"Shut up! I hate you both!" Rina began to cry as she turned away from the boys, dropped the shoeshine box and ran all the way back to Laura's place.

* * *

Rina refocused on the present for a brief moment as she sat next to Steve in the pew at church, waiting for the service to begin. She stared at a candle on the altar, mesmerized by the flickering flame and the melting wax as it slowly liquefied and ran down onto the brass candle holder. Rina was sent back into yet another recollection from her childhood. This was her most painful memory of them all. It was the day when her world completely crumbled.

CHAPTER 24

CITY OF ROCHESTER
JANUARY 1974

Rina came home from school to find her mother crying one afternoon. "Mommy, what's wrong?" she asked with genuine concern.

Dorothy wiped her eyes, "Nothing! Go to your room!" she responded angrily.

A few minutes later, Rina heard her mother on the phone. "I can't believe it Lisa! Bert is breaking up with me," Dorothy said before bursting into tears again.

Shortly after Dorothy hung up the phone, she came into Rina's room to let her know that Lisa was going to take her out later that night.

"Is Bert going, too?" Rina asked.

"No, we won't be seeing Bert anymore," Dorothy proclaimed angrily.

"Why?" Rina said sadly.

"I don't know, probably because of you. I have baggage and guys don't want *baggage!*" Dorothy said mockingly.

"Baggage? I'm sorry, Mommy." Rina's eyes began to well up with tears.

"Listen, I just want you to know I'm going out tonight with Laura and Lisa. You and Jessica are in charge."

"I'm going to be alone?" Rina said her eyes wide with concern.

"Jessica is just upstairs," Dorothy replied.

"I'm scared, Mommy."

"Don't be ridiculous. You're eleven-years-old now and can stay by yourself for a couple of hours. Besides, you'll be sleeping anyway and won't even know I'm gone."

Later that night, just as Dorothy said, Rina was sleeping when a scream woke her from her slumber. The noise was coming from the back staircase that led up to Lisa's apartment on the second floor. At first, Rina thought she was dreaming and she couldn't quite make out what she was hearing. Then she realized it was Jessica screaming from upstairs. *"Fire! Fire!"*

Rina shot up in bed frozen in shock. She wasn't sure how she was going to get out. Then she thought about the kids upstairs, how was she going to get them out? She panicked and didn't know what to do, when she looked over to her nightstand at her music box from Hun.

She heard fire trucks in the distance. The sound spurred her into action. She remembered what she had learned at school about how to escape a fire. She crawled like a soldier under a barbed wire obstacle course, across her bedroom floor and out into the kitchen. It was dark, but she made her way toward the door that led to the back staircase. She felt the door first to see if it was hot before opening it, just as she had learned in school. Once she was in the smoke-filled hall, she covered her mouth and nose with her pajama top. She attempted to go upstairs to help the other kids escape but was prevented from doing so by the flames she could see at the top of the stairs. She feared the worst for her friends as she ran outside and around to the front of the apartment building with her cherished music box held tightly in her grip. She was relieved to see the neighbors outside with their arms around Jessica and her two younger brothers. Rina joined them and they all stood there in shock as they heard the crashing sound of the windows breaking in the upstairs apartment. Flames shot out of them. Flashing red lights surrounded them as the fire trucks filled the street. The firemen began to unload their hoses and instructed the next-door neighbor to escort the kids into her house. Rina knew the neighbors, and they were all mesmerized as they watched the flames pour out of the windows.

Rina noticed her mother out of the corner of her eye. Dorothy was running toward their apartment when she was stopped by a fireman. As she was frantically waving her arms in the air, gesturing toward the building in obvious distress, the fireman pointed to the neighbor's house, calming her worst fears.

"Mommy! Mommy!" Rina shouted as she came running out.

"Rina, are you okay?" Dorothy said with relief as she bent down and hugged Rina tightly. Rina felt loved and cared about, a feeling she hadn't experienced in a very long time.

CHAPTER 25

CITY OF ROCHESTER
JANUARY 1974

Dorothy picked up the phone in the kitchen at Laura's house and dialed the operator. "I'd like to place a collect call to Louie Rosello from Dorothy Rosello."

Dorothy had just told her daughter that they were going to be staying at Laura's for a few weeks, and then they would be moving to a new apartment. That meant a new school with new friends for Rina. It was unwelcome news, something that made her feel sick to her stomach. Once Louie accepted the charges, Dorothy filled her parents in on the unfortunate events that happened before handing the phone to Rina, whose face lit up with joy. "Hi, Hun!" Rina squealed.

"Rina! Oh, my goodness, I miss you so much, my little sweetheart. How are you doing?" Hun said, affectionately.

"We had a fire in our apartment building last night!" Rina blurted out.

"I heard. That must have been scary."

"It was, Hun, but I'm okay."

"Thank goodness you're okay. I don't know what I would do if anything ever happened to you."

"I learned what to do at school," she stated matter-of-factly.

"That's wonderful, I'll have to send the folks at school a note and thank them for that!" Hun said.

It reminded Rina that she would not be going back to her school. "Hun, can I come live with you now?" She asked.

"I'm working on it," Hun replied, sounding disheartened.

"We're staying at Laura's for a while, and I have to go to another school and make all new friends, Hun."

"I know, I am sorry, sweetheart," Hun said, trying to hide his disappointment. He was avoiding having to tell her that he had no legal rights or grounds to take her from her mother. It was even more complicated, since he was now living in another state. He thought it was best to wait a few more years until Rina turned 14, then she could make her own decision about where she wanted to live.

"Hun," she whispered with her hand over the mouthpiece of the phone, "I'm scared."

With concern, Hun said, "Are you worried about another fire?"

"No. Not that."

"What is it Rina? What are you afraid of?"

"I think I'm going to get raped and murdered," she answered. The boys had been teasing her about it, convincing her that she was going to be the next victim. Perhaps the fire was a just a sign that something bad was about to happen to her.

Hun was stunned. What could an eleven-year-old girl know about murder, let alone rape? "Jesus, Rina! What the hell is going on up there?"

"I have double initials."

"Yes, you do, so what about it?"

"There is a bad man out there raping and killing little girls with double initials, and the kids said that I'm going to be next."

"What?" He was completely confused at this point.

"It's true, Hun."

"Listen to me," Hun said sternly. "That is not going to happen. You don't need to worry about that anymore. I am wiring some money up to your mom so that you both can move to a better area and away from all the nonsense of living in the city."

"But I want to come live with *you*, Hun. Please come get me, pleeeaaase!" she begged as she started to cry.

"I'm working on it," he said with a lump in his throat, "but until I can make that happen, please promise me that you will always follow your heart, be true to yourself and, most importantly, remember what I told you, trust your gut. Do you understand me?"

"Yes, Hun. Trust your gut. You taught me that. It is the feeling you get that tells you something isn't right and, if it doesn't feel right, then it isn't." Rina said, recalling his words.

"That's my girl! You need to trust that feeling, *always*!" Hun emphasized. "Promise me!"

"I promise, Hun," she said. Dorothy entered the kitchen, pointing to her watch.

"Time to say good-bye, Rina," Dorothy said.

Rina pouted at her mother. "I guess I gotta go, Hun," she said sadly.

"Hey, keep your chin up. Everything happens for a reason and, although you may not know why now, someday you will look back at this time in your life and it will all make sense."

"Hun, I . . ." Rina said, as a tear escaped her eye and streamed down her cheek. "I really miss you. Can you please come get me?"

With his heartbreaking, Louie tried to calm her, "Hey, do you remember the song I used to sing to you when you were a little girl?"

Rina wiped her eyes with the back of her hand, "Yes, I do." she said, smiling through her tears. "Please sing it for me, Hun."

He started out humming, then began to sing softly to her, *"Let me call you sweetheart, I'm in love with you. Let me hear you whisper that you love me too."*

She smiled, closed her eyes and swayed her head from side to side as she tightly clutched the phone receiver in her hand. She reveled in the sound of his voice. She remembered the many times he sung that song to her. That was the happiest time in her life. She sang along with Hun for the second verse.

"Keep the love light glowing in your eyes so blue," Rina smiled. *"Let me call you sweetheart, I'm in love with you."*

"Good-bye, my sweetheart. I love you," Hun said.

"Good-bye, Hun," Rina said and just as the call ended, she whispered into the receiver, "I love you too . . ."

Later that night, Rina was sleeping when she thought she heard the bedroom door creak. Did someone just enter the room? She sensed there was a male presence and that he was familiar to her. She tried to open her eyes but she couldn't. Then she felt the man lying on her, suffocating her with his heavy body. Who was this horrible man on top of her? She knew him but she couldn't see him. She tried to fight. She struggled to breathe. She wanted to scream, but she was paralyzed with fear.

The brightness of the light caused her to squint and everything around her was white. She thought she died and was in Heaven. Then she saw Hun sleeping in a chair.

He looked just like he always did when he used to nap in his favorite reclining chair with his arms folded and his chin to his chest. Her heart was filled with joy as she recognized his full head of wavy gray hair and the deep wrinkles in his face. She perked up and hopped down from the bed and quietly walked over to him, careful to not to wake him. She paused for a moment, soaking in his presence, smiling happily as she stared at him. She looked down at his hands. Hun's wonderful hands, oh how she missed the man whose hands she was now looking at. As Hun slept peacefully in the chair, Rina softly placed the palm of her hand on Hun's hand, feeling the shape of his raised veins, just as she had done when she was younger. She couldn't believe that he was here. Hun was here, and she was actually touching him. Without moving or opening his eyes, Hun smiled at her and, even though it had been a while since she last saw him, it was as if she had just seen his smile yesterday. A wonderful feeling of peace, joy, and happiness came over her. She cried out, "Oh, Hun! Yeah! You're here! *You're here!*"

Just then, the sound of her own voice jarred her into consciousness. She opened her eyes and, still disoriented, she jolted up.

"Hun!" She called out before she noticed the early morning sun beginning to shine through the bedroom window. That was when she realized she had dreamt everything.

But the nightmare, it was so vivid, so real, so terrifying. She patted the sides of her neck expecting to feel something, perhaps pain, but she didn't. Anxious to put her nightmare out of her mind, she lay back down, trying desperately to fall back into her dream about Hun. She kept picturing him sleeping in his chair and she wanted more. She wanted him to come back to her, and this time she wanted him to open his eyes, talk to her and hug her. But as hard as she tried she couldn't conjure the image. She could see only what she had already dreamt. Regardless, she still felt a certain sense of protection and she cherished the image of Hun in her mind as she drifted back to sleep.

Rina awoke a short time later that morning still reeling from her dream experiences. She went down the stairs and as she turned the corner to go into the kitchen, she was surprised by the sight of her mother crying with Laura behind her rubbing her back, trying to console her.

"Mommy?" Rina said with hesitation.

"Oh, Rina, you startled me," Dorothy said, trying to stifle her tears.

"Why are you crying?"

"Rina, please come here," she said gently. "I have some bad news."

"I'll give you some privacy," Laura said as she patted Dorothy's shoulder and looked down sympathetically at Rina. "I'll be in the next room if you need me."

Dorothy nodded at Laura and tried to compose herself before she told Rina that she received a call from her brother, Louie Junior.

Apparently, Hun had suffered a massive heart attack and had died sometime during the night. After Hun got off the phone with Rina, he went out to putter around in the yard. He went into his shed to find a tool and was reaching across his workbench when he felt a painful pinch on his hand. He looked down, saw a scorpion, and swiftly shook it off. Later, at dinner, Hun had claimed to have some shortness of breath. He told Phyllis he was going to lie down, as he wasn't feeling well. After Louie appeared to be asleep for a very long time, Phyllis went in and tried to wake him, "Louie, are you okay?" she had said, as she shook him.

When her attempts to wake him failed, she called for help and Hun was flown by an air ambulance to a hospital in Phoenix. They tried for hours to save him but unfortunately, he did not survive.

"Rina, did you hear me?" Dorothy said, "Rina?"

Rina stared into space, refusing to look at her mother.

"Rina, I said Hun died. Did you hear me?"

"No! *No!*" Rina shouted angrily.

"Oh, Rina," Dorothy said, as she burst into tears.

"It's not true! He's not dead, he's just sleeping," she said. "He's coming to get me and he's gonna take me to Arizona to live with him!"

Dorothy, consumed with her own pain, didn't have the patience to deal with Rina's. "He's not sleeping Rina. He's gone! He died and he is not coming to get you!"

"I don't believe you. *You're lying!*" Rina screamed as she hit her mother with her fists. "You're lying! He's not dead! *He's not dead!*" Rina kept yelling as Dorothy held her arms in an attempt to stop her hysterical outburst.

A distraught Rina wriggled her way out of her mother's grasp and ran out of the kitchen and into the front room where she collapsed on the floor in a heap.

Rina was inconsolable. Her pitiful wailing was so loud that it woke Bobby and Alex. The boys came running down the stairs at the sound of the commotion and were shocked to see their friend lying on the floor wracked with misery. They didn't know what to do. They just stood there staring.

* * *

"Rina?" The sound of Steve's voice brought Rina back to the present as he waved his hand in front of her face. "Where are you? You are a million miles away," he said, handing her the program for the church service.

"I was just thinking of Hun and how I was so mad at God when he died," she said, as her eyes began to well up with tears.

"I understand," Steve said, placing his hand on her knee. "I know how much he meant to you. I really wish I could have met him. He sounds like he was a wonderful man."

"He was. I will be forever grateful to him for leaving all that money in trust for me for my college education," Rina said.

"I am certain Hun is in Heaven smiling down on you with pride for all you've accomplished and for the person you have become. I'd also say that I am sure he is happy that you have made such good use of the money he left you."

Rina smiled at the thought, as that was all she ever wanted—to make Hun proud.

The church bells rang out, signaling the call to worship and the start of the morning service. But Rina couldn't focus on the sermon, and her mind continued to drift into daydreams of her past.

CHAPTER 26

CITY OF ROCHESTER
FEBRUARY 1974

After Louie's funeral, the reality that Rina was never going to see Hun again began to set in. The pain and heartache was overwhelming for her and there was no sympathy from her mother. All Dorothy seemed to do was lay on the couch in a state of depression and sleep. In fact, she was even meaner than ever towards Rina.

It was lunchtime when Rina emerged from her bedroom. She saw her mother lying on the couch so she decided to surprise her and make them something to eat. She opened the cupboard and pulled out a can of tuna fish. She opened the can, dumped the tuna into a bowl and added the mayonnaise. She stirred it carefully before taking out four slices of bread and placing them on paper plates. Feeling proud of her accomplishment, she was certain her mother would be pleased when she brought the sandwich, along with a glass of milk and a napkin, into the living room.

"Mommy, I made us lunch," she said.

Dorothy sat up, took the plate from Rina and bit into the sandwich. Abruptly she stopped chewing and wrinkled her nose. Before swallowing, she took off the piece of bread from the top of the sandwich and looked down with disapproval. "What the hell! Didn't you squeeze out the oil, Rina?" she said spitting the contents from her mouth into the napkin.

"The oil?" Rina said with confusion. "What do you mean by the oil?"

Dorothy shoved the plate back at Rina. "That is disgusting Rina, you are supposed to squeeze the oil out of the tuna fish can before you add the mayonnaise to it."

"I didn't know that," Rina said as she lowered her head in disgrace and went back into the kitchen with the sandwiches.

"You are pathetic! You can't even make a tuna fish sandwich!" Dorothy snapped.

Rina threw the sandwiches in the trash can and ran to her room. Once inside, she collapsed onto her bed and burst into tears, her head buried deep in her pillow.

Her mother's words resonated in her head. *"You are pathetic! You can't even make a tuna fish sandwich!"* As she cried she began to believe that her mother was right. Perhaps that was why her mother didn't love her, she thought, because she was a complete disappointment to her. If her own mother didn't love her, how would anyone else ever love her? Her cries continued, and she lifted her head for a moment and looked at her dresser where her porcelain music box rested, and she thought about Hun. She reached over, took the lid off and twisted the turnkey. Normally the sound of the song that played was a joyful reminder to her, but this time it caused her more heartache because now Hun was gone. She was never going to see him again. All of a sudden, the pain and devastation she felt became unbearable. She was unlovable, no man was ever going to want to marry her, her mother hated her and the one person that meant the most to her in her life was dead.

Rina cried until she had no more tears left. She sat up in her bed and stared without blinking, out the window. She felt so alone. With her cherished music box in hand, she walked up to the bedroom door and slowly opened it. Her mother had fallen back to sleep on the couch and Rina quietly walked by her towards the bathroom. She entered the bathroom, softly shut the door behind her and locked it. She stepped up to the sink and stood there for a few moments just staring in the mirror. Her face was blotchy, her blonde hair disheveled, her normally bright eyes, red and puffy from crying so much. She opened the medicine cabinet. Band-Aids, aspirin, mercurochrome, calamine lotion and a prescription bottle. Her eyes fixated on the pill bottle that was prescribed to her mother right after Hun's death. She picked up the bottle and read it. Diazepam. The directions read: Take one to two pills by mouth every 4 hours as needed for pain, anxiety and depression.

Pain was certainly what Rina was feeling. She set the pills on the side of the sink and reached for the paper cup dispenser as she turned on the water faucet. She pushed down on the cap, opened the pill bottle and poured out a handful of round yellow pills from the half-empty pill bottle into her hand. Perhaps her mother would be happier without her, she thought. She felt hopeless, that she had nothing to live for. She thought about not feeling pain anymore, she thought about life after death as she learned in church. She thought about Hun and about being with him again in Heaven, just as they said at his funeral Mass.

She brought the handful of pills to her mouth and swallowed, choking them down with the water. *There, it's done!* She thought as she stood staring at her reflection in the medicine cabinet mirror. After several minutes passed, she began to feel dizzy. She was still staring at herself when her eyelids grew heavy and her head drooped. She reached for her music box and as her legs grew weak, she stepped back against the wall and slid down onto the floor. She carefully took off the lid of her beloved music box, turned the key and then set it back down. She listened to the music play and when she couldn't hold the weight of her head up any longer, she laid down on the cold tile floor. She looked up with blurred vision as the music slowed. She smiled as she imagined how happy Hun was going to be to see her. She felt her breath becoming shallow as she was getting weaker and drowsier.

"Hun!" she called out to the man in the distance. "Hun, it's me, Rina!" she yelled at the figure as it walked away from her. "Hun, wait up! Where are you going? Hun, don't walk so fast, please wait for me!" She shouted as she ran after him. Finally, she caught up to him and gripped his arm, turning him around to face her. "Hun, why are you walking away from me?"

As he turned around she couldn't make out his face as it was fuzzy, but she knew it had to be Hun. "Hun, I'm so happy to see you!" she said, but her smile faded as she could sense that Hun was not happy to see her. He looked down at her with his arms crossed shaking his head. She could see the look of disappointment, just as she had when she was a child and was being scolded for misbehaving. She hated disappointing Hun, and what was even worse was she could also see tears on his cheeks, just like the ones she saw when they moved to Arizona and left her behind. Then, without saying a word, he walked away from her and disappeared into the distance.

Rina opened one eye and could see the white claw-foot on the porcelain tub. She was lying on the bathroom floor and couldn't move, when suddenly she panicked at the thought of dying. *What have I done? I don't want to die! I DON'T WANT TO DIE!* She thought. She wanted to yell for her mother to help her, but she was extremely weak and couldn't speak. Somehow, she gathered her strength and lifted herself up to the toilet where she brought her hand up, placed her finger in her mouth and down her throat.

After throwing up several times, she filled a cup with water, drank it, and then lay back down on the floor. She slept for a while before she was able to sit up and drink some more water. She stood up and had to balance herself along the sink to walk to the door. She left the bathroom and noticed that her mother was now awake.

"You were in the bathroom for a long time Rina, what were you doing in there?" Dorothy asked from the living room.

"Uh, nothing . . ." She tried to think of something she could tell her. "I don't feel good, I . . . have a stomach ache," she said.

143

"You do look very pale, come here," Dorothy said, putting her hand on Rina's forehead. "You are a bit clammy also. Lie here and I'll bring you some ginger ale and make you some soup."

"Thanks, mommy," Rina said as she lay back against the armrest on the sofa.

Later that night Phyllis called.

Rina picked up the receiver. "Hello?"

"Hi Rina, how are you?" Phyllis said.

"Hi Grandma, I'm okay," Rina replied.

"Are you sure, you don't sound right," Phyllis said with concern.

"I just don't feel good," Rina answered.

"Okay, I hope you feel better."

"Thanks, Grandma."

"The reason I called, Rina, is that I need to tell you something," Phyllis said. "You know that you were very special to Hun and me?"

"Yes, I know," Rina said, hoping that Hun wasn't upset with her for what she did earlier.

Phyllis's tone became serious. "Rina, what I wanted to tell you is that Hun tried really hard to get you to be able to come and live with us, but he wasn't able to fight the court systems. In the end, the judge made the final decision that there was not any legal reason to award us custody."

"What does that mean?' Rina asks.

"It means the law said you had to live with your mother."

"Stupid law!" Rina said with disgust.

"But what I really wanted to let you know is that Hun had put aside some money for you to use for college someday. It is in trust for you at the bank and that money is for your college education and no one, not even your mother, can touch it," Phyllis told her.

"Does my mom know about it?" Rina asked.

"Yes, she does and she isn't very happy about it, so please don't bring it up to her."

"Okay Grandma, I won't," Rina promised.

CHAPTER 27

CITY OF ROCHESTER
MARCH 1978

S oon after Hun's funeral, Rina went to a new school. It was tough starting in the middle of the school year, but Rina quickly made friends with a nice girl named Wendy who sat next to her in class. Wendy was the youngest of seven children. She was a bubbly brown-haired girl, with a chubby face and a friendly smile. Her mother, Mrs. Peevey, was the lunchroom lady and she was the most wonderful woman Rina had ever met. Mrs. Peevey was a jolly woman, caring and considerate, with short strawberry blond hair and warm brown eyes. She was a soft-spoken natural mother with nurturing instincts, and she was loved dearly by all the children at school. Rina and Wendy became fast friends and it was that friendship that became a turning point in Rina's life.

Rina and Wendy were best friends well into high school, and throughout those years Rina often shared with her friend the stories of the tempestuous relationship she had with her mother. It seemed Dorothy and Rina fought constantly, and as Rina got older, she became combative in return. One afternoon, Wendy was over waiting in Rina's bedroom while Rina and her mother were in the living room arguing about Rina's phone privileges. Rina was allowed to give their home phone number to only two friends and could talk on the phone for only ten minutes at a time. Dorothy was very strict about her rule and would time Rina's conversations. At nine minutes Rina would get a warning that her time was almost up. If she did not hang up at the ten-minute mark, Dorothy would press the disconnect button on the phone.

Rina knew the rules and, therefore, gave the number only to her friends Wendy and Dawn. Unbeknownst to Rina, Dawn wasn't aware of the rule and had apparently given the number to Sandy, another friend from school. It was on this day that Sandy called and asked to speak to Rina.

"Rina! Telephone!" Dorothy called from the kitchen.

"Coming, Mom!" Rina said as she came out of her room.

"Who's Sandy?" Dorothy asked angrily, with her hand covering the mouthpiece on the handset.

"My friend from school," Rina answered. "Why do you ask?"

"What is she doing with this phone number?"

"I don't know. I didn't give it to her," Rina replied nervously.

"Tell her you cannot talk right now," Dorothy said through clenched teeth.

"Mom, please! You're embarrassing me," Rina said under her breath, knowing that Sandy probably heard the whole conversation. She clutched the phone and spoke quietly into the receiver. "Hello?"

"Hi, Rina. Is everything okay?" a bewildered Sandy asked.

"I can't really talk right now, Sandy," Rina said as she looked over at her mother's livid gaze.

"Gosh, I'm really sorry, Rina," Sandy said.

"Don't be, you didn't do anything wrong. I'll see you at school tomorrow."

"Okay, bye!"

Rina had no sooner put the phone on the cradle when Dorothy began to yell at her. "It looks like you will now lose your phone privileges for a month!"

"What? Are you serious? That's not fair, Mom!"

"You know the rules! And you better make sure your friends know that they are not to give out your phone number ever again."

"You're ridiculous! No one else's parents are like this, and they have a lot more freedom than I do."

"Freedom?"

"Yeah, *freedom!*" Rina said sarcastically. "You know, this is America!" Rina stood up straight, put her hand on her heart and condescendingly began to sing "My country 'tis of thee, sweet land of liberty—"

Whack! Dorothy smacked her across the face. Rina's cheek burned. "Jesus mom, what the hell is wrong with you?"

"You disrespectful little brat!" an angry Dorothy said as she lifted her hand up to slap Rina again.

"Please, not the face!" Rina tried to block another slap. She didn't want to have to explain marks on her face at school. But Dorothy kept slapping and punching her until Rina was able to escape and ran to her room. Once inside, she saw a shocked Wendy sitting on the bed. Rina latched the hook to lock her bedroom door.

"Let me in, Rina, or I'll break this door down!" Dorothy shouted as she furiously pounded on the door.

Rina looked at Wendy, over to the open window and then back to Wendy as Dorothy kicked at the door. It would be only a matter of minutes before she would get through so Rina made a quick decision to escape. She jumped out the window onto the hood of the car parked in the driveway next door. She slid down the hood, onto the ground and ran down the street, leaving a shocked Wendy behind.

The bedroom door burst open and there stood a red-faced, infuriated Dorothy. "Where is she?" she shouted angrily. Mortified, all Wendy could do was point towards the window and tell Dorothy that she had to go home as she rushed past her and out the door.

A few moments later she caught up to Rina down the street. "What the hell was that?" a wide-eyed Wendy asked.

"Welcome to my life," Rina answered.

"Holy shit, that was heavy!"

"That was actually pretty mild, she's usually worse."

"Wow!" Was all a dismayed Wendy could say.

"Yeah, well, I think she hates me."

"Geez, Rina! You have a red handprint on your face."

"Damn it! I hope it goes away before school tomorrow."

"Come on, let's go to my house. You can't go back there right now."

"Yeah, you're probably right." Rina conceded.

Later that evening, Mrs. Peevey called Wendy downstairs and asked her what had happened to Rina. Wendy filled her mother in on the incidents that Rina had shared with her in the past, including what she had witnessed earlier that day. Mrs. Peevey offered to call Dorothy and to let her know that Rina could stay at their house for a few days, hoping that this would allow her mother to settle down a bit.

After a few days had passed, Rina went back home expecting that her mother would be more reasonable. For a few weeks, things seemed to be better between Rina and her mother. Unfortunately, the truth was, the only reason Dorothy was being nice was because if Rina didn't live there, her mother would not be able to collect welfare.

Rina was soon to learn that everything happened for a reason and as the relationship between Rina and her mother deteriorated, it became more explosive than ever. It was after a particularly intense fight that left Rina with a black eye that Mrs. Peevey extended the offer for Rina to come live with them permanently.

Rina, now fifteen years old, made the decision to take them up on their offer and she happily moved in with the Peevey's. A couple of months later, Dorothy and Laura moved to Texas. Even though Rina and her mother didn't get along, Rina still felt saddened by her mother moving away. She was also often embarrassed, having to answer the constant questions as to why she lived with Wendy's family.

Rina settled in nicely with the Peevey's and they treated her as their own. She now had the family life she had always wanted, with two parents, a big house with a pool, family dinners and a neighborhood full of friends. Rina spoke to her mother over the phone on occasion, but it wasn't often, and it was almost as though she had been adopted by the Peevey's and they were her family now.

Rina thrived in her new environment and was an excellent student throughout high school. Ever since she had learned that the law would not allow her to live with her grandparents, she was determined to become a lawyer so that she could help people. It was Wendy's older brother Kelly who affirmed Rina's decision to be a lawyer. Kelly also assisted Rina with her school selection, the college entrance paperwork and choosing the proper curriculum as a prerequisite for law school. He even helped her study for the Law School Entrance Test when the time came. It was thanks to his support, in addition to the money Hun left her that Rina went off to Albany University and eventually Albany Law School. Rina's past, including her memories of the double initial murders, was all but forgotten. That was until now.

* * *

Rina was jarred out of her daydream when the minister held up both his hands, gesturing for the congregation to stand as he delivered his Benediction prayer. "May the Lord bless you and keep you. May the Lord make his face to shine upon you and be gracious to you. May the Lord lift up his countenance upon you and give you peace. Amen."

CHAPTER 28

MONROE COUNTY COURTHOUSE
SEPTEMBER 1991

After two days of jury selection, the first day of the trial had finally arrived. A stalwart bailiff stood proudly at the front of the courtroom, clearly reveling in his moment in the sun with the eyes of so many paying such close attention to him. "All rise!" he said, puffing out his chest. "The U.S. District Court for Monroe County is now in session, the Honorable Judge Crandall presiding."

Right on cue, Judge Crandall emerged from his chambers and surveyed the courtroom before him. There was a lot of pressure on him, presiding over a case that had, at one-time, garnered national attention, a cold case that had lain dormant for almost two decades. His expression was pensive. He wanted to make certain that justice was served, that the jury would hear a fair trial and that all of the evidence in the case would effectively sway the jury one way or the other.

Rina's mood was anxious that morning. She was not sure if she was ready to face this seemingly insurmountable challenge. She felt as though she had the weight of the world on her shoulders. It was a feeling that she had been dealing with for two months now, since the moment she had received the case files. Today, she would have to try to overcome the extreme heart palpitations, the labored breathing and the sweaty palms. Today, she would begin to fight the battle of her life. Today, she was determined to see that justice prevailed.

In contrast, her opponent, Thomas Cugino, was quite sure of himself. He was beaming confidently as he stood across the aisle from Rina. He wasn't worried. He had years of trial experience in his favor and he looked forward to this day when he would have the opportunity to do what he did best. He looked at his competition across the courtroom floor and was quite certain he would soon have yet another victory to add to his list of courtroom accomplishments.

Rina stood nervously, and as the jurors began to enter the jury box, her eyes were drawn to the big gold words on the wall above the judge's bench. "In God We Trust." She did trust in God. She trusted in God to ease her own suffering from time to time. She had trusted in God to give her the strength to leave her mother. She had trusted God to provide her with the stamina to get through law school. And today, she trusted in God to give her the acumen she desperately needed for this trial.

"Please be seated," Judge Crandall instructed the courtroom and then turned to address the jury. "Jurors, this is a criminal case brought by the State of New York, charging the defendant, Mr. Burns, with three counts of kidnapping, rape, and murder in the first degree. It will be your duty to decide if Mr. Burns is guilty or not guilty of the crimes he is charged with. I'd like to impress upon you that the burden of proof lies on the prosecution and, in order for you to find the defendant guilty, you must be certain of his guilt beyond any reasonable doubt. It is also important that you make your decision based on the evidence you are presented with during this trial and not on any personal opinions or anything you have heard in the media." Judge Crandall said. He looked at Rina for her to proceed with her opening statement. "The prosecuting attorney, Ms. Rosello, will begin."

Rina took a deep breath, stood up, and glanced quickly out into the audience. The courtroom was crowded with observers of this high-profile case. Steve caught her eye and nodded confidently. She smiled briefly and then her face became serious. She pulled her shoulders back and addressed the courtroom in a professional manner.

"Your Honor, counsel, and ladies and gentlemen of the jury, my name is Rina Rosello and I am representing the people of New York State against the defendant." She directed her attention toward the jury as she continued with her opening statement.

"On November 16, 1971, at around 4:40 p.m., ten-year-old Carmella Candelario left her home to walk two blocks to the drug store, to refill a prescription for her mother. She handed the pharmacist the empty pill bottle along with her mother's Medicaid card. She told the pharmacists that she would be back to pick it up. Unfortunately, she never did make it back, because an hour later, on Interstate 490 near the Churchville exit ramp, as traffic was traveling in a typical rush-hour fashion, Carmella, who was naked from the waist down, was furiously attempting to escape her killer. She was running toward the traffic in sheer terror and waving her arms desperately while the car on the side of the road was backing up towards her.

"Unfortunately, no one called about what they had seen until three days later, after her violently raped and horribly battered body was discovered." Gasps could be heard in the courtroom. Rina looked loathingly at the defendant then back at the jury as she continued.

"Then on April 2, 1973, the defendant struck again when eleven-year-old Whitney Walkowski ran an errand to the corner store for her mother to pick up some groceries and diapers for her younger sister. But Whitney did not return home on that ill-fated day. Instead, while her frantic mother was desperately trying to find her, Whitney was being brutally and heartlessly sexually assaulted before she was strangled to death. The next day a traveler noticed his dog in the distance sniffing something white that stood out from the gloomy gray ground cover. It was a little girl's bare legs. A girl later identified as Whitney Walkowski, lying face down on the cold wet ground." Rina paused for a brief moment. She looked down and pinched the bridge of her nose to prevent the tears from falling from her eyes.

"Carmella and Whitney both weighed less than sixty-five pounds and they didn't stand a chance. Unfortunately, for Maria Mancuso," Rina said, "the defendant wasn't finished with his reign of terror yet. It was November 26, 1973, only ten months after the body of Whitney was discovered, when Maria Mancuso, just days after her eleventh birthday, didn't return home after school. When she was not home by five, her distraught mother called the Rochester Police Department. She was so distressed that she could barely speak as she reported her daughter missing. Two days later her horribly bruised and viciously raped body was found in a ditch in Macedon. Just as he had done with Carmella and Whitney, he also strangled Maria with a belt and heartlessly left her on the side of the road as if she were trash." Silence filled the courtroom. Rina cleared her throat.

"Jurors, you will be shown evidence and hear testimony from several witnesses in this trial. The first witness you will hear from is Mrs. Gaezzer, who was Whitney's friend and the last person to see Whitney alive.

"The next witness is Mr. Ellis who will tell you about his altercation with the defendant just hours before Maria was murdered and her small lifeless body was dumped in a ditch less than a mile from where the witness had seen the defendant.

"You will hear from forensic scientist Mr. Gaspar, who will explain the forensic evidence that links the defendant to the crimes. Finally, the prosecution will bring you Carmella Candelario's mother, Lauren Candelario, who will verify that Mr. Burns was acquainted with Carmella. She will also describe her visit with the defendant just days before he brutally raped and murdered Carmella."

Rina then paused and walked over to the prosecution table to take a sip of water, leaving the jury a moment to digest what she had just said.

"I am confident that the evidence will show beyond a reasonable doubt, that not only was the defendant acquainted with all the girls, but there is also overwhelming evidence in this case pointing at the guilt of the defendant, including the identification of him and his vehicle.

"Ladies and gentleman," she said, knowing that her narrative was coming to an end, "we are all in the presence of a heartless serial killer who is sitting in this very courtroom and, at the end of this trial, I know that you all will agree that the defendant, Mr. Burns, is guilty on all counts of these heinous crimes."

CHAPTER 29

MONROE COUNTY COURTHOUSE
SEPTEMBER 1991

Tom rose to address the jury after a nod from the judge. Even though he and Judge Crandall had quite a long history together, the two of them had to be sure they didn't let their relationship interfere with the trial as neither of them wanted a mistrial. They couldn't risk tarnishing their reputations, so they put on their professional facades and proceeded.

The attorney cleared his throat and began his opening statement. "Good morning and thank you all for being here. I am Thomas Cugino, and it is my privilege to be defending Mr. Burns here today. I'd like to start by saying thank you to Ms. Rosello for representing the state in this case.

"Wow! That was quite a story we all just heard!" Tom said boisterously as he shook his head. "I have a young daughter myself and just as everyone else in this courtroom, I too am very disturbed by the horrible crimes that were committed against Carmella, Whitney, and Maria in the early 1970s. However, this case is not as simple as the prosecuting attorney, Ms. Rosello, would lead you to believe. Instead, this is a clear case of misidentification, coincidence and circumstantial evidence." Tom slowly walked over to the defense table, where he paused for a few seconds before he continued.

"Ladies and gentleman, what you are seeing in front of you is an innocent man." He said pointing at Mr. Burns. "My client is a devout Catholic who has a clearly documented track record of being a positive role model for children. He had a long, prosperous career as a public servant for Monroe County and he was a contributing member of the community.

"Now, I'm not going to take up a lot of your time. I'm not going to tell you things that are irrelevant to this case, and I'm not going to embellish on the realities here. But I am going to tell you the simple truth and present the facts that will put a reasonable doubt in all your minds and prove that my client, Mr. Burns, did not commit these crimes." Then he walked confidently over to the jury box. He made eye contact with each juror and smiled charmingly at the middle-aged woman who was smiling, obviously enamored of him. *Perhaps she thinks I'm handsome*, Thomas thought to himself. That's just what I need.

"We are all going to hear testimony in this case representing both the prosecution and the defense. I urge you to consider the credibility and reliability of the witnesses, especially those identifying the defendant from what they believe they had seen a long time ago. On behalf of Mr. Burns, the defense will call to the stand Mr. Nicholson, the former manager of Mr. Burns, who will attest to his exemplary performance, impeccable reliability and dedicated service while he worked for him. You will also hear from Mr. Gallipeau, the technician who administered a polygraph test to my client.

"Lastly, and most importantly, as a testament to his own innocence, you will hear from Mr. Burns himself in his defense." It was the aspect of the case Cugino was least thrilled about. Naturally, he had advised his client not to testify on his own behalf. But Mr. Burns insisted. He looked forward to the cross examination from Rina, and after several attempts to change his mind, the attorney relented. In the mind of Mr. Burns, he presumed he would be able to intimidate Rina as if she were still a young girl and thus cause her to slip up, helping his case.

Thomas continued. "I ask you all to keep an open mind in this case. Please consider all the evidence that is being presented and, most importantly, do not be swayed by emotions." Thomas walked over to his client, placed his hand on the defendant's shoulder and then sat down beside him.

"Thank you, Mr. Cugino," Judge Crandall said, and looked over at Rina. "Is the prosecution ready to present its case?"

"Yes, Your Honor. I would like to call my first witness, Mrs. Gaezzer," Rina said.

The courtroom deputy swore in the witness, and Rina began her direct examination. Mrs. Gaezzer wrung her hands in her lap. Even though it had occurred so long ago, her normally jovial personality and pretty face were showing signs of nervousness and of grief over the murder of Whitney. The fact that she had been so young when it happened had added to her distress.

"Mrs. Gaezzer," Rina said, "thank you for being here today. Will you please tell the court about the last time you had seen your friend Whitney Walkowski?"

"Um," She said nervously. "It was a rainy day in April back in 1973. I was walking down the street in our neighborhood with another friend when we saw Whitney walking behind us."

"What was Whitney doing?" Rina asked.

"She was walking home from the store."

"What makes you believe she was walking home from the store?"

"She was carrying two brown paper bags that appeared to be full of groceries."

"Please continue, Mrs. Gaezzer," Rina said.

"I wanted to wait up for her, but because it was raining we wanted to get home, so we kept walking."

"Then what happened?" Rina asked.

"It was raining a little harder, so we began to run. That is when I turned around again and saw Whitney had stopped to lean up against the fence and she was balancing one of the bags with her knee. I presumed it was to get a better grip on it."

"Did you notice anything else?"

"Yes. I also saw a car driving by her slowly."

"Can you describe the car?" Rina asked.

"It was a long car, a Lincoln Continental."

"That is a pretty specific make and model. Can you tell the court what makes you believe that it was a Lincoln Continental?"

"As it drove by us I could see that it had a wheel-shaped half circle on the trunk with the word Continental in silver letters written on it."

"As the car drove past, did you notice anything else?"

"I saw Whitney in the front seat. I just assumed she got a ride home from a friend or family member."

"What made you believe it was Whitney?"

"Because when the car drove by, I turned around quickly and saw that Whitney was gone. And the girl was wearing a pink coat like the one Whitney was wearing that day."

"Thank you, Mrs. Gaezzer. Let the record show that the witness described a Lincoln Continental driving by with Whitney, wearing the pink jacket that was found at the scene, in it. The prosecution also submits into evidence the Department of Motor Vehicle records showing that a 1969 Lincoln Continental Mark III was registered to Mr. Burns in June 1972."

Rina turned and walked away from the stand. "Your witness, Mr. Cugino," she said.

"Mrs. Gaezzer," Thomas said anxiously as he rose from his chair. "How old were you in 1973?"

"I was eleven, the same age as Whitney," Mrs. Gaezzer answered.

"As you know, it is now 1991. Eighteen years is a long time. Isn't it fair to say your memory could be a bit fuzzy?"

"I remember that day very well, sir, because I still feel guilty that we didn't wait up for her." It was truly a day she had relived over and over in her mind. The constant what-ifs. The pangs of guilt that bubbled up when she thought back to that day.

"The car you describe, the Lincoln Continental. Wasn't it one of the most popular cars of the 1970s?"

"Objection!" Rina interjected. "How would the witness know the popularity of a car, Your Honor?"

"The relevance," the attorney retorted, "is that Lincoln was a very popular vehicle manufacturer in 1973, and I'm pointing out that the witness must have seen a lot of them back then."

"I'll allow it," Judge Crandall said, giving the matter very little thought. "Please continue, Mr. Cugino."

"Thank you, Your Honor. "Mrs. Gaezzer, would you say that you had seen a lot of Lincolns in the '70s?"

"I guess they were popular back then, I really don't know, though."

"Mrs. Gaezzer, you said you had seen Whitney in the car, the Lincoln Continental, as it drove by, is that correct?"

"Yes, it is."

"And you said she was wearing a pink jacket?"

"That is correct."

"Can you please explain to the jurors how you could see the jacket?'

"Excuse me, but I'm not sure what you mean."

"I have a thirteen-year-old daughter myself, Mrs. Gaezzer, and I have to say that when she sits in the front seat of my car, her head is the only thing that can be seen in the window, so I find it a bit hard to believe that you would be able to see what the little girl in the car was wearing that day, wouldn't you agree?"

"I—I thought I saw the pink jacket, but . . . I don't know."

Rina put her head back and closed her eyes. *SHIT! I didn't even think of that. How could I be so stupid?* She thought. This was her strongest witness testimony and the thought of losing the jury so early in the game made her heart begin to race. But Thomas Cugino wasn't done yet. He wasn't about to let it go that easily. He wanted to be sure the witness testimony was completely disregarded.

"And didn't you also say it had begun to rain a little harder?"

"Yes."

"Were the windows fogged up?"

"The windows?"

"Yes, the windows of the car. Typically, when it rains, car windows tend to fog up a little bit. You know, because of the condensation building inside the cabin? Were the windows of the car you had seen that day fogged up?"

"I guess, maybe a little bit."

"With the rain, *and* foggy windows, how can you be certain there was even a little girl in the car?" Thomas gave the jury a suspicious stare, as a signal that he was onto something that they should pay very close attention to.

"I assumed it was her, because when I turned around she was gone."

"So," the attorney said with a long, dramatic pause, "let me get this straight. You recall seeing a car, one of the most popular cars of the 1970s, a Lincoln Continental, drive by with what you assumed was your friend Whitney inside of it, but you didn't actually see Whitney get into the car? And it was raining that day? And you were only eleven years old at the time? Perhaps your memory is a bit fuzzy?" The attorney's condescension was palpable.

"That is not what I said. I said—"

"No more questions, Your Honor!" Tom interrupted. He put his hand up to the witness to signify that he was done and smiled confidently at Rina as he walked by her on his way back to his seat.

"Thank you, Mrs. Gaezzer, you may step down." Judge Crandall said. "Ms. Rosello, please call your next witness to the stand."

"Yes, Your Honor, the State calls Mr. Ellis to the stand." Rina watched the shaky old man as he slowly made his way to the stand. He rested his walking cane up against the back wall and carefully sat down. He was in his late seventies now, and Rina hoped that he had remembered everything they had discussed prior to the trial. It was very important that his testimony go off without a hitch for the slightest mistake would give the defendant's attorney the opportunity to take a stab. She was already feeling less hopeful now that Thomas Cugino had destroyed her first witness's testimony. She figured that if he used the same aggressive nature to attack all of her evidence, it may take an act of God to pull this whole thing off.

"Hello, Mr. Ellis."

"Hello," the man said with a hoarse voice.

"Please tell the court what happened on November 26, 1973." Rina continued.

"Yes ma'am," he said clearing his throat. "I was traveling on Route 350 in Macedon around five-thirty p.m., on my way home from work, when I noticed a vehicle pulled over on the side of the road. I slowed down thinking that the car had a flat tire."

"What else did you see?"

"As I slowly drove past the man standing there, he pushed a young chubby girl behind him. Then he stepped in front of his car as if he was trying to block both the girl and his license plate from my view."

"Did you think that was odd?"

"Yeah, I did, but the man stepped aggressively toward my vehicle with his fists clenched in a threatening manner." Mr. Ellis paused to take a sip of water.

"What did you do next Mr. Ellis?" Rina asked.

The man hesitated, visibly upset as he answered. "Regrettably, I drove off." He looked down at his hands nervously as he continued. "I thought that perhaps he was just letting his daughter out to go to the bathroom and I didn't want a confrontation. I had no idea that a young girl was missing and, honestly, to this day, I have never been able to forgive myself for not doing something," he said, as his eyes grew wide with sadness.

"Mr. Ellis, do you recognize the man you saw that day here in the courtroom today?" Rina asked.

"I believe that is him over there." Mr. Ellis said, pointing in the direction of the defendant. "He looks a bit older, but I am pretty sure that is the guy I saw that night with the little girl."

"Thank you, Mr. Ellis," Rina said.

"Your witness, Mr. Cugino," Judge Crandall said.

Thomas Cugino stood up, ready to tear into Mr. Ellis like a lion with a piece of meat. "Mr. Ellis, you said you were coming home from work, is that correct?" the attorney asked.

"Yes, that is correct." Mr. Ellis answered.

"So about five-thirty in November?"

"That sounds about right."

"Isn't it dark by then?"

The witness thought for a moment. This wasn't one of the questions he and Rina had discussed, but he did remember Rina's plea to remain calm. "I guess it was dusk and starting to get dark at that time." Mr. Ellis answered.

Thomas couldn't help but let out a faint laugh, saying, "I don't know about you, Mr. Ellis, but it always appears to me, thanks to daylight savings time when we put the clocks back an hour, that it is dark by five p.m. just as I am getting out of work. Taking that into consideration, wouldn't you agree that it may have been too dark for you to see the man clearly?"

"It was getting dark, but I got a pretty good look at him," Mr. Ellis answered.

"A *pretty good look*?" Thomas questioned sternly.

"Yes," the witness replied confidently.

"Let me just clarify that eighteen years ago in November you were coming home from work. It's dark out at five-thirty, as it typically is that time of the year, when you approached a car on the side of the road with a man and a young girl, and you *think* you see the man in the courtroom today?" His facial expressions were exaggerated for dramatic effect. It was part of his act, much like what young actors are taught shortly before they first venture onto the stage: make your movements larger than life so people can read your emotions. He wanted the jury to consider it unlikely that someone could remember what a stranger looked like at night so many years ago. The jury waited patiently for the witness to answer.

"That is correct," Mr. Ellis said.

"Mr. Ellis, I must say you have a better memory than I do, to be able to recognize a man you saw on the side of the road for a moment *almost two decades ago* when it was dark out. That is very impressive." The attorney looked over at the jury with a sarcastic sneer.

"Objection, Your Honor!" Rina shouted. "He's badgering the witness."

"Withdrawn. No further questions," Thomas stated.

"Thank you, Mr. Ellis, you may step down. At this time, I'd like to take a brief recess. Court will resume in thirty minutes." Judge Crandall announced.

CHAPTER 30

MONROE COUNTY COURTHOUSE
SEPTEMBER 1991

Rina burst through the ladies' room door and made a beeline for the sink. She turned on the faucet and splashed cold water on her face to try to calm herself down. "That son of a bitch!" she said with clenched teeth to her reflection in the mirror. She buried her face in her hands and tried to talk herself out of a full-blown panic attack. She was no match for Thomas Cugino and she was quickly losing all hope. Just then, the door opened and a woman walked in. Rina quickly composed herself, brushed herself off and left as the woman entered an empty stall.

Steve was outside waiting for her as she came out of the restroom. "Are you okay?" he asked with concern.

"No. Quite honestly, I am *not* okay!" she snapped back.

"I know you are upset, but please, just try to calm down."

"That is easy for you to say! You're not the one getting your ass kicked in there!"

"I know, you're right. I'm just worried about you."

"Don't worry about me, save it for the families of the victims who are reliving their worst nightmare, only to watch tha walk."

"Now Rina, you don't know that is what is going to happe

"At this point, it isn't looking good. I think I made a mist is too big for me and I'm not sure I am cut out for this."

"Don't sell yourself short, you're a great attorney."

"Yeah, sure. Well, I have to get back in there and get beat more," a dismal Rina replied.

* * *

"Your next witness, Ms. Rosello," the judge stated as ᴜᴜᴄ ᴜᴀᴉ resumed.

Rina stood, glancing over at Thomas Cugino. *Hopefully, he can't crack this one,* she thought. "The prosecution calls expert witness Mr. Gaspar to the stand."

The man made his way to the stand, adjusting his glasses as he walked. He was wearing a dark-colored blazer and a light blue dress shirt underneath. His back was straight as he peered out over the assembled crowd. "Mr. Gaspar," Rina began, "can you please tell the court where you work and how long you have been there?"

"I am a forensic scientist for the Rochester Crime Lab and I have been there for about five years." Mr. Gaspar replied.

"Thank you," Rina said. "Can you please tell us about your report on the evidence in the murders of Carmella Candelario, Whitney Walkowski, and Maria Mancuso?"

"Yes, of course. In June we received a hit on a partial fingerprint found on one of the buttons of Carmella Candelario's sweater. Mr. Burns was arrested in California for an unrelated crime and his fingerprint came up in our database, which effectively reopened the cases." Mr. Gaspar explained.

"What else can you tell us about the cases?" Rina asked.

"We know that all three of the victims died of asphyxiation with the same object, presumably a belt. We also know that all three victims had eaten within two hours of their deaths. The stomach contents of Carmella revealed a milkshake. It appeared that Whitney had eaten custard and Maria had been digesting a cheeseburger. Additionally, all three victims had white cat fur on their clothing." Mr. Gaspar explained.

"White cat fur?" Rina asked.

"Yes, white cat fur was found on all three victims, but none of them had owned a cat," the expert witness responded.

"One last question, Mr. Gaspar. In your expert opinion, if all three girls had white cat fur on them, and none of them had owned a white cat at the time of their deaths, would it be safe to say that not only were all three victims killed by the same man, but that either the killer had a white cat, or he was in frequent contact with one?"

"Yes, absolutely," the man agreed.

"Thank you very much, Mr. Gaspar. No further questions, Your Honor," Rina concluded.

"Your witness, Mr. Cugino," Judge Crandall instructed.

"Mr. Gaspar, you said that the fingerprint found on Carmella's sweater was that of my client, Mr. Burns?" Tom asked. He was in a near sprint towards the witness stand.

"Yes, that is correct."

"Mr. Gaspar, my client does not deny that he was at the home of Lauren Candelario and that he knew Carmella. In fact, he admits that he was at their house just a few days before Carmella was murdered and that it was a cold fall day. He claims that when she was going out to play, he helped her button up her sweater before she went outside."

"Objection! He's leading the witness, Your Honor!" Rina retorted.

"Sustained. Is there a question for the witness, Mr. Cugino?" Judge Crandall inquired.

"Yes, Your Honor. Mr. Gaspar, in your expert opinion, would you say it was possible for that fingerprint to have been there from a few days prior?" Tom asks.

"I guess it's possible, but it's not likely," Mr. Gaspar answered.

"Please, Mr. Gaspar, do us all a favor and answer the questions with a yes or no. I'll ask that again. Is it possible for a fingerprint to have been on the button of Carmella Candelario's sweater from a few days prior?"

Mr. Gaspar paused. "Yes."

"Can you please say that a little louder for the jury, Mr. Gaspar?" Thomas said, once again gesticulating for the benefit of the jury and the audience that was sitting behind him. He placed his right hand behind his ear, as if trying to hear more clearly what the man was saying.

"Yes, it's possible," Mr. Gaspar said, this time in a much louder voice.

"No further questions, Your Honor," the confident attorney said as he returned to his seat

"Ms. Rosello, are you ready for your next witness?" Judge Crandall asked.

"Yes, Your Honor. The State calls its final witness, Lauren Candelario, the mother of Carmella Candelario, to the stand," Rina responded as sounds of people shifting in their seats could be heard.

Lauren Candelario's eyes bore years of suffering and agony. She approached the witness stand, hoping against hope that what she was about to say would in some way help to put this man behind bars for the murder of her daughter. It would not ease the suffering, but at least she could heal on some level and close a chapter that had remained open for far too long.

All eyes were on Lauren as she took the stand and was sworn in.

"Good morning, Mrs. Candelario," Rina began. "First off, I apologize for you having to endure this process, given what you have already been through. All those painful memories," she said sympathetically. Lauren tightened her lips. She had since run out of tears over the loss of her daughter.

"Can you please tell us what happened on November 16, 1971?" Rina asked.

"It was the worst day of my life," Lauren responded. "It was the day my daughter, Carmella, was taken from me."

"Yes," Rina agreed. "I know, and I am so very sorry. Please continue by telling us what happened that day," Rina said.

"I needed medicine for the baby." Lauren smiled for a moment as she recalled the spirited nature her daughter had possessed and then went back to telling the story. "Carmella was always eager to please, so she happily offered to go to the drugstore to fill the prescription for me. She urged me to let her go alone. It was only two blocks away, so I didn't see the harm in letting her go. I have lived with guilt and regret ever since," Lauren said as she bowed her head and closed her eyes.

"Do you know the defendant?" Rina asked.

"Yes," Lauren responded with disgust as she looked up and over at the defendant.

"How do you know him?"

"I met him out one night."

"Did you and Mr. Burns date?" Rina asked.

"No, we went out a few times, but it was more like a friendship," she responded.

"I don't mean to get personal, but were you and Mr. Burns ever romantic with each other."

"We were not. He was more like a brother to me. He would come over and we'd just talk, or he'd play with the kids and sometimes he'd take me to the store. I didn't have a vehicle, you know."

"When he took you to the store, did he pay for your groceries?"

"Sometimes he did."

"Did he expect anything in return from you?"

"If he did, he never acted like it. I just always thought he was being nice because he knew I was on public assistance and he wanted to help me out."

"Since Mr. Burns had been at your house several times, did Carmella know him?

"Yes, she did."

"Do you recall the last time he was at your house?"

"Yes, it was a couple of days before . . ." the bereaved mother said before stopping to take in a lungful of air. She fought back her tears. "Before Carmella was raped and murdered."

"I know how painful this is for you Ms. Candelario but can you please tell the court about that last visit?"

"Mr. Burns was always very nice to Carmella, like an uncle, and he seemed to pay extra special attention to her whenever he was over. At first, I thought he was just a very caring and compassionate man, but this last time seemed . . . different."

"Can you please explain what you mean by 'different' Mrs. Candelario?"

"The phone rang, and I went into the kitchen to answer it, leaving Carmella in the living room with Mr. Burns. I was only gone for a few minutes and when I returned, Carmella was sitting on his lap and he was caressing her cheek.

"At first, I was startled by what I saw, but he quickly explained that he was saying a prayer for Carmella. I brushed it off, thinking that it was very nice of him."

"A prayer? Are you Catholic, Mrs. Candelario?"

"Yes."

"Interesting coincidence. Whitney and Maria were also Catholic, just like Carmella and oh yeah, Mr. Burns is Catholic too," Rina said.

"Objection!" the attorney fired off. "Is there a question, Your Honor?"

"Sustained! The jury will ignore that last remark from the prosecution," Judge Crandall instructed. "Be careful, Ms. Rosello."

"I apologize, Your Honor. No further questions," Rina said as she turned and walked back to her seat.

"Mr. Cugino, your witness," the judge announced.

"Thank you," the attorney said. "First off, I'd like to offer my condolences, Mrs. Candelario."

Lauren nodded respectfully and responded with a barely audible, "thank you."

"You stated that Mr. Burns was at your house a couple of days prior to Carmella's disappearance, is that correct?'

"Yes."

"Did Carmella express any discomfort or fear toward Mr. Burns during or after that visit?" Tom asked.

"No."

"And you didn't feel the incident was worth reporting to the police?"

"I guess I didn't think that was necessary."

"Perhaps because he was just a nice man who showed compassion, who showed kindness toward a young girl who was living an underprivileged life and whose mother was on welfare because she couldn't afford to provide for her own children," Thomas said with only a hint of sympathy in his voice.

"Objection!" Rina shouted as she stood up.

"Sustained. Counsel, please approach the bench, both of you!" Judge Crandall ordered sternly. "Ms. Rosello and Mr. Cugino, may I remind you both to stick to questions pertinent to the case and do not use my courtroom to promote your personal views, do you understand?"

"Yes, Your Honor," they said in unison. Rina had at that point felt vindicated. She had succumbed to the perils of poverty and welfare, to the gut-wrenching guilt she had felt at not having enough money when she was growing up, and she knew that talk of that nature had no place in the courtroom.

"Mr. Cugino, do you have any more questions for the witness?"

"No further questions, Your Honor," Thomas responded.

"The witness may step down," Judge Crandall said. "Ms. Rosello, does the prosecution have any more witnesses?"

"No, Your Honor," Rina answered.

"Very well, I'd like to adjourn for the day," Judge Crandall said as he looked at his watch. "Court will resume tomorrow at nine a.m. when the defense will begin calling its witnesses. Court adjourned!"

CHAPTER 31

MONROE COUNTY COURTHOUSE
SEPTEMBER 1991

At nine o'clock sharp, Rina and Tom were seated at their respective tables when the courtroom doors opened and the spectators began to file in. The defendant was still in holding by the court deputy. Thomas looked over at Rina. He was intrigued by her and equally impressed by the skills he observed in her as an attorney.

Judge Crandall entered from his chambers and took his seat behind the bench. He called court into session and instructed the defense to call its first witness. Thomas Cugino stood up and called Mr. Nicholson to the stand.

"Good morning, Mr. Nicholson. Thank you for taking time out of your retirement to be here as a witness today."

"No problem," he replied with a nod.

"How do you know my client, Mr. Burns?"

"I was his manager for about six years, from 1968 to 1974."

"And what type of employee would you say Mr. Burns was?"

"He was always dependable, reliable and dedicated. A model employee. He was very passionate about his job. Honestly, the best employee I ever had."

"How did you feel when Mr. Burns left?"

"I was very disappointed to see him go, but I understood that he had a great opportunity to work with his cousin in California."

"Thank you, Mr. Nicholson. No further questions, Your Honor."

"Your witness, prosecution," Judge Crandall said without lifting his eyes from a collection of papers that were spread out in front of him.

"Mr. Nicholson, what were Mr. Burns' hours when he worked for you?"

"His hours?"

"Yes, his hours. What time did Mr. Burns start work and what time did he finish work?"

"I believe his hours were from eight a.m. to four-thirty p.m., the same as mine and everyone else's in my department."

"Thank you. No further questions, Your Honor," Rina said.

Having expected more questioning of the witness, Thomas and the judge exchanged a curious glance. "No further questions? Are you sure, Ms. Rosello?" Judge Crandall asked.

"Yes, Your Honor, no further questions," she said.

"Okay," the puzzled judge remarked. "Let's proceed then. Will the defense call its next witness, please?" Judge Crandall said.

Surprised at having to call his next witness so quickly, Thomas hesitantly said, "The defense calls to the stand Mr. Gallipeau."

"Hello, Mr. Gallipeau."

"Good afternoon, Mr. Cugino."

"Please tell the court why you are here today."

"I was the technician who administered the lie detector test to Mr. Burns when he was first extradited back here to Rochester as a suspect in this case. I'm actually surprised to be testifying, as typically lie detector results are not admissible in court."

"That is correct, however, the prosecution has allowed it in this instance," the attorney said. He thought that it was a big mistake on Rina's part to allow the results to be read in court, especially since his client volunteered to take the test to prove his innocence and had passed it.

"Ms. Rosello, can you please confirm for the court that the prosecution accepts the polygraph test as admissible evidence in this case?" Judge Crandall asked.

Rina stood up to respond. "Yes, Your Honor, the People accept the testimony regarding the polygraph test."

"Okay," Judge Crandall replied with surprise as he too felt this was an error on her part. "Please continue with your witness, Mr. Cugino."

"Thank you, Your Honor. Mr. Gallipeau, please explain to the court what a polygraph test is and how it works."

"A polygraph, usually referred to as a lie detector test, measures, and records several indicators such as blood pressure, pulse and respiration while the subject is asked, and answers, a series of questions. It is designed to analyze the physiological reactions when the subject gives deceptive answers that can be differentiated from those associated with non-deceptive answers."

"And you performed the polygraph test on Mr. Burns?"

"Yes, I did, sir."

"Please tell us about that."

"I hooked Mr. Burns up to the monitors and began by asking him the control questions."

"For those that don't know, will you please explain what control questions are?" the attorney asked his witness.

"Certainly. Those are simple questions to which we know the answers. For example, what is your name? What is your birthdate? What is your mother's name? Questions of that nature."

"Understood. Please continue."

"Once I established his responses to the control questions, then I began to ask him various questions pertaining to the crimes. I asked him if he had anything to do with the rape and murder of each girl individually and his answers to each one was no."

"Were there any measurable physiological differences regarding the answers that Mr. Burns provided?"

"There was a slight difference in the graph."

"Mr. Gallipeau," Thomas said, interrupting him, "again, I ask if there were any *measurable* differences?"

"No, nothing measurable showed on the data."

"In your expert opinion, would you say that Mr. Burns passed the lie detector test?"

"Yes, in my opinion, he passed the test."

"Thank you. No further questions, Your Honor."

"Your witness, Ms. Rosello," Judge Crandall announced.

"Mr. Gallipeau, you said that Mr. Burns passed the lie detector test, is that correct?" Rina said as she stood up.

"Yes."

"What does that mean exactly?"

"That means that there was not any measurable difference in physiological response between the control questions and the questions regarding the murders."

"But you mentioned there *was* a slight difference?"

"Yes, but that is normal."

"Did Mr. Burns have a normal heart rate and blood pressure during the test or would you say it was a bit elevated?"

"Gee, I guess I would say it was a bit elevated. But again, that is normal as most people get very nervous being hooked up to all the electrodes and wires we use."

"Is it possible to trick the test?"

"Trick the test? I'm not sure what you mean by that."

"Let's say the person was in physical discomfort or pain. Is it possible for someone in pain to have an elevated heart rate when answering the control questions, such that it would confuse the test when a deceptive answer is given?"

"Ms. Rosello, I assure you that Mr. Burns was comfortable and not in pain when I performed the test."

"Was Mr. Burns wearing a long-sleeve shirt that day?"

"Objection! What was he wearing? Really? Is this a joke, Your Honor?" The attorney shouted, flailing his arms in the air for dramatic effect.

"Overruled," Judge Crandall responded, curious as to where Rina was going with her line of questioning. "Ms. Rosello, I hope you have a point. Please get to it."

"I do, Your Honor," Rina said. "Mr. Gallipeau, please answer the question."

"I guess he may have been wearing a long-sleeve shirt."

"So, you did not see his right arm."

"I'm not sure, but I don't recall specifically seeing his right arm. We had an armband on his left arm but nothing on the right."

"Did you know that he had a pretty severe burn on his right forearm?"

"No, I did not know that."

Rina walked over to the prosecution table and picked up a file folder. She opened the folder and pulled out a piece of paper, looking at it briefly before she walked it over to the court recorder and handed it to her. "The prosecution would like to submit to the court the jail infirmary log showing that Mr. Burns was treated for a burn on his right forearm from an apparent spill of hot tea the day before the administering of the polygraph test."

"Mr. Gallipeau," Rina continued, "if you asked Mr. Burns his date of birth, and if at the same time Mr. Burns pressed his wound against the edge of the table, would that cause an elevation in his heart rate, pulse, and blood pressure?"

"Objection!" The attorney again shouted. "Ms. Rosello does not have any proof that the defendant caused himself any pain during the test."

"Your Honor, Mr. Gallipeau is an expert witness and I'm asking him his opinion, hypothetically speaking," Rina said, defending her line of questioning.

"Overruled. Mr. Cugino, since the witness is an expert in his field, I'll allow it. Please answer the question, Mr. Gallipeau." Judge Crandall said as Thomas sat down in his chair, rubbing his temples in frustration.

"Pain could possibly cause some physiological elevations."

"Would you say, in your *expert* opinion," Rina said as she looked over in Thomas's direction, "that those elevations would be equal, or close to, the elevations of telling a lie?"

"I believe that the elevations would be comparable."

"That being said, I'd like to ask you again, Mr. Gallipeau, is it possible that Mr. Burns tricked the polygraph test?"

Thomas was flushed and sweating under his suit and tie. He appeared to be nervous as the witness answered the question.

"Yes, I would have to say if Mr. Burns was somehow inflicting pain on himself while we were administering the test, he could definitely confuse the results."

Rina smiled. "Thank you, Mr. Gallipeau," she said, satisfied with the witness's testimony. "No further questions."

Judge Crandall pursed his lips and nodded. This was his first case with Rina, and he was impressed with this young assistant district attorney. The next and final witness was to be Mr. Burns himself, so Judge Crandall felt it was good timing to call a recess for the day.

Everyone exited the courtroom, leaving Thomas and Rina alone. Rina had her head resting on her hand and was concentrating intently on her case files. She hadn't even realized that Thomas was the only other person still in the courtroom. He thought it was the perfect time to approach her.

"Nice job, Rina," he said.

Surprised by his voice, she jumped. "Geez, you startled me Mr. Cugino! I didn't realize anyone was still in here."

"Please forgive me, I didn't mean to startle you. I just wanted to take this opportunity to tell you that you are really doing a great job on this case. I must admit, when I heard they assigned you to this case, I thought this was going to be an easy win for me. I am not easily impressed, but you remind me of myself, and I'd like you to give me a call, please, after this is over." Thomas reached in his inside suit jacket pocket, pulled out a business card and motioned for her to take it.

Rina looked up at him. "Call you?"

"Yes, I would like to talk to you about the possibility of joining my firm. I could really use someone like you on my team."

"Thank you, I'm flattered and honored, Mr. Cugino," she said, reluctantly taking the card from his outstretched hand. "But I feel I should tell you that I'm not interested in being a defense attorney. I don't think I can defend pieces of . . ." She paused, choosing to respond in a more professional manner. "Let me rephrase that. I don't think I can defend *guilty* people, like your client, Mr. Cugino," she stated plainly.

He laughed out loud at her naiveté. "Believe me, I used to say the same thing. That was until I realized that there is a lot more money on the defense side of things. Listen, all I ask is that you just think about it."

"Mr. Cugino, I don't mean to sound rude, but I didn't choose to be a lawyer for the money, and this is neither the time nor the place for a job offer. If it's all the same to you, I'd really like to get back to my files now. You'll have to excuse me, as I have only one thing on my mind right now, and that is a guilty verdict for your client."

"Understood," Thomas said with a nod as he turned away. He smiled admiringly, thinking that her abrasiveness toward him was just one more quality that would work in his favor should he convince her to accept his offer.

CHAPTER 32

MONROE COUNTY COURTHOUSE
SEPTEMBER 1991

It was the morning of what was expected to be the last day of testimony. After a sleepless night, Rina rose before the alarm went off to get ready for what could be the biggest day of her career. She was in the shower when Steve walked into the bathroom. "Happy Friday!" he said as he set the mug, filled with Rina's favorite morning drink, half coffee, half hot chocolate, on the bathroom vanity.

She pulled back the shower curtain and peeked around the opening at him. "You're the best! Thank you," she said with a smile.

He could see just enough of her naked body through the curtain to become aroused. "Why don't you come back to bed for a few minutes after your shower?" he said with a wink.

"Hmmm, I suppose I could certainly use something to take the edge off today. I just may take you up on your offer." She said as she teasingly rubbed the soap across her breasts, down her stomach and in between her legs.

Before long, Rina would find herself hopping back in the shower once more. She spent the next thirty minutes as she got ready for work focusing on her questions and the cross-examination of Mr. Burns. This caused her nerves to be so raw that as she put on her makeup, she had to steady her shaking hand with the other. *What if I make a mistake? What if he doesn't respond as I am expecting him to?* She knew he was guilty, but she couldn't help but worry as all these questions went through her mind. She was starting to second guess herself. *Stop it! He's guilty and you know it! You can do this, Rina!* She could hear Hun in her head, scolding her for doubting herself. She closed her eyes and could see him with his arms crossed, nodding at her. It was then that a song popped into her head. It was their song and she felt Hun's presence, his strength and his belief in her.

* * *

The time had come and there was a full courtroom when Mr. Burns was ushered in from holding. His handcuffs were removed, and he smiled arrogantly at Rina as he rubbed his wrists. He looked as though he was actually going to enjoy this. *I can't wait to wipe that smug smile off that face of yours you guilty son of a bitch!* Rina thought as she looked away in disgust.

The Judge entered the courtroom and instructed everyone to be seated. Now it was time for the big show. The defendant himself, Mr. Burns, the one who was standing trial for the murder of three young girls, would take the stand to defend his name and, in his mind, his sacred honor. Just a few minutes prior, his attorney had tried desperately to convince the man that it would not serve him well to testify in his own defense. No good will come of it, he whispered to his client, but the defendant refused to let any of Thomas's words persuade him, his mind was made up.

For the defendant's part, he was sure that he could convince the jury that he was innocent, that he was a good man, a religious man and a community servant. Mr. Burns thought he would look innocent to the jury by showing the affable expression in his deep-set eyes, by his careful attention to the line of questioning. He was certain he would evoke a sense of virtue with his proven record of dependability in his career and devoutness in his faith. He felt confident that they would see him as a person who could never have done something so sinister.

"The defense calls to the stand the defendant, Mr. Burns," Thomas stated. There was a low drone of chatter in the courtroom with fingers being pointed and muted rustling as people adjusted in their seats.

Mr. Burns rose self-assuredly from his seat, sliding it back with his foot. The gaze between Rina and Mr. Burns was impenetrable as he walked to the witness stand. The court deputy instructed the defendant to place his hand on the Bible and the other over his heart as he was sworn in. "Do you swear to tell the truth, the whole truth and nothing but the truth, so help you God?"

"I do," Mr. Burns replied.

"Mr. Burns, do you understand that under the Fifth Amendment you have an absolute right to not testify here today?" Thomas began his direct examination of the defendant.

"I understand," Mr. Burns replied.

"Are you speaking here today against my advisement as your attorney not to testify?"

"Yes, I am."

"Can you please tell the court why you wanted to take the stand here today?"

"Mr. Cugino," he said self-assuredly, "I wanted to testify to let the court know that I am innocent. I am a good man, a hard worker, and a devout Catholic. I love children and would never hurt them."

"We all heard from your former boss at your full-time job that you were a model employee for your entire tenure there. Can you tell the court what you did on the weekends?"

"I love children, but unfortunately I had an injury when I was younger, and I could not have any children of my own. I used to work at Seabreeze Amusement Park on the weekends. I drove the train."

"You worked all week long and, out of your love of children, you worked at an amusement park on the weekends too, is that correct?"

"Yes, that is correct."

"Why?"

"Because I longed for a child and couldn't have one, it brought me joy to be around them and to drive them around on the train making them laugh and seeing them happy." Mr. Burns bowed his head as he wiped a tear from his cheek. He paused and, with sadness in his eyes, he looked over at the jury in hopes that his story would garner some sympathy.

Rina faked a dramatic coughing spell and all eyes moved from Mr. Burns to her. She held her hand up, still coughing, and said, "I apologize, excuse me!" She coughed a few more times before she cleared her throat and took a sip of water. "Again, I'm sorry, please continue." She said as she coughed one final time.

Thomas pursed his lips and glared at her. Even though he didn't appreciate her little ploy, he was secretly impressed as he, too, was known to engage in these sorts of courtroom antics to undermine a witness's testimony.

"Mr. Burns," the attorney continued, "you said that you are a devout Catholic. Please elaborate on that."

"Certainly, I'd be happy to." He paused for a moment as if praying for the right way to answer the question. "I was raised with a strong religious belief. I went to Catholic schools and to church every Sunday. I know God and I serve him in this world."

"How did you serve God, Mr. Burns?"

"I was an altar boy at Mass on all Sundays and Holy Days of Obligation. I would fast and abstain on appointed days, I confessed my sins, I received Holy Communion and I contributed to the support of the church."

"It sounds as if you were very devoted to your faith."

"Yes, sir," the defendant said with a nod.

"Thank you, Mr. Burns. No further questions, Your Honor."

Thomas was convinced that he had painted the type of picture that would swing the jury in his favor. Many people hid behind their religious beliefs, the highly successful attorney was keenly aware, so it wasn't a stretch to think that it could tug at the heartstrings of the faithful, and for those who were less devout, it would give them an excuse to pass the defendant off as some fanatic who was too convinced of his own purity to commit such a sin.

CHAPTER 33

MONROE COUNTY COURTHOUSE
SEPTEMBER 1991

Rina was as ready as she'd ever be. There she stood, like the biblical David, slingshot in hand, ready to do battle against the celebrated attorney. Like Goliath, Thomas Cugino was a towering giant in the legal world. Like David, Rina knew that the odds were against her and that the scales of justice were not likely to tip in her favor. Regardless, she would have to rely on her wits, and she would fight with everything she had.

"Your witness, Ms. Rosello," Judge Crandall stated.

Rina approached the witness stand, employing a slow, methodical and confident gait. The defendant smiled at her, oddly pleasant. He didn't want to give the impression of being antagonistic to the jury. Instead, his smile was kind, as if he were trying to convey the essence of Christian charity, of loving one's enemies. Rina was representative of the enemy, and he just needed to find a way to appear unruffled by her accusations and questions. On the outside he seemed unconcerned, knowing that she couldn't possibly have any definitive evidence against him.

"Good afternoon, Mr. Burns."

"Good afternoon, Rina, I mean Ms. Rosello. It's been a long time. My goodness, you sure have grown up, it's nice to see you again," Mr. Burns said. Whispers and murmurs filled the courtroom.

"Order! Order in the court!" Judge Crandall shouted.

The gallery complied, and Judge Crandall instructed Rina to continue.

"Great, I'm glad we got that out of the way. You remember me then?" Rina said.

"Why yes, of course, I do."

"We will get back to how you and I know each other later, Mr. Burns, but first off, please tell us about your childhood."

"My childhood?"

"Yes, your childhood. Tell me about that."

The defendant wasn't quite prepared for this question. He was sure that the young ADA would concentrate on his current life, on how connected he was with the church, how he had had a laundry list of experience working with and caring for children.

"I grew up in a Catholic orphanage and was raised by nuns."

"That must have been difficult for you Mr. Burns."

"Not at all. I am not ashamed. God is the father of orphans and his bounty in Heaven will be shared with us." He caught the nod of a juror, a woman, who was wearing a necklace with a gold cross on it.

"Why were you in an orphanage?"

"My mother was single, and she couldn't afford to take care of me, so she felt it was better for me there."

"What about your father?"

189

"I don't know him." He answered with an obvious emotional detachment.

"Did you ever see your mother after she left you at the orphanage?"

The defendant was starting to get uncomfortable. The little he knew about legal proceedings had convinced him that his attorney was resting on his laurels while he should have been up in arms, firing, "Objection! Objection!" But Thomas knew what he was doing. He was allowing the questioning for a reason.

"Why are we talking about my mother? Do I have to answer that?" he asked as he peered over at the judge.

"Yes," Judge Crandall replied, making a motion with his hand to encourage the man to continue.

"She came to visit me occasionally at first, then her visits became fewer and far between until eventually, they stopped altogether."

"When was the last time you saw your mother?"

"I guess it was just before my eleventh birthday."

Rina looked over at Thomas. Not a peep. Thomas was concentrating on the jurors, some of them showing visible signs of sympathy. It was just the type of thing he was hoping to see in them during his own questioning of the defendant and of the character witnesses, but it appeared that the defendant himself was doing a much more effective job.

"Did you know that would be the last time you would see her?" Rina continued.

"Yes, she told me she was moving away and that she could not afford to take me with her."

"What did you do?"

"I did what any young boy would do. I cried and begged her to take me with her. I said that I'd get a job to help her, but she said I was too young and that her new boyfriend did not want any children."

"Wow that sounds very traumatic for an eleven-year-old. Would you say you were angry with your mother for abandoning you?"

"Yeah, I guess, but it was a long time ago and I've forgiven her. Certainly, I couldn't call myself a servant of the Lord if I held resentment against my own mother."

"What was your mother's name?"

"Her name? Why are you asking that?"

"Just curious, what was your mother's name?"

"It was Barbara."

"Barbara? Barbara Burns?"

"Yes."

She turned quickly and paced in front of the jury box as she continued. "So, the woman who left you even after you begged her to take you with her, just before your eleventh birthday, your mother, had double initials?"

"Objection!" Thomas shouted. Even he hadn't thought to do that much digging into the man's past. How could he not have known that the guy's mother had double initials? Not that it was anything more than coincidence.

"It is okay, no need to answer the question, Mr. Burns," Rina said as she turned and walked over to the prosecution table, pretending to look at her notes. She was waiting for the jury to digest her last thought-provoking question. She walked back over to the witness stand and continued. "You mentioned an injury that prevented you from having children. What happened?"

"Objection!" Thomas cried out again. "Relevance, Your Honor? What does what happened to prevent Mr. Burns from having children have to do with this case?"

"Your Honor, I request permission to approach the bench," said Rina.

Judge Crandall agreed and waved them both toward him.

"What is going on here, Ms. Rosello?" Judge Crandall asked.

"Your Honor, the injury the defendant sustained is relevant as it shows the state of mind and establishes his psychological health," Rina protested.

"Okay, I'll allow it, but this better not be any more of your antics."

"Yes, Your Honor," she said. Both attorneys returned to their tables. Thomas Cugino was starting to show signs of uneasiness.

"Mr. Burns, I repeat the question: what was the injury that prevented you from having children?" Rina asked sternly.

"It was when I was at the orphanage. I got hurt in the shower."

"How?"

The defendant hesitated and looked over to the jury.

"Mr. Burns, how did you get hurt in the shower?" Rina asked again.

"Do I have to answer that, sir?" Mr. Burns asked Judge Crandall.

"Yes, please answer the question, Mr. Burns."

"I was attacked by a couple of the older boys while taking a shower one day."

"Mr. Burns, I need you to tell the court what the boys did to you."

"They came up to me from behind, they kicked me down there and as I fell I hit my head on the floor."

"Then what happened, Mr. Burns?"

"I was in and out of consciousness, so I don't really remember much."

"Mr. Burns, remember you are under oath, so you need to tell the truth. What happened after you fell to the floor?"

"I don't know, I really don't know, but I was . . ."

"You were what?"

"Sore . . . and bleeding."

"I know this is very difficult for you but where were you sore and bleeding from?"

He looked down ashamedly, and nearly inaudible, answered, "My . . . rectum." Gasps could be heard from the courtroom. Thomas looked around and was pleased that his client was getting some compassionate looks from the crowd and the jurors. He felt sure that Rina's inexperience was working as he had hoped, so he sat back and let it play out.

"How old were you when that happened, Mr. Burns?"

"I believe I was about eleven, maybe ten."

"Hmmm, interesting coincidence, Carmella, Whitney, and Maria were all ten and eleven years old."

"Objection! Relevance?" Thomas declared.

"Sustained! Ms. Rosello, do you have a question?"

"My apologies, Your Honor," Rina said simply. "Mr. Burns, did you know me when I was a little girl?

"Why yes, Ms. Rosello, yes, I did know you," he said, happy to change the subject.

"Did you also you know Carmella, Whitney, and Maria?"

"I believe you already know that I was acquainted with Carmella."

"What about Whitney and Maria?"

"Maybe I knew them. In my job, I came across a lot of children. I can't possibly remember them all."

"Okay, so you mentioned church and that you are a devout Catholic. Did you know that Carmella, Whitney, and Maria were also Catholic?"

"Yes. Obviously, I knew that Carmella was, because I was friends with her mother and we went to church together a couple of times."

"That's right, I remember now, her mother testified that she had walked in when you had Carmella sitting on your lap as you were *praying* for her, isn't that correct?" she asked mockingly.

"Objection!"

"Sustained!"

"Mr. Burns, did you ask Carmella to call you 'Uncle'?"

"Yes, I did. So what, is having a young underprivileged girl calling a man Uncle a crime?"

"No, not a crime, just interesting, that is all."

"Objection!" Thomas called out.

"Sustained! The jury will ignore the last remark made by the prosecution," Judge Crandall stated. "Ms. Rosello, I advise you to stick to the questions relevant to the case and not your opinionated, sarcastic remarks."

"Forgive me, Your Honor," Rina said as she continued.

"Mr. Burns, why didn't you have a romantic relationship with Carmella's mother?"

"I don't know. She wasn't my type, I guess."

"Is that because your type was little girls?"

"Objection!" Thomas said loudly.

"Overruled. I'll allow it," Judge Crandall stated. "The witness may answer the question."

Looking a bit flustered, Mr. Burns asked, "Um, what was the question again?"

"Was Ms. Candelario not your type because you liked little girls?" Rina repeated.

"That is absurd!" he said, visibly upset.

"You didn't answer the question, Mr. Burns."

"Of course not."

"I'm looking for a yes or a no answer," Rina said. She leaned in to look him right in the eyes.

"No!" he shouted.

"Okay, so you said you were a hard worker, and your former boss certainly had all good things to say about you. He said you were dedicated to your career—never missed a day, in fact—which is pretty impressive, I must say."

That statement produced a smile on the defendant's face. He felt better that Rina was getting back to his stimulating career.

"We also know that you worked every Monday through Friday until four-thirty and never missed a day, is that correct Mr. Burns?"

"Yes, I had a perfect attendance record."

"Did you know that all three girls were abducted between four-forty-five and five-thirty p.m., all during the week, which would have been after you got out of work?"

"That sounds like a coincidence to me."

"Perhaps," Rina said. "Mr. Burns, would you say you loved your job?"

"Yes, I did," he said, puffing out his chest. He adjusted his blue tie proudly.

"If you loved it so much, why did you quit?"

"Excuse me?"

"You heard me. Why did you quit a job you loved so much, Mr. Burns?"

"It was like my boss said. I had an opportunity to move to California to work with my cousin. He was starting a business."

"Your cousin?"

"Yes, my cousin."

"Did your cousin stay in contact with you while you were at the orphanage, Mr. Burns?"

"What do you mean?"

"If your cousin lived in California, I'm just curious as to how he was able to connect with you if he didn't stay in contact with you while you were at the orphanage?"

"We were actually really close friends. We grew up in the orphanage together and we used to pretend we were cousins. You know, because neither of us had any family."

"I see. More fake family members, just like the fake uncle you wanted kids to call you."

"Ob-jec-tion!" Tom interjected.

"Sustained. The recorder will strike Ms. Rosello's last comment. Ms. Rosello, again I ask you to stick to questions and not your comments. This is your last warning."

"Yes, Your Honor. Mr. Burns, can you please tell the court why, if you had a great job that you loved, a job in which you had a good income, and a job in which you were well respected, then why would you want to leave?"

"I don't know."

"You don't know why you would leave a job you loved?"

"I don't. Maybe I just wanted to get away from the weather up here," he snapped sarcastically.

"Or maybe you sold your car and ran away to California a week after the murder of Maria because you were afraid that the police were closing in on you, after Mr. Ellis described your car, and the sketch of a man that strongly resembled you was printed in the paper?"

Before Thomas could get out his objection, Mr. Burns, visibly agitated, shouted out, "That wasn't me! That was that fireman guy. I remember reading about it in the paper! He was the one who killed those girls and then he shot and killed himself."

Rina recalled reading in her transcripts that a fireman was initially one of the suspects in the murders of Carmella, Whitney, and Maria. He was also responsible for a series of other rapes in the area. The difference was those rapes were of older girls, all of whom were raped but not killed. On his last rape attempt, he tried to abduct a young woman at gunpoint. However, the woman caused such a commotion that her neighbor called the police. Taken off guard, the fireman ran to his car and managed to escape. But he knew that a witness got his license plate number and that it would lead the police right to him, so he shot himself in his apartment where his body was discovered a few days later.

What Mr. Burns obviously did not know was that in 1985 the fireman's body was exhumed and his DNA was tested against the semen on Whitney's clothing. It turned out that he was not a match and was therefore exonerated as a suspect.

"I hate to burst your bubble, Mr. Burns but the fireman's DNA was not a match to the semen found on Whitney's clothing."

"DNA? Se-men?" He said slowly.

"Yes DNA, it's a new science. It stands for deoxyribonucleic acid. It is a molecule that carries the genetic information of everything. For example, blood, hair, bodily fluids and, in this case, semen. And the best part is that they can match it to the person it came from."

Mr. Burns didn't speak, as his mind was racing. He thought back to when they arrested him and they put a large cotton-tipped stick in his mouth. He recalled them mentioning something about a DNA swab, but he didn't really know what it meant. He didn't know there was any evidence left on any of the victims and especially not semen. He wondered if there was something to this DNA thing Rina was talking about and if there was a way it could somehow tie him to the murders.

"I have no idea what you are talking about," the defendant said, shrugging his shoulders as he looked away, trying to hide his uneasiness.

"You didn't know there was semen found on Whitney's clothing?" she said patronizingly. She wasn't about to let the defendant know that a flood in the basement storage area of the crime lab several years prior had destroyed many of the boxes containing cold case forensic evidence. It was unfortunate that one of the boxes happened to be the one that contained some of the evidence from the Whitney Walkowski case and, therefore, they couldn't compare the DNA of Mr. Burns with what was found.

"What am I thinking? Of course, you wouldn't know that Mr. Burns, after all, it wasn't public knowledge and it wasn't printed in any of the papers." Rina said. "But how about the fact that the girls all had the same white cat hair on them. Do you remember reading about that in the papers, Mr. Burns?"

"White cat hair? Hmmm, I don't recall."

"Okay, we'll talk a little more about the cat hair later," she said. She was purposely changing the subject to create some confusion and anxiety in him. "Please tell us what you did for a living, Mr. Burns?"

"I worked for the Department of Social Services as an investigator."

"Did you have access to privileged information and files for families that were on welfare?"

"Yes, it was part of my job."

"You had access to names, addresses, religious affiliations, and just about anything else there was to know about whoever was collecting social services?"

"Again, as I said, it was part of my job."

"Did you ever make home visits?"

"Yes, I did. I made visits to be sure that everything was legit and that the children were being properly taken care of with the money their mothers were getting."

"You would meet the children?"

"Sometimes. If they were home from school when I conducted an investigation."

"Did you ever offer any of the children money, ice cream, candy or food?"

"Maybe, I don't remember."

"We know you asked Carmella to call you Uncle. But what about other children? Did you ask any of the other children you visited to call you that also?"

"There were a few children that I felt extra compassion towards. But, again, that isn't a crime. I just wanted them to feel comfortable with me."

"Comfortable enough to feel safe about getting into your car with you if you offered them a ride or something to eat?

"Objection!" Thomas shouted.

"Sustained," Judge Crandall said.

"Mr. Burns, when we first began here today, you admitted to knowing me, is that correct?"

"Yes, I knew you as a young girl."

"How old was I when you knew me?"

"I don't know, I presume around nine, maybe."

"You also know that my mother was on welfare, I was Catholic and that I also had double initials just like Carmella, Whitney, and Maria, correct?" she said. The jurors began looking at one another quizzically.

"What's your point?" he answered.

"Just testing your memory, I guess. Remember earlier I mentioned that white cat hair was found on all three of the girls?"

"Yes, what does that have to do with me? I didn't have a cat!"

"You didn't have a white cat, Mr. Burns?"

"Objection! He's already answered the question, Your Honor, he didn't have a cat!" Thomas burst out with annoyance.

"Sustained. Please move along, Ms. Rosello."

Rina walked over to the prosecution table to look at her notes and suddenly the courtroom doors opened. Normally, Rina would not even look up, as people entered and exited the courtroom all the time during trials, but this person immediately caught her eye. As the petite blonde woman entered quietly, she ducked down in an attempt not to disturb anyone. She slid into the first empty seat she could find. It was Rina's mother, Dorothy. She looked strikingly attractive for her age, despite her hardships.

It had been many years since Rina had last seen her mother. However, this case had stirred up many bad memories, hurt feelings and mixed emotions for Rina which led her to call her mother, and they talked about some of the things that had happened in the past. It was during this conversation that Dorothy opened up to Rina about how she was conceived and for the first time, Rina felt a shred of empathy towards her mother.

Rina turned back to the defendant who had also seen Dorothy make her entrance into the courtroom. His face had drained of its color. Rina looked back and smiled at her mother. The shocked and worried expression on the defendant's face was priceless, and Rina knew exactly how she was going to proceed.

"You don't look so good, Mr. Burns. Are you okay?" Rina said, taking pleasure in seeing him look so uncomfortable.

Mr. Burns just stared at Dorothy without answering. "Mr. Burns? Are you ill?" Judge Crandall interjected.

A perplexed Thomas looked up and around with curiosity as he was unsure what happened to cause the sudden onset of his client's "sickness".

"Uh, may I have some—some water?" Mr. Burns stammered.

Rina smiled to herself as she went over to the table, poured water from the pitcher into a fresh paper cup, and walked back over to give it to the defendant. "Here you are, Mr. Burns!" she said sweetly as she handed him the glass.

"Thank you, Rina, I mean, Ms. Rosello."

"You're welcome *Bert* — I mean Mr. Burns," she said mockingly. "Well, now that you mentioned it, since we established early on that you know me, can you please tell the jurors *how* you know me?"

He cleared his throat and said, "As you know, I used to date your mother."

Thomas Cugino was listening intently to the cross-examination and was unsure as to where it was going. He knew that his client had briefly dated Rina's mother a long time ago, but he felt it was inconsequential to the case, and in retrospect, he felt it could possibly intimidate Rina and be favorable to his client on the stand. Thomas considered objecting to the line of questioning, however, his own curiosity was piqued now, and he could not see any harm in it.

"That is correct, Mr. Burns. You dated my mother. How long did you and my mother date?

"I don't know exactly," he said as he looked out into the courtroom in Dorothy's direction, "perhaps around two, maybe three years?"

"How did you meet my mother?"

"I met her when she applied for social services. I reviewed her application and, as part of my job, I scheduled a home visit to verify her eligibility."

"Did you visit all applicants for social services?"

"No, of course not. There were too many, I couldn't check them all. I selected only a few at random."

"At random?"

"Yes."

"How did you select them randomly?"

"I just put them in a pile and selected one," he said matter-of-factly.

"You didn't select them based on who had a young Catholic girl with double initials did you?" she asked suspiciously.

"Objection, Your Honor. Speculation!" Thomas shouted.

"Sustained," Judge Crandall agreed.

"Withdrawn," Rina stated calmly. "When was that, Mr. Burns?"

"When was what?"

"When was it that you and my mother started dating?"

"Objection! What is this line of questioning about, Your Honor? When my client dated the ADA's mother?" an irritated Thomas said, his voice rising.

"Your Honor, I am establishing a timeline here."

"Okay. I'll allow it, but Ms. Rosello, please get to the point, *Asap!* Mr. Burns, please answer the question."

"I don't know. It was a long time ago."

"Perhaps I can assist you Mr. Burns. My mother applied for public assistance in August of 1971, right after my grandparents moved to Arizona. Does August 1971 sound about right?"

"I guess."

"And then you dated her until January 8, 1974. I remember the date because it was the night of the fire in our apartment building. It was also the day that you abruptly and unexpectedly broke up with my mother, which is why she went out, to begin with that night. Does that sound about right, Mr. Burns?"

"If you say so," he replied with a shrug.

"How did you feel about me, Mr. Burns?"

"What do you mean by that? I was always very nice to you."

"Yes, I do recall you were always very nice to me."

"Exactly!" He said as he threw his hands in the air. "What is your point with that question?"

"Were you nice to me so that I would feel comfortable with you?

Perhaps so you could abduct me?"

"Objection!" Tom shouted.

"That is ridiculous! You were different!" Mr. Burns answered, ignoring his attorney's objection.

"I repeat my objection, Your Honor!"

"Overruled," Judge Crandall stated.

"What exactly do you mean by I was different, Mr. Burns?"

"You were different from the other girls . . . I mean the other *children* that I came across in my job."

"Different how?" She asked curiously.

"You were obviously going to amount to something someday. And looking at you now, I see I was right!"

"I was going to amount to something? You mean in your opinion Carmella, Whitney, and Maria were not going to amount to anything?"

"I didn't say that. You're twisting my words," he retorted angrily.

Rina walked slowly past the jury box. She paused briefly so they could digest what was just said, then abruptly turned on her heel and continued. "Mr. Burns, you and my mother dated for a few years, so you obviously had sex with her during that time, is that correct?"

"Yes, of course," he looked out in the audience and winked at Dorothy. Dorothy looked away, cringing in disgust.

Thomas's curiosity got the best of him, and he couldn't help turning to look at who his client was staring at. That is when he caught a glimpse of Dorothy. He turned back around but couldn't get the image of the woman out of his mind.

"Is it true that you insisted that my mother shave her private area, something that was very uncommon back in the '70s?" Rina continued.

"How do you know that?" Mr. Burns asked with embarrassment.

Rina smiled smugly. "Let's just say my mother and I had a nice long conversation about you recently, Mr. Burns. Now please answer the question."

"Oh. Yeah, I did. I liked a clean look."

"Didn't you also demand that she dress up like a Catholic schoolgirl?"

Thomas didn't object. Consumed with his own thoughts, he had momentarily lost his focus on the trial.

Meanwhile, the defendant continued to answer Rina's questions uninterrupted. "So what, I liked her to dress up in a Catholic schoolgirl outfit. Is there a crime against a man having his woman dress up for him? It's fun and I'm sure your boyfriend likes it when you dress up for him too, Rina. I think most guys are especially fond of that outfit in particular, wouldn't you agree?" he said as he leered at her.

Rina blushed uncontrollably. She saw Steve in the audience out of the corner of her eye and recalled him liking the time that she had put on a short red, white and black checkered miniskirt, with knee-high socks, pigtails, and a crisp white shirt conveniently unbuttoned just far enough down to show off the tops of her breasts. She caught the defendant smiling at her embarrassment, and, repulsed by his vile demeanor, she shook the recollection from her mind and returned to her questioning.

"Mr. Burns, isn't it true that you had trouble performing sexually with my mother unless she shaved her privates and dressed up like a Catholic schoolgirl?"

"Objection! Conjecture!" Thomas shouted as he awakened from his daydream.

"I'll rephrase the question, Mr. Burns. Did you ever have sex with my mother when she wasn't dressed to suit your sexual fantasies?"

He shifted uncomfortably in his chair as he looked out at Dorothy once more. She was staring right at him as if she were daring him to lie. He looked away, refusing to answer.

"Mr. Burns, as you are aware, I know the answer to this question, so I remind you again that you are under oath and that you put your hand on the Bible earlier today when you swore to tell the truth, the whole truth, and nothing but the truth. I'll ask you this again, Mr. Burns. In the years that you had dated my mother, between August 1971 and January 1974, did you refuse to have sex with her unless she was fully shaven in her private area and dressed like a Catholic school-girl?" Rina, with arms folded, demanded.

Mr. Burns remained quiet and rubbed his hand across his mouth as the spectators awaited his answer.

"Mr. Burns, you need to answer the question," Judge Crandall insisted.

"Yes," he said quietly as looks of disgust crossed the faces of the jurors.

Feeling satisfied, Rina turned to walk toward her seat, pretending to be finished with her questions. Instead, she snatched a photo from the table. "Oh, I almost forgot to mention one last thing, Mr. Burns," Rina said as she turned towards the witness stand. "Does the name Tiffany ring a bell?"

"Tiffany?" he said inquisitively, "I don't know anyone named Tiffany."

"Interesting. Okay, perhaps you remember our expert witness Mr. Gaspar mentioning the white cat hair that was found on all three of the victims, Mr. Burns?"

"Oh, good grief, we are back to the cat again? I told you before, I didn't have a cat and I never have. I hate cats."

"You never had a cat, Mr. Burns? Not even at the orphanage?"

"Oh, that cat. Yeah, the orphanage had a cat but so what, certainly you don't think the hair from the cat in the orphanage when I was eleven showed up on those girls!" he said, as he let out a loud sarcastic laugh.

"You're right, Mr. Burns, that would be impossible, wouldn't it?"

"Of course, it would be."

"Is that because that cat was found dead in the trash can behind the orphanage when you were about thirteen years old?"

"What?" Mr. Burns asked.

"Weren't there several dead cats found behind the orphanage, around the neighborhood and in trash cans while you were at the orphanage?"

"I don't know what you are talking about."

"I'd like to remind you that I visited the orphanage and spoke with Sister Bonacorso. She told me that the neighbors were complaining that their cats were missing or found dead, and they were convinced that it was someone at the orphanage."

"First of all, Sister Bonacorso is a very old woman. I'm sure her memory has deteriorated. Second, there were many violent boys in the orphanage that could have done that to those cats."

"Okay, you're right, it was a long time ago and perhaps her memory of what happened is a little hazy. Now I remember you said you didn't have a cat, but I just want to ask you again about Tiffany, Mr. Burns?"

"Listen, I told you before that I don't remember anyone named Tiffany, and I am getting very annoyed that you keep asking me about her!"

"I apologize, Mr. Burns, but I do have something to show you," she said as she handed him an old Kodachrome photo with a date stamp on the back that read April 1973. "What do you see in this photo, Mr. Burns?"

"This is silly. I don't understand."

"Mr. Burns, I'll ask you again to please tell the court what you see in this photo."

"It's a cat sleeping in an orange-colored chair."

"That is correct. Do you recognize that chair, Mr. Burns?"

"No, should I?"

"It was a recliner that used to be my grandfather's. It was his favorite chair. He gave it to my mother when he moved to Arizona, and we used to have it at our apartment. It was the nicest piece of furniture we had, and you always sat in it when you were over. As I recall, you used to comment all the time on how comfortable it was."

"Oh yeah, I do remember that chair now and, yes, it was very comfortable. I used to sit in it after work while I read the paper and had a beer. What does that stupid chair have to do with anything?" he asked.

"That *stupid chair* was also Tiffany's favorite chair. My cat, Tiffany. You must remember her now, the cat that you used to shoo out of the chair when you came over, so you could sit in it. Do you remember my *white* cat Tiffany now, Mr. Burns? The cat that used to sleep in the same chair that you just admitted to sitting in many times when you were over?"

His eyes widened with fury as he realized what she had just got him to admit to. But Rina wasn't finished yet. She had him right where she wanted him, and she was going to plunge the wooden stake deeper into his heart.

"Mr. Burns, there is something else I'd like to share with you. The night of the fire, when you were probably on your way to California, we were fortunate that our apartment had only minor damage, and we were able to salvage most of our belongings. I have two possessions from my grandfather that I have had with me all these years. One is a music box and the other is his favorite chair. That same chair just happened to be my cat Tiffany's, and *your* favorite chair. It's old and doesn't go with any of my décor, but for me it's sentimental, so I've kept it in storage, wrapped in plastic all these years. Thanks to the development of DNA analysis, I was able to have my chair forensically tested, and I think you must know at this point that the cat hair from my grandfather's chair was a perfect match to the cat hair found on Carmella, Whitney and Maria."

Rina could not contain her elation any longer as she smiled broadly. *BAM!* She knew that this single piece of evidence was stronger than any eyewitness statement or anything else in this case. She reached over, took the photo from Mr. Burns, and brought it over to show the jurors. "I'd like to show you all this photo of my white cat sleeping in a chair. The same chair that the defendant just admitted to frequently sitting in during the time he dated my mother between the years of 1971 and 1974 when the murders happened."

The defendant's face contorted with rage. He began to mutter to himself.

"Mr. Burns, I didn't hear that. What was it you just said?" Rina asked.

He angrily blurted out, "I said, why do you care so much about those girls anyway? Their mothers couldn't take care of them, and they were on welfare, draining the system. They were never going to amount to anything aside from being a burden to society, just like their mothers. They were living a lifestyle that would be perpetuated from generation to generation. God's will was to spare them from the disadvantaged lives they were destined to live." The crowd stirred and the mood in the courtroom shifted from shock to anger.

Rina turned aggressively toward him and looked directly into his eyes. "You keep hiding behind your religious righteousness, Mr. Burns, but it's very evident that you have made a career out of justifying your demented actions so that you could *play* God. Well, the truth is, you are a sadistic preferential child molester who is only attracted to preadolescent young girls because you are sexually immature and cannot perform properly with an adult woman."

"Objection! Objection!" Thomas Cugino shouted, but his protest fell upon deaf ears and the enraged defendant spewed vitriol like a volcanic eruption violently discharging its molten rock.

"How dare you! I was always so nice to you and I even defended you to your mother!" Mr. Burns shouted as he stood up, pointing at Rina. "You ungrateful little bitch! *I should have killed you when I had the chance!*"

The courtroom burst into chaos and a defeated Thomas sunk down in his chair. He knew it was over.

"Order! Order in the court!" Judge Crandall shouted as he slammed his gavel several times, "Order in the court!" Once everyone settled down, Judge Crandall continued. "Is there anything further, Ms. Rosello?"

"Yes, just one more question, Your Honor."

Wondering what more she could possibly need at this point, Judge Crandall held out his hand and said, "Okay, Ms. Rosello, what is your final question?"

"Thank you, Your Honor. Mr. Burns, I'm just curious as to where were you planning on dumping my badly beaten body after you raped and killed me? Would it have been right here in Rochester? That starts with an 'R'!"

There was another explosion of pandemonium as Rina looked at Mr. Burns then at Judge Crandall. She smiled triumphantly. "No further questions, Your Honor!"

It took many bangs of the gavel before Judge Crandall gained control of the courtroom and dutifully addressed Thomas and Rina. "Ms. Rosello and Mr. Cugino, I must say this has been a very dramatic testimony. I realize that emotions and tempers are high right now, but we do have to move on, so I need to ask, do either of you have any more witnesses in this case before we begin the closing statements?"

Rina stood up confidently, "The prosecution rests, Your Honor," she stated.

"The defense also rests," Thomas echoed halfheartedly.

"Thank you, we'll continue with the closing statements, beginning with the prosecution, after a recess. I think we all could use a break right now," Judge Crandall said.

CHAPTER 34

MONROE COUNTY COURTHOUSE
SEPTEMBER 1991

About an hour later, as court resumed, a confident Rina picked up her folder, stood and walked to the podium in front of the jury box to deliver her closing statement. She paused briefly before she looked up from her notes and addressed the jury.

"Good afternoon, ladies and gentlemen of the jury. Thank you for your time and attention in this case. I feel I must say that it's not unusual for an attorney to begin a closing argument by thanking the jury for their time. However, this case is unique, and I think we all can agree that your service here has been much more difficult than in most cases. You all have had to hear about the shocking and violent deaths of three defenseless young girls. One can only imagine the horror those poor girls experienced in their last hours of life having been sexually violated, badly beaten, and then thrown away on the side of the road as if they were trash." Rina paused to compose herself before she continued. It seemed all too real to her, the fact that she could have been the man's next victim, the fact that the defendant, her mother's ex-boyfriend, had at one time seemed to be a father figure, someone to look up to, and someone upon whom she could rely.

"I believe we all know that a serial killer is someone who commits a series of murders following a certain predictable behavior pattern. Serial killers choose victims with similar characteristics. They are usually servicing an abnormal psychological gratification, and the murders typically take place over a period of time with a significant break, or a cooling off period, in between. With less than three percent of the population having double initials, and with the miles driven to dump the bodies in areas that also had the same initials as those murdered, it is no coincidence that the killer methodically chose these three young girls. So obviously what we have in this case is the true definition of a serial killer.

"But I'm sure you all wonder, as do I, what does a serial killer look like? First off, serial killers are very hard to identify. They often wear a mask of sanity and many times they project a very non-threatening, attractive and charming public image. Additionally, statistics show that the typical serial killer is a single white male with an average or above average intelligence. He is organized, he is charismatic, and he possesses the interpersonal skills sufficient to enable him to develop both personal and romantic relationships. Does this description sound like anyone in this room?" Rina asked the jury as she looked over at a stone-faced defendant.

"What makes a serial killer tick? What made Mr. Burns become a monster? Was he born that way? The truth is that the most common predisposition to violent tendencies in serial killers is due to brain injuries, loneliness, isolation, and/or psychological abuse during childhood. This is where I'd like to point out a few things about the defendant that we all learned during this trial." Rina walked over to Mr. Burns, and as she stood in front of him, she turned around to face the jury.

"Mr. Burns told us of a brutal attack when he was only eleven years old in the shower at the orphanage. Perhaps it was during that fall that he suffered a brain injury to his temporal lobe, which is the part of the brain that, if damaged, could account for uncontrollable aggression and an unregulated hormonal system. Maybe that, combined with the sexual abuse he suffered, contributed to his loss of control over his primary emotions such as fear and rage. But most importantly, one can only imagine the psychological effect it would have on an eleven-year-old boy who was abandoned by his mother, even after he pleaded and begged her to take him with her. That same lonely and isolated young boy was then attacked, beaten, and raped. It's no wonder that he chose young girls who were around ten or eleven years old because that is how old he was when he was sexually abused and stopped maturing sexually. It is also around that time that he began taking out his aggression on animals, the orphanage cat and the neighborhood cats who were found tortured and strangled in the trash can behind the orphanage. It's a disturbing statistic of convicted serial killers that ninety-nine percent of them admit to acting out their fantasies on animals before graduating to humans.

"I'm looking around at all of you and I can see some tears and some sympathetic looks on your faces. I can relate to how you are feeling, as I too am a compassionate person. But regardless of what happened to Mr. Burns that turned him into a vicious murderer, we cannot forget that he committed three very brutal and horrifying crimes against Carmella Candelario, Whitney Walkowski, and Maria Mancuso. Three young girls, who had double initials, just like his mother Barbara Burns. Additionally, Barbara Burns was from Brockport and, interestingly, he left his victims in a town with the same first letter as the initials in their names.

"What we have proven in this case is that Mr. Burns is the true definition of a psychopathic serial killer who had opportunity and motive. He chose his victims who had double initials like himself and his mother. He chose victims who were underprivileged and could be easily lured by his promises of fast food, frozen custard and other treats. He chose victims who were eleven years old, the same age he was when he stopped maturing sexually, due to the sexual abuse he suffered. Additionally, he chose victims with the same religious affiliation as his own because somewhere in his twisted mind he believed that he was actually doing God's work and saving those girls. Perhaps he wished he had been killed himself and spared the abuse he suffered. I will agree that it's hard not to feel sympathy for Mr. Burns, however, we cannot forget about the horrific crimes that he has committed regardless of what happened to him.

"I know you will all agree that the most convincing proof of the defendant's guilt is the white cat hair. This one piece of evidence should be more convincing than anything else you've heard or seen in this case because it makes it overwhelmingly clear that the defendant, Mr. Burns, is guilty beyond any reasonable doubt.

"You all have a very difficult decision to make, and, quite frankly, I don't think any of us will ever be the same after this case. It is very unfortunate that we have had to be here in this courtroom to deal with what we have heard and seen, the shocking photographs and the unspeakable acts committed against three defenseless young girls. At least you and I can feel some relief that our lives will never be as irrevocably affected as those of the victims' families." Rina paused briefly.

"Ladies and gentlemen, we must remember that there is one thing that needs to happen here today and that is justice. Justice for three innocent young girls whose lives were unmercifully taken. Justice for their heartbroken families, and justice for a community that was shattered by such horrifying crimes. I realize it was a long time ago, but it is never too late for justice. You all have the opportunity here today to bring justice for Carmella, Whitney, and Maria. So now it is up to you, ladies and gentlemen of the jury, to do your part and return a guilty verdict." The courtroom was silent. Rina closed her file folder and returned to the prosecution table.

Judge Crandall paused before he spoke, breaking the silence. "Mr. Cugino," he said, clearing his throat. "Are you ready for your closing statement?"

"Yes, Your Honor," the beleaguered attorney said. He had planned on a much longer and more elaborate closing statement for his defense, but after all that had happened, after he had been slain by the virtually unknown attorney Rina, he knew it would be a pointless exercise. Regardless, Thomas dutifully stood up to deliver his closing statement. "Ladies and gentlemen of the jury, I would also like to start off by thanking you for your time. Ms.

Rosello paints a picture of the man that she would like you to see, however, the man she describes is not my client.

"While admittedly my client grew up in an orphanage due to his mother's inability to care for him, there is no evidence that he suffered a brain injury, was sexually abused, or that he acted out violently against animals. There is no evidence whatsoever that he hurt the other cats in the neighborhood as there were other older boys in that orphanage who could have committed those crimes. As for the cat hair, that could just be a coincidence, after all, we know that Mr. Burns made home visits and isn't it possible that the cat hair was transferred from him to each of the girls on those visits?

"The real Mr. Burns is a devout Catholic who dedicated his life to public service. He chose his career because he could relate to children who were underprivileged and he felt a need to help them. But Mr. Burns is also human, and what you heard here today was an infuriated man who felt betrayed, disgraced, and humiliated by someone he once cared about. Ms. Rosello not only discredited his strong faith, but she also attacked his integrity and questioned his manliness. We all have our breaking points, and I ask who here today hasn't said 'I'll kill you' or wished someone dead in a moment of anger? My guess is that many of us have said or thought that at some point in our lives, I know I have."

Tom looked directly at a young man whom he knew from jury selection was a single man about thirty years old, whose name was Jerry. All Thomas needed was one juror to find his client not guilty and he'd have a hung jury. He believed that because of his age and his good looks, Jerry might be the best bet. The attorney figured that he'd be the most likely to be able to relate to the defendant in his angry outburst and especially in regards to the schoolgirl sexual fantasy. He believed this man could be his only hope for an acquittal at this point, so he chose to focus most of his efforts on this young man.

"My client was a hardworking man with strong religious beliefs. After many years of working for social services, he came across many unwed single mothers who needed public assistance. It wouldn't be unusual for him to have formed a negative opinion about some of those cases. Additionally, he was a healthy young man at the time who happened to like his girlfriends to dress up like Catholic schoolgirls as part of his sexual fantasies. So what? That, after all, does not make him a rapist and murderer." Thomas said as he paused briefly in front of Jerry before he continued.

"Today, you are all faced with a preposterous amount of circumstantial evidence and theories rather than facts. My client is charged with a heinous crime. He faces a life in prison sentence. You have a tremendous duty here today, and you hold a man's life in your hands. I remind you all that the defense does not have to prove innocence. The burden of proof is on the prosecution, and you must know that the state did not prove beyond a reasonable doubt that Mr. Burns committed these crimes. Therefore, a conviction in this case would be a travesty. I urge you all to think long and hard about all the facts in this case, and in doing so I am confident that you will return a *not* guilty verdict." The attorney picked up his papers from the podium before he walked over to his client and patted him on the shoulder.

"Ms. Rosello and Mr. Cugino, is there anything further?" Judge Crandall asked.

"The prosecution rests, Your Honor," Rina said standing up quickly then sitting back down.

"The defense rests," Thomas said as he too stood and sat hastily.

"Very well then, I will excuse the jury for deliberation and call an adjournment pending a verdict," Judge Crandall announced.

CHAPTER 35

MONROE COUNTY COURTHOUSE
SEPTEMBER 1991

After one hour, the court was called back into session. Thomas knew that if the jury had already come up with a verdict, it was not a very good sign for his client. Unbeknownst to Thomas, the young man he thought would relate to the defendant's sexual fantasies was gay. Jerry, the juror, had remembered being distressed over the rapes and murders of Carmella, Whitney and Maria, when he was a young boy. This trial had evoked in Jerry the memory of his own sisters and how fearful his family was, and he was therefore not empathetic toward the defendant at all. In fact, he had become, at the time of the jury deliberation, the staunchest advocate for a guilty verdict.

Everyone was ushered back into the courtroom and the jury entered from the deliberation room. As they took their seats in the jury box, Judge Crandall asked, "Has the jury reached a verdict?"

The jury foreman, an older woman named Carolynn, rose. "Yes, we have, Your Honor."

"Very good, will the defendant please rise and face the jury?" Judge Crandall commanded.

Thomas and his client rose as instructed and the courtroom was quiet. Rina held her breath for what seemed like an eternity until the foreman opened the folded piece of paper she was holding.

"On the charges of the rapes and murders in the first degree of Carmella Candelario, Whitney Walkowski, and Maria Mancuso, we the Jury find the defendant—guilty as charged!" No sooner was the word *guilty* spoken, then the courtroom erupted in shouts of approval, support and applause for the conviction. Rina raised her clenched fists and whispered an exuberant, *"Yes!"* while Thomas bowed his head in disappointment. Just as in the story of David and Goliath, the underdog took on a seemingly unbeatable opponent and defeated him.

"Thank you for your service, ladies and gentlemen of the jury. You are now dismissed, and court is adjourned." Judge Crandall slammed his gavel one final time.

The court deputy walked over, handcuffed the defendant, and escorted him into custody. As Mr. Burns was ushered past Rina, he looked at her loathingly and through clenched teeth he snarled at her, "You ungrateful little bitch. I spared you and this is how you thank me?"

"Mr. Burns," the triumphant ADA began, "I know you are a religious man, and since you are obsessed with double initials, I have a couple for you. They are H-H and they stand for Holy Hell, which is the place that you are going to be spending the rest of your life." The infuriated defendant lunged and spit at her in defiance, nearly hitting her face. She calmly smiled at him as he was tugged back by the court deputy and roughly escorted away. Rina watched intently as he was shoved through the door and disappeared from her sight.

The courtroom doors opened, and in a whirlwind of chatter, the spectators left the gallery spilling out into the hallway as the jurors were led from the jury box into a separate room off the courtroom until the crowd dispersed. Thomas Cugino looked over at Rina and before he could congratulate her, he saw her smile and wave at Dorothy in the audience. Thomas glanced at the woman whom

Rina waved to and he could clearly see the resemblance between them. He already knew they were mother and daughter, but even if he hadn't, he would have made the obvious connection. He went back to gathering his things when something strange occurred to him. He looked up again and back at Dorothy. This time instead of allowing his mind to wander and his focus to drift, as it did during Rina's cross-examination, he focused his gaze more intently on her. That is when his heart began to beat fast and adrenalin surged through his veins. He couldn't believe his eyes as he stood there, overwhelmed by his realization. In his mind it was as if he was watching a movie in a fast-forward mode when that day came back to his memory in full force.

It was June in 1962 when he first met her. Thomas and his buddies had been drinking in the park that day, enjoying the weather and eager about their upcoming graduation from high school. Tommy, as everyone called him back then, was popular, handsome and smart. He had already received his acceptance letter from Cornell University and there was nothing that was going to get in the way of that.

It was on this early summer day at Durand Eastman Park, when Dorothy, and her younger sister Linda, came walking past, happening upon the boys and their party. When the boys spotted them it seemed harmless to call out and invite the attractive young girls to join them. Linda appeared apprehensive and resistant at first, but Dorothy must have convinced her it was okay, because the girls made an about face and walked towards the pavilion.

Dorothy, the stunning young blonde, shy, unassuming, innocent and soft-spoken, captured Tommy's attention immediately. He was used to getting any girl he wanted. He was used to girls being infatuated with him, and Dorothy was no exception.

"Hey gorgeous, what's your name?" he said to Dorothy as he handed her a beer.

"My name is Dorothy," she replied as her cheeks flushed. She looked away, nervously biting her bottom lip.

"Nice to meet you Dorothy, I'm Tommy. How about we do a shot of Jack Daniels together?" he said with a wink and a smile. She timidly nodded in agreement.

Tommy was instantly attracted to Dorothy. He took her hand and led her over to a corner of the pavilion for some privacy. Dorothy's back was propped up against the post of the covered shelter with one-foot pressed flat on it, her knee bent up and outward. Tommy was leaning into her with one hand on the post above her head, his body close to hers. They were getting along nicely, talking about school, college and their dreams for the future.

Tommy gently touched the side of her cheek and, when Dorothy looked up with a smile, he bent down, giving her a soft kiss. He could see in her eyes that she wanted more so he placed his hand on the small of her back and gently pulled her closer to him. After a long and passionate kiss, he pulled back and he looked down at her perky breasts. He could see her hard nipples through her tight-fitting t-shirt, and it was clear that she wasn't wearing a bra. He leaned in, kissing her again, and this time he reached up under her t-shirt. As he lightly fondled her breasts, he could feel her kisses becoming deeper, more sensual, and he himself was now fully aroused.

"I really want to be with you," Dorothy whispered breathlessly in his ear as he was kissing her neck. "But . . . ."

"But what, gorgeous?"

"It's just that I'm—I'm saving it."

Tommy had heard this objection before, and in his experience, no really meant yes. "Don't worry, there are other things we can do," he replied with a wink.

"I knew you would understand," she said as she grabbed his t-shirt and pulled him in for another kiss.

They were oblivious to anything or anyone around them. They were lost in a world of their own, a world that was ablaze with passion, when without warning, an irritated Linda shouted.

"Get your hands off me, you pig!" she cried.

Tommy and Dorothy saw that one of Tommy's buddies had his arm around Linda's shoulder and was trying to put his hand up her sundress.

"Leave me alone!" Linda cried out, slapping his hands down.

"Aw come on, you know you like it," he badgered.

Having had several shots, Dorothy was drunk, but she snapped out of it when she saw what was happening and went rushing to the aid of her sister, pulling the large guy off Linda. "Hey jerk! You keep your hands off my sister!" Dorothy shouted at him as she placed her hands on his chest and pushed him back.

Dorothy looked over in the direction of Tommy, disappointed that he wasn't coming to her defense. Instead, he looked away from her in an obvious attempt to hide the smirk on his face.

"Come on Linda, let's go!" an angry Dorothy said as she looked at Tommy in disgust and turned to leave.

"Now, come on, Dorothy, don't be so dramatic, they're all just having a little fun." Tommy finally chimed in, grabbing her arm.

"Don't touch me!" Dorothy responded, yanking her arm from his grip.

"Seriously? A few minutes ago you were practically begging me for it and now all of a sudden you don't want me to touch you?" Tommy said with annoyance. "What are you, some kind of cock teaser?"

"You're disgusting, please get out of my way," Dorothy said, pushing him aside to clear a path with her sister in tow.

"Where do you think you are going?" one of the bigger guys said, as he detained Dorothy by holding her arms behind her back.

"I'm going home, now get your hands off me, asshole, or else!" she shouted.

He laughed mockingly, "Or else what?"

"I'll scream!" And just as she was about to, he quickly covered her mouth. "Shhhh!" he said in her ear from behind her, "Don't cause a scene or you'll be sorry"

Dorothy started to kick frantically, taking the guy by surprise. He released her briefly which was long enough for her to shout to Linda. "Run, Linda, run! Go home and get dad!" Linda paused for a second, not wanting to leave her sister behind. "Don't worry about me, go *now!*" Dorothy yelled out, just before her mouth was quickly covered again. Linda turned and, before any of the other boys could react and grab her, she ran away as fast as she could.

"Okay guys, that's enough, let her go," Tommy said to his friend, who, upon command, released Dorothy. With a look of sheer loathing on her face, she brushed her wrinkled t-shirt down with her hand.

Dorothy was turning to leave when Tommy stopped her. "Come on Dotty, don't be mad," he said, trying to charm her once again. He knew she was into him. She wanted him. He could see it in her eyes.

"I'm leaving," she said angrily.

"But we were having such a good time . . ." Tommy responded.

He reached for her hand and she pulled away from him, a disgusted look on her face. He was upset seeing her look at him that way. From there, everything went fuzzy, and he got carried away. He knew that he went too far. He should have just let her go, but he had too much to drink and wasn't thinking clearly. His buddies were drunk too. They egged him on. He knew it was wrong, but he justified it in his mind that he was giving Dorothy what she wanted. After all, every girl wanted him. She clearly did too. He heard her say it. She said she wanted him. His friends knew it too. That is what they kept telling him, *"She wants you, Tommy! Give her what she wants, Tommy! You're the man, Tommy!"* They chanted as they held Dorothy down and watched as

Tommy had his way with her.

It had taken Thomas many years of counseling for him to get past the biggest regret of his life. He felt so much shame and guilt over what he had done all those years ago when he was young, drunk, and full of himself. He never knew what happened to Dorothy, but he had always hoped that she was okay. He hoped that she met a nice man, got married, had children and lived a happy life. He didn't know that what he did that day had a lasting effect on Dorothy's life and that she never recovered from the ordeal as she had a constant reminder, his daughter.

Rina, who was deep in thought and anxious to put this gut-wrenching case behind her, stood up, collected her files, and slung her briefcase strap over her shoulder in preparation to leave the courtroom.

Thomas sprinted up and grasped her arm to stop her as she rushed towards the exit. "Rina," he began, "Please stop, we need to talk."

"Mr. Cugino, I'm flattered, but I already told you that I am not interested in working for you as a defense attorney," she said as she put her hand up and continued walking towards the exit.

"Wait! Please, stop for a minute. It is not about that, it's . . ." Tom stuttered unable to find the words.

"What is it Mr. Cugino?" Rina asked quizzically.

"It's urgent! You really need to call me. We need to talk, but not here." he said seriously as he looked around.

"Okay, okay I will call you," she conceded, thinking it would stop him from badgering her any further. Then she made her way out of the courtroom to face the barrage of cameras and news reporters who were eagerly awaiting her first public statement.

CHAPTER 36

As Rina and Thomas left the courtroom, they were swarmed by a crowd of people. "There they are!" someone shouted and soon the two were surrounded. It was difficult to see with all the people and lights, but Rina could make out Steve and her mother at the far end of the crowd. Steve was leaning up against a wall waiting patiently for her. They were both beaming with pride.

"Ms. Rosello, excuse me, Ms. Rosello?" one of the reporters shouted out, shoving a microphone in her face. "Congratulations on the verdict, Ms. Rosello!" the reporter said, pushing his way to the front of the crowd with his cameraman in tow.

"Thank you, but I could not have done it without the help from the witnesses who testified in this case. They are the ones who truly deserve the recognition," a fatigued Rina said humbly.

"How does it feel to be responsible for finally bringing justice for Carmella, Whitney, and Maria after all these years?" another reporter asked.

"I'm obviously very pleased about the conviction in this case.

However, I can't truly be happy because three young girls were taken from their families, brutalized, and suffered a very gruesome death."

"You appeared to be struggling in the beginning but managed to bring it around. How did you do it?"

"I can only answer that by saying that luck was on my side. Other than that, I guess the one thing about the bad guys is that sometimes they don't see the good guys coming!" she said with a smile.

"That is a good way to put it, Ms. Rosello. So please tell us, was it difficult for you to face this man who may have considered doing the same to you that he did to the others?"

Rina shuddered at the thought of the horror that those young girls went through in their final hours and how close she came to the same fate. "Yes, to say it was difficult is an understatement," she replied.

Rina looked past the reporter and saw Steve. He was the one person in her life who could steady her when her world was spinning. He was Heaven-sent, arriving in her life unexpectedly, and at a point when she needed him most. She thought of Hun too. When she was a young girl, Hun was her everything, her mentor, her inspiration. And now he was her guardian angel. She touched the side of her briefcase, feeling the lump in the pocket. Inside, it held her most valued possession, the little music box from Hun. She had put it in her briefcase that morning before court for strength, and to remind her that Hun was with her. It was a little worn from age, a few chips in it and the pink flowers a bit tattered now, but remarkably it still played music, their favorite song, which she could hear playing in her mind.

Rina smiled at the memory and, anxious to be done with the questions, she said, "I'm sorry, no more questions, please, excuse me." She pushed past the reporters and toward the love of her life, Steve, who had been waiting patiently for her to navigate the media firestorm.

As she walked through the crowd, Lauren Candelario touched her arm to stop her. "Ms. Rosello?" The thin frail woman, who had aged beyond her years, said with tears in her eyes. "I just want to say thank you!"

"Ms. Candelario, there is no need to thank me. I was just doing my job," Rina replied gently.

There was a hint of light in the eyes of Carmella's mother and peacefulness in her demeanor. She had finally seen justice for her daughter and that was enough to give her closure and comfort.

"But it was more than just a job for you, Ms. Rosello. You had a passion, unlike anything I've ever seen. As I watched you, I thought of Carmella and how she would be around the same age as you. It made me think that maybe if . . ." she choked back the tears as Rina placed her hand on the woman's shoulder, trying to give her the strength to finish. "Maybe if that monster hadn't murdered her, perhaps she would have grown up to be a lawyer like you."

"Ms. Candelario, I have no doubt that your daughter would have grown up to be someone very special. Again, I am truly sorry for your loss."

"Words seem hardly enough for what you've done for me and my family." She said softly and smiled as she wiped the tears from her cheeks. "I want you to know that for the first time since November 16, 1971, I will sleep tonight, knowing that my little angel will now rest in peace."

"I'm happy to hear that."

"Thank you, again."

Rina bowed her head, "You are very welcome, Ms. Candelario."

Alfredo, Carmella's now-grown younger brother, who was the one needing medicine that day, nodded at Rina in approval as he put his arm around his mother and walked away with her.

Rina's eyes fell on Steve. A huge smile lit up her face and she had to hold herself back from running towards him and jumping up into his outstretched arms.

"Congratulations honey! You did it, you did it!" Steve said, beaming with pride when she eventually made her way to him. "That was amazing!"

"Thank you!" Rina said, as he wrapped his arms around her petite frame and hugged her tightly. It was such a relief for Rina to be embraced by this man who truly loved her. Someone with whom she could feel complete and safe. He told her when she met him that if she would give him a chance, he'd make her happy. She took a chance, placing her faith in something much greater than herself, and true to his word, he made her happier then she had ever been in her life. Now as she stood there, she knew that things in life transpire at just the right moment, and the sweet wonder of it all was that everything happens exactly as it is meant to.

Steve released Rina and she turned toward Dorothy. "Hi, Mom, it's so nice to see you," Rina said.

"Oh my goodness Rina, you look wonderful," Dorothy said. In fact, she looked more than wonderful. She looked regal to Dorothy, almost saint-like. What she had just done in the courtroom not only put a nearly-two-decade-old mystery to rest, but it also gave Dorothy an opportunity to close a chapter in her own life. She had surely had her struggles with men, and in her attempt to find someone who was able to help her take care of her daughter, she seemed to invite only people who would break her and her daughter's hearts. It had made her cynical, unwilling to see the good things in life, and the pressure of that way of living made young Rina's life utterly unbearable. The courtroom victory provided further proof that Rina had turned out all right, despite what Dorothy may have done to her, consciously or unconsciously.

"Thank you, Mom, and I really appreciate your coming all that way to be here for this."

"I'm glad I made it too and sorry I was late but unfortunately, my flights were delayed," Dorothy said.

"Actually, Mom," Rina said, recalling the look on Bert's face when Dorothy had entered the courtroom, "your timing was absolutely perfect." She let out a buoyant laugh.

"Gosh, I can't even begin to tell you how incredible it was for me to be able to see you in action like that!"

"I am glad you were here, mom. Thank you for all your help. I couldn't have done it without you," Rina said with a grateful smile.

Dorothy leaned in to hug Rina, and as she did, she caught a glimpse of a stunned Thomas Cugino staring in their direction. She froze, instantly recognizing his face. Dorothy had blocked out his name and image, along with the memory of him and what happened that day, for twenty-nine years. He took advantage of her and he ruined her life, and now there he was right in front of her.

The memories of that day came flooding back to her all at once. He wasn't a model, but he could have been, and the chemistry between them was intense. She could still smell the clean cotton scent of his pristine white t-shirt. She could still hear his deep, masculine voice. She could still see his broad shoulders, his radiant smile, and his spellbinding hazel eyes. She touched her lips with the tips of her fingers, remembering the yearning she felt when he kissed her. His kisses left her breathless, his touch made her shiver, and her desire for him was overwhelming. Dorothy was smitten. It was love at first sight for her and she envisioned them together forever.

But then, it all went terribly wrong. She tried to fight, she cried for help, but they overpowered her. Pinned to the picnic table by two of the boys, she was helpless as Tommy pulled off her shorts, then her panties, and methodically penetrated her repeatedly.

Dorothy had always hoped that he had somehow paid the price for what he did. She hoped that his karma was unbearable and excruciatingly painful. But now, much to her disappointment, it was obvious that he didn't suffer at all. He went off to college and became a very successful attorney. How unfair life was. Dorothy wanted to scream. She wanted to go over to him and slap him in the face. She wanted to kick him in the balls, over and over and over again, and leave him lying there in agony, traumatized and heartbroken, just as he did to her that day.

But then the irony of what had just happened made her smile. The over-confident, arrogant lawyer just lost this case, unknowingly to his very own daughter. *HA!* She thought, reveling in her belief that his defeat today must have felt like a kick in the balls for him.

"Mom?" Rina said interrupting Dorothy's trance. "I see you staring at Mr. Cugino. Please don't do that. He is so damn cocky and I'm sick of seeing women fawning all over him. It makes me sick!"

Realizing that Rina had no idea what was going on in her head, Dorothy responded reassuringly, "you don't have to worry about that Rina, he's not my type anymore."

Rina stood back in surprise, giving her mother a puzzled look. "Anymore? What do you mean by that? Mom! Do you know him?"

"I met him once, but it was a long time ago," Dorothy said. She knew the day was quickly approaching when she would have to divulge her secret to Rina, but that day was not going to be today. Thomas Cugino had already taken too much from them, and she wasn't about to allow him to take the joy of her daughter's big victory and their happy reunion.

"Oh my God, are you serious? Where on earth did you meet him?" Rina's voice was elevated in surprise.

"It was back in high school. I'll tell you all about it someday, but right now I just want to look at you." Dorothy said in her best attempt at changing the subject. She stepped back and put her hands on her daughter's shoulders as she looked into her eyes. "You look so beautiful Rina, and so grown up. I'm in awe!"

"Thanks, Mom." Rina smiled. She wasn't used to hearing such compliments from her mother, and the feeling made her forget all about the arrogant Thomas Cugino for the moment.

Dorothy's smile was replaced by a forlorn look. Her eyes welled up with tears as she spoke softly. "Listen Rina, I have to tell you that I am so very sorry for everything." She looked over in the direction where Mrs. Candelario had just been standing and thought about how that could have been her. She could have been the mother of one of the victims. "I should have been a better mother. To think that what happened to those poor girls could have happened to you, Rina. I can't believe I didn't see it. Dear God, I had that horrible man in our home! How could I have been so stupid?" Dorothy said ashamedly. "Rina, will you please forgive me?" she asked with pleading eyes.

Rina pursed her lips and nodded thoughtfully at her mother's apology. She could certainly understand that things were not easy for Dorothy back then. After all, Dorothy was raped, but the one thing that Rina could never comprehend for her entire life was why her mother wouldn't just let her go to live with her grandparents? If Dorothy didn't want her, didn't love her, and couldn't care for her, why wouldn't she just let her go? After all, that is what Hun wanted. That was what Rina wanted and she begged her mother constantly to go live with Hun, but Dorothy wouldn't let her leave.

For years Rina had carried resentment towards her mother for that, and it wasn't until she was older when she realized that the reason her mother wouldn't let her live with her grandparents was that Dorothy needed a child to collect welfare. Without Rina, she wouldn't qualify for the government benefits. This enraged Rina, but eventually, she learned to bury those feelings deep inside her. But feelings buried alive never die and now she could feel that anger rising up, allowing the bitterness to be resurrected. Rina drew in her breath and let it out with a heavy sigh.

"Mom . . . I . . ." Rina choked back her angry words. Part of her wanted to tell her mother *No! No, Mom, I don't forgive you and I never will!* But the other part of her looked at her mother with compassion. Dorothy was older now, seemingly a changed person, and perhaps she truly was remorseful. Rina thought that maybe her mother deserved a second chance as her apology certainly appeared to be genuine. However, forgiving her mother would be difficult and Rina wasn't ready for that just yet, especially not today. "Mom, I think this subject is one that you and I will have to table for now and revisit another day."

"Oh, yes of course, I understand. You're right, this is a happy occasion." Dorothy said as she leaned over, wrapped her arms around Rina and hugged her like she never had before. As the mother held her daughter in an affectionate embrace, she finally said the words Rina had so desperately longed to hear for her entire life, "Rina, I love you, and I am so very proud of you!"

Rina was hesitant. There was a time in her life when she would have given anything to hear those words from her mother and although part of her wanted to say, *"It's too little, too late!"* instead, she responded with a simple, "Thank you, Mom."

"I think a celebration is in order!" Steve shouted out, as he put his arm around Rina.

The three turned, and as they walked towards the exit, Rina looked back over her shoulder and saw the courtroom doors being shut. She paused at the symbolism, and thought about how, as those doors closed, she too was closing a few doors of her own, the doors to her past. She was walking away with dignity, with her head held high, and she was confidently stepping forward into the next chapter in her life.

EPILOGUE

It had been a month since the Double Initial Murder trial, and Rina had become one of Rochester's iconic and celebrated figures, a local heroine. After scores of interviews on the local television stations, and newspaper reporters filling up her secretary's voicemail with requests for interviews, the buzz had finally shifted from a rolling boil to a slow simmer. It was truly a treat for Steve to see his girlfriend weave through the media attention with such grace and poise. He couldn't help but feel it was ironic that of all the cases she could have been assigned, she had gotten that one. It was as if she had been meant for it all along, as if she didn't choose her career path, it chose her.

Dorothy had extended her stay in Rochester to be with her daughter, and it was during this time that Rina and Dorothy had begun going to counseling to work on repairing their severely damaged relationship. Rina was finally able to tell her mother how she felt and, in doing so, she felt the weight slowly lifting and the healing begin. Dorothy was also able to recognize her mistakes and admitted that her behavior towards her daughter was abusive. The two still had a long way to go, but they were getting along nicely.

One day they had gone down to the lake for a walk and Dorothy felt the time was finally right for her to tell Rina about her father.

"I'm so happy that I've been able to spend this time with you and I feel we've come a long way together," Dorothy began, "but I have something very significant to tell you."

"Sounds serious, what is it?" Rina asked. She could sense the anxiety in her mother's voice and it made her uncomfortable. The breeze along the lakeside was picking up, and there was an autumn chill in the air, hinting of the winter yet to come. "Please, don't tell me its bad news."

"No, not exactly, but it's something I think you should know, and I'm not really sure how you're going to take this," Dorothy said as she clutched Rina's arm tighter.

"Mom, you're scaring me, what is it?" Rina inquired, her heart starting to beat fast as she gave her mother a worried glance.

"In the courtroom that day I didn't want to spoil your moment when I realized it. Please forgive me for waiting this long to tell you, but . . ." Dorothy hesitated.

"Mom! Please, just tell me!"

"It's about Thomas Cugino."

Rina stopped in her tracks for moment, "Thomas Cugino?" Every muscle in her stiffened at hearing his name mentioned by her mother.

"Yes, Thomas Cugino," Dorothy affirmed.

"That's right. I forgot you said you knew him, what about him?"

"We went to high school together." Dorothy blurted out.

"Oh my God mom, I can't believe you knew him in high school, I had no idea. How well did you know him?" Rina asked hesitantly.

"Everyone knew of him, he was the most popular guy in school. Quite honestly, I think I would have done anything to get his attention back then. But I never would have imagined . . ."

Dorothy looked as if she was about to cry. Rina was starting to suspect a dark secret and urged Dorothy towards a nearby bench to sit down.

Rina sat silently as an emotional Dorothy told the whole story, about the time in the park, about how she and Tom had an undeniable chemistry, and about how things went awry that day.

Rina sat there silently, staring wide-eyed off into the distance. For a moment, her face was frozen in an expression of stunned surprise. Rina bit her bottom lip as the realization of what she just heard hit her. "Are you saying what I think you are saying mom?" Rina said when she finally spoke. She knew the answer but she needed her mother to say it, almost as if it wasn't spoken then it couldn't possibly be true.

Dorothy sighed heavily. "I'm saying that Thomas Cugino . . . is your father."

Rina covered her mouth with her hand and watched the lapping waves against the waterfront. She thought about how there was something about the man that captivated her early on when she first learned that she would be going toe to toe with the legal giant. All in all, even though she didn't want to like him, she couldn't resist the feeling of admiration and an innate desire to want to know more about him—his process, his pathways to success. It was all starting to make sense to her, but never had she imagined the man was, of all things, her *father*.

"I am utterly shocked and quite honestly, I really don't know what to say to that," Rina said as she was still processing the news she had just been given.

"I wanted to tell you right after the trial but the timing just never seemed right."

"Does he know?" Rina asked without looking at her mother.

"I can't say for certain, but the way he looked over at us that day, well, he's a pretty smart guy so my guess is he might have figured it out."

"That certainly explains a lot," Rina said with a heavy sigh.

"What do you mean by that?"

"He's been calling my office relentlessly for the last month. I've returned a few of his calls but kept missing him. I assumed he was just trying to get me to work for him, but now I'm thinking that perhaps he has a different reason for being so persistent."

Dorothy looked at her daughter and suddenly years of shame and guilt, years of trying to cover up a very dark part of her past, were starting to melt away. "I'm so glad you turned out okay, in spite of everything that has happened."

"To say it has been a rough road is an understatement, Mom, but thankfully, I've had some very good people around me. Steve has been especially supportive. I'm so grateful for his confidence in me and for giving me the strength to get through the difficult times. Speaking of Steve," Rina said, "we should be getting back home. He has dinner plans for us later, and we don't want to keep him waiting!"

A few hours later, there was nothing but scraps left of the roasted chicken and fettuccini that Steve had made. Steve was a great cook and Rina teased him often about quitting his day job to become a full-time chef.

"That was delicious, Steve, thank you very much. Handsome and a great cook, boy my daughter sure is lucky." Dorothy said with a chuckle.

"I'm glad you liked the dinner I prepared," Steve said, noticing the satisfied looks on both Dorothy and Rina's faces. "But I have one more surprise in store for you Rina." Before the women could respond, Steve darted into the living room.

Steve returned, holding something behind his back. "I just so happened to come across a travel agency today and picked up these," he said as he pulled around his hand that was holding two fanned out tickets."

"What are those?" Rina asked with curiosity.

"These, my love, are two tickets to paradise!" He answered with an ear to ear grin.

"Paradise?"

"Yes, a Caribbean cruise. We leave next Saturday."

"What? Oh my goodness! Are you serious?"

"Yes! And I've already called Lynn. She said you don't have any trials for the next few weeks, so work shouldn't be an issue."

"Wow! I can't believe it! I've never been on a cruise, I'm so excited!"

"Me too," Steve said, beaming with anticipation.

"I've got to call Joanne, wait until she hears about this!" an elated Rina said as she ran out of the kitchen to make a call to her best friend.

Steve was pleased with Rina's enthusiasm, and as soon as she was out of earshot, he looked over at Dorothy with a glow of excitement.

"Steve, you look like the cat that just ate the canary, what is going on?"

"If you can't tell, I'm madly in love with your daughter. So much so that it is my lifelong goal to protect her, provide for her, support her and most importantly, always be true to her for as long as I live."

Dorothy could hardly contain herself and she held both her hands up to her face nearly covering the huge smile she was displaying underneath.

"I plan on asking Rina to marry me," Steve said with a grin.

A tear rolled down Dorothy's face as she reached over to hug

Steve. She couldn't think of a more perfect match for Rina, and she was thrilled that her daughter had found true love, despite her traumatic past, despite the upset she had endured, despite the shame that had crippled her in her youth, and despite the fact that she quite possibly could have been a victim of the double initial killer. All of that washed away, the tears were washing it away. The tears were righting the wrongs.

It was on the flight to Miami to catch the cruise ship that Rina finally had the opportunity to fill Steve in on the details surrounding Thomas Cugino. Naturally stunned at the revelation, just as Rina was, but in typical Steve fashion, he supported Rina in however she decided to handle the situation. Rina had discussed everything with her psychologist and decided to wait until after their vacation to return Tom's calls.

Several days later on the cruise ship, after a formal captain's night dinner, Steve, dressed in his tuxedo, and Rina, in her elegant long black evening gown, took a walk to the back of the ship. The moon shone brightly in the clear starlit sky and its soft shimmery glow reflected on the tranquil water. A warm breeze blew the blonde wisps of hair from Rina's face as she breathed in, smiling as she took in the peaceful sight. It was the perfect opportunity, the one that Steve had hoped for as he grabbed her hands and turned her to face him.

"Rina, I truly believe that I knew ever since I laid eyes on you that first night in the Old Toad, that you were special. The past few years we have spent together have really affirmed my faith in humanity, in life itself, for here before me stands the most beautiful woman I have ever known." Rina looked up into his loving eyes, reveling in his compliments as he continued. "I am completely and wholeheartedly in love with you and . . ."

Steve knelt down and reached for his pocket. Rina's eyebrows raised, and her jaw dropped at the sudden realization at what he was doing. Her hand covered her open mouth and she stared at Steve as he continued.

"I can think of no other way to show how much you mean to me than to ask you if you would do me the honor of being my wife." Then he produced a black velvet ring box. He opened it and turned it towards Rina, displaying a two-karat round diamond engagement ring. "Rina Rosello, will you make me the happiest man in the world and marry me?"

All the brilliance of the sparkling diamond reflected back at her and she gasped in disbelief. More than any other time in her life, she knew that she had finally found the love of a lifetime and for all the struggles she had ever gone through in her life, this day would be a new beginning and allow her to truly put her past behind her.

"Steve," Rina said finally after wiping away a few tears that had escaped from her eyes. "You are definitely the best thing that has ever happened to me and I never want to imagine a day in my life without you in it." Rina stared lovingly into his eyes and choked back her tears as she answered, "Yes, Steve. *Yes*! I'll marry you!"